RAVEN'S CURSE
RAVEN'S CLIFF
BOOK FOUR

ELLE JAMES
KRIS NORRIS

TWISTED PAGE INC

Copyright © 2025 by Elle James & Kris Norris

All rights reserved.

No part of this book may be reproduced in any form or by any electronic or mechanical means, including information storage and retrieval systems, without written permission from the author, except for the use of brief quotations in a book review.

Without in any way limiting the author's [and publisher's] exclusive rights under copyright, any use of this publication to "train" generative artificial intelligence (AI) technologies to generate text is expressly prohibited. The author reserves all rights to license uses of this work for generative AI training and development of machine learning language models.

ISBN EBOOK: 978-1-62695-670-4

ISBN PAPERBACK: 978-1-62695-671-1

To Jen — for that one diabolical scene.

To Chris — for knowing that Earl had to die.
(Sing it with me!)

To Elle — for trust and confidence.
This is truly a bittersweet ending.

To Kris — for all the heart and soul you put into this project.
Your light truly shines in this body of work.

AUTHOR'S NOTE

Raven's Cliff Series
Elle James with Kris Norris

Raven's Watch (#1)
Raven's Claw (#2)
Raven's Nest (#3)
Raven's Curse (#4)

RAVEN'S CURSE

RAVEN'S CLIFF BOOK #4

New York Times & USA Today
Bestselling Author

ELLE JAMES
&
KRIS NORRIS

RAVEN'S CLIFF

RAVEN'S CURSE

NY TIMES BEST SELLING AUTHOR
ELLE JAMES
KRIS NORRIS

PROLOGUE

Eastern Europe
Classified rescue mission
Five years ago…

"Thirty seconds to infil. We've got massive resistance so, we're going in hot."

Chase Remington shifted in beside his buddies as Foster Beckett's voice sounded through his comm unit. Though, for Foster to comment on the conditions, the situation had to be worse than usual. Which meant their intel had been lacking. Again.

Zain Everett and Kash Sinclair — along with Kash's partner, a feisty German Sheperd named Nyx, strapped to his chest — moved in beside him. Chase shook his head. And Kash thought Chase was crazy carrying his medic bag.

The helicopter swooped in low, rotors thundering through the night, nothing but a hint of moonlight guiding their way. The doors slid open, a mix of mountain air and incoming rain spilling into the cabin. A thick canopy of trees rushed beneath them, the tops black against the indigo sky.

Foster banked the chopper, skimming the treetops before the forest disappeared, the off-grid compound rising before them like a monolith. A large wall surrounded the collection of buildings, smoke rising from a couple chimneys.

He didn't slow, eating up the distance before flaring off the speed — bringing the machine into a high hover. Dust kicked up beneath them, their ropes snapping in the downwash as they dropped out of the chopper, the ends pooling on the roof of the building.

Green tracer fire streaked across the sky as gunfire popped through the air. Bullets ricocheted off the struts, their gunner, Rhett Oliver, returning fire.

Rhett waved them on. "Get your asses out the damn door before they're filled with lead."

Zain rolled his eyes, then leaped out, racing down the line face first — firing off rounds as he went. He hit the clay tiles all of five seconds later, Kash a step behind him. Chase brought up the rear, boots slamming against the rooftop, the rope slipping free as Rhett reeled it back in. Chase scoured the area for wounded, the voice inside his head poking at him. Based on the amount of resistance, he doubted the mission would go off without injuries.

Zain took up his position as overwatch, already scoping the area as Chase and Kash dropped to the ground, his buddy catching Nyx as she followed him off the roof. Alpha team waved them over, two of the Green

Berets taking point. Laying down cover fire as Chase and Kash closed in. After a few hand signals, they took off, hoofing it across an open stretch, then behind one of the peripheral structures. Some kind of shed that creaked as the chopper roared overhead, banking hard to the right before disappearing into the night.

Master Sergeant Eric Dalton, Alpha's squad leader, wove his way across the compound, stopping at the main building. A red door sat recessed amidst the wood and stone, the frame giving against the force of Dalton's boot.

He grabbed a canister off his vest, then chucked it inside. The grenade skipped across the floor, each impact sending out a tiny vibration. It spun to a halt, everything freezing for one agonizing moment before it detonated.

Lights and sound filled the air, smoke billowing out the end. Shouts rose above the ear-piercing wail as people poured out of the rooms, barely taking a couple steps before crumpling.

Dalton twirled his finger, and his team exploded into the building, night vision goggles covering their eyes, rifles notched in their shoulders. Quick, sharp bursts echoed through the space, scattering anyone not already down. Chase followed suit, the night vision's eerie green hue painting the interior. They swept through the main section and continued down a long hallway, clearing rooms, then moving ahead. Chase covered their six, gun at his shoulder, ready to charge ahead if anyone got hit.

Dust filtered through the air, glowing in the soldiers'

small beams cutting through the darkness. Boots tapped the floor as the men entered a large area, photos and maps pinned to the far wall. Kash jogged ahead, giving Nyx enough slack to work the room. She stopped at a shelving unit, then pawed at the floor, glancing up at Kash.

"Good girl." Kash reeled her in as Dalton and his weapons' specialist, Caleb Rios, shouldered up.

They muscled the shelf to the side, exposing a thick, metal door. Some C4 tacked to the hinges, and the door exploded, clattering to the floor as more smoke filled the air. Shouts echoed from inside, the hostages clutching each other as the team swooped in.

Chase gave them a quick once-over, bodily lifting one woman who wouldn't budge, gaze fixed straight ahead. Clothes torn. Alpha's medic, Royce Carver, hiked the woman onto his shoulder, following the rest of his team back through the corridors as Chase swept behind them.

Rios veered off at the next junction, covering an adjoining hallway when gunfire erupted from the shadows, catching Rios in the neck. He fell hard, blood arcing off the ceiling and walls, his legs spasming.

Chase took off a heartbeat later, vaulting over a chair before sliding under more rounds. Two seconds flat, and he had his hand cinched around the wound, his bag spread out beside him. Bullets whizzed past, hitting an inch from his head, kicking up bits of wood as they pinged off the floor and walls.

He kept working, clamping off one of the bleeders before packing the whole mess with sponges and gauze

— prepping Rios for medevac. More gunfire erupted in the next room, shouts and grunts prickling the hairs on Chase's neck when his comm unit clicked.

Zain's voice crackled over the line, steady. Unyielding. "Enemy reinforcements inbound. Get the lead out."

Chase tied off the bandages, packed up his bag, then lifted the man fireman style, weapon still grasped in one hand. He booked it down the hallway and out the door, scouring the landscape.

The hostages stumbled their way across the grounds, Kash and the others picking up any stragglers. Chase trailed after them, Marcus Hodges, Alpha's comm tech, guarding his six. Keeping a path open as they raced for the landing zone.

Gravel crunched in the distance, those reinforcements bumping along the main road — headlights slicing through the darkness. His teammates angled right, staying on the periphery, Zain picking off anyone trying to flank them.

Chase sped up, Rios groaning with every jostle when a band of hostiles stepped out of the shadows, rifles spitting out rounds.

The group separated, Kash and two others veering right — corralling the hostages against the wall as they hauled ass toward the rendezvous site. Dalton and Carver returned fire, until a grenade landed nearby.

The two men hit the ground, the frag exploding a second later. Dirt and shrapnel flew through the air, dust choking off the area in a smothering debris cloud. Chase raced ahead, firing off rounds before he and

Hodges ducked behind another small building. Chase eased Rios onto the ground, then chucked out a few canisters, emptying his mag until everything erupted into chaos.

The grenades detonated, a blinding flash slicing through the darkness as an ear-piercing shrill echoed through the air.

"Cover me." Chase didn't wait for Hodges to start shooting, just darted out, dodging gunfire and tripwires before grabbing Dalton and dragging him behind a wall. Chase braced his shoulders against the shed, then raced over to Carver, taking a hit to his vest as he carried the man back.

Hodges took point, doing his best to cover every angle as Chase piled more supplies on Dalton's legs, quickly triaging the injuries. Carver had multiple shrapnel injuries, the worst chunk poking out from his thigh. Blood dripped from the wounds, soaking into the ground in an increasing black puddle. Dalton had a GSW to his upper shoulder, just outside his vest. No exit wound.

Chase went to work, pouring on clotting powder, doing his best to plug the holes — ready them for medevac. Hodges was on the comms, calling in another chopper, going through his mags in an effort to keep the forces at bay. Rotors sounded in the distance, the deep resonance vibrating through the ground.

Footsteps pounded near the wall, two hostages doubling back — hitting the ground amidst more gunfire. Chase tensed, glancing at the soldiers, then back to the civilians, aware he couldn't carry them all.

Couldn't save everyone.

Dalton gave him a shove, hand falling to his lap as if the simple movement had drained his strength. "We're not dead yet, Remington. We can drag our asses to the medevac chopper. Hodges has our backs. Get them and go."

Chase clenched his jaw, staring at the increasing pool of blood. The unfocused eyes staring back at him. He readied his rifle, glanced at Hodges, then over to Dalton. The man was already fading, eyes drooping, his weapon resting in his lap.

Dalton coughed, blood splattering across his fatigues. "I said, go."

Chase pushed down the riotous roil of his gut. The cold reality that he might not make the return trip in time. "I'll double back once they're onboard. Ride home with you."

"Only if we don't get onto that other chopper, first."

"You'd better." Chase took a step — looked back. "I'm sorry."

He took off, sprinting across the short section — grabbing both women without really slowing. He slung one over his shoulder as he wrapped his arm around the other's chest — half-carrying her as he bolted for the aircraft. Shouts carried on the wind, grenades and gunfire following in his wake as he picked up speed.

Foster's chopper waited in a small clearing, the rotors damn near hitting the trees, Rhett rattling through ammo as he cut through the adjoining forest, cracking branches and scattering more forces.

Chase hit the opening at a dead run, Zain curling in

behind him when some asshole popped up off to their right, catching Chase twice in the vest. He managed to twist before he hit the ground, keeping the hostages from landing beneath him. A couple reports popped next to him, Zain appearing out of the night as he grabbed the women.

He snagged Chase's collar — yanked him upright. "Run."

Chase shook his head, glancing back. "I can't leave Dalton and the others. Go. I'll catch a ride with them."

He took a few stumbling steps, willing his damn lungs to inflate against the fire in his ribs when a whoosh soared overhead.

White light filled Chase's view, the missile strike bowling him backwards. He cartwheeled across the ground — stars, dirt, repeat. Over and over before he landed on his back, dust and gravel swirling through the air. Smoke burned a line down his throat. A deafening roar sounded in his head.

He coughed, blacked out, rousing when a hand grabbed his vest. Loud pops boomed around him, the odd casing flicking across his body.

Rhett lifted him onto his feet, snugging his arm around Chase's chest as he kept firing. "Are you nuts?" Rhett backed up, clipping anything that moved, dragging Chase with him.

Chase shook his head. "Dalton..."

He barely got the man's name out without puking. Nearly collapsing right there on the ground.

Rhett tightened his grip, catching another tango

when he stepped out of the forest. "Medevac's almost here. They'll grab anyone still breathing."

"Rhett, I can't—"

Rhett stopped next to the chopper, looking Chase dead in the eyes as he heaved him inside. "There were multiple hits." He swallowed, closed his eyes. "I'm sorry. I don't see how they survived. Regardless, you're in no shape to rescue anyone, not even yourself. So, plant your ass on the floor, and try not to fucking die before we get you back to base."

Rhett took up his position, still firing as Foster picked up the chopper, tossed it off to one side and roared out, the doors open as he whizzed overhead, punching through flames and smoke before heading off.

Chase slumped against the bulkhead, blood smeared on his skin. He stared out at the carnage as it faded into the distance, an emptiness settling in his gut.

I'll double back...

His own words looped in his head, the hollow tone following him into the darkness.

* * *

"Look who's still alive."

Chase chuckled, then grunted, holding his ribs as Rhett sauntered into his hospital room, a ridiculously large pink teddy bear clutched in his hands. He plopped the bear on the end of the bed, looking more than amused with himself.

Chase rolled his eyes. "Seriously, jackass? That had better be for the cute nurse."

Rhett glanced at the bear and shrugged. "Thought you might get lonely in here all by yourself, seeing as you're taking your sweet-ass time to heal."

"I had a collapsed lung."

"Yeah, like three days ago." He nodded toward Chase's ribs. "Chest tube's already out."

"This morning." He cursed when his broken ribs ground against each other. "Trust me, I hate this."

"You PJs are always the worst patients." Rhett leaned in. "Heard the entire staff bitching about you wanting to double check every med, every procedure. Hell, you questioned a sponge bath with that brunette." He shook his head. "You've got serious issues, brother."

"With meds. And the brunette's hands are like freaking ice. Not the kinky act you're imagining."

Rhett laughed, then sobered. "Sorry about Dalton and his crew."

Chase swallowed the bitter taste of defeat, toying with the edge of his blanket. "Not your fault. You're not the one who left them behind."

"Neither were you." Rhett stopped him with a hard stare. "Chase. You nearly died twice on the flight here. If Kash hadn't spent the past six years watching you treat people, you'd be dead. Guy deserves a damn medal. As do you because I know, without a doubt, if I hadn't forcefully dragged you into the chopper, you would have staggered to your feet and gone looking."

Rhett slapped Chase's thigh, ignoring Chase's resulting grunt. "You wouldn't have made it more than twenty feet, tops, but you would have tried. Would have died before you admitted you were too compromised to help. So, if you need to blame anyone, blame me. I can shoulder it."

Chase snagged Rhett's hand. "You're an ass. And I owe you. Huge." He shoved Rhett's hand away as Foster and the others walked in. "Hey, Beckett, please tell me you reamed Rhett a new one for leaving the chopper. I mean, is that even allowed?"

Foster crossed his arms, shaking his head. "It's not the leaving that scared me, it was him yelling at Sean to man the machine gun." Foster gave Sean a clap on the back. "Have you seen the man fire anything that powerful? It's sad."

Sean flipped off Foster. "At least, I wasn't yelling at Chase to get up, as if he could hear me from inside the cockpit." Sean batted his eyelids. "You two have such a bromance. Folks are talking. You know that, right?"

"Shut up." Chase looked at Foster. "So, they really didn't find anyone else alive?"

Foster sighed. "Nothing, yet. The joint task force is considering another assault based on what the survivors told them. They want to take down the entire cell... but it's doubtful anyone survived that missile strike."

"And we're sure it was that extremist group — the Legion — who initiated it? Because I have a hard time believing they had the resources, let alone the balls to blow up half their own compound."

Foster shuffled over. "How about you focus on getting your ass out of that bed, and let me deal with the bureaucrats."

Chase huffed, closing his eyes as pain shot through his ribs and into his chest, scattering dots across his vision when he finally looked up at his buddies. "That's not an answer."

"It's the best I've got." Foster glanced at Chase's IV. "Are you taking any of the meds?"

"You know how I feel about that."

"Buddy, you're not your father. You can take the damn morphine and not kill anyone."

Chase clenched his jaw, the mere mention of his dad sparking another kind of pain no amount of narcotics could ever touch. "You can't guarantee that."

"Damn straight we can." Kash moved in on the other side. "Hand to God, I'll tackle your broken ass to the floor if you so much as twitch. Or at least, toss the freaking stuffy at you." He scrunched up his face, glancing at Rhett from the corner of his eye. "Did you win this at a carnival back in the nineties?"

Rhett shrugged. "I've been saving it for the right moment."

Zain waved them both off. "Ignore them but take the meds. You're a damn bear at the best of times. Trying to manage all this pain... People are talking, and it's not kind."

Chase breathed through the next stabbing jolt. "You'll keep my ass in this bed?"

"Guaranteed." Zain tapped him lightly on the shoulder. "We ordered pizza. We'll go grab it and camp out for the night. Prevent one of the staff from putting a hit on you."

"Fine." Chase snagged Rhett's hand as his buddies darted from the room. "I meant what I said."

Rhett shrugged it off. "Yeah, yeah, you owe me, like

you haven't saved all of us at some point. Rest, we've got your back."

Rhett stepped aside when the nurse came in carrying a syringe. She gave Chase an evil eye, waiting until he begrudgingly nodded before injecting it into the IV tube.

Chase eased back in the bed. He'd give himself a few days to kick the pain to the curb, then he'd be back. Looking for the next win. Something to dull the voice in his head still screaming at him.

Some form of redemption he wasn't sure he'd ever find.

CHAPTER ONE

Raven's View Lodge
Present day

"C'mon, Rhett, enough screwing around. Just open your eyes."

Chase leaned across the bed, looking for any hint Rhett was improving. Some small sign. A tremble in his fingers. A twitch of his mouth. Anything other than the same blank expression he'd had for the past year.

Instead, all he got was a telling silence broken only by an incessant beeping in the background. Proof Rhett hadn't slipped away just yet. A glimmer of hope that slowly leached the life out of them.

Kash braced his hip against the end of the bed, shaking his head. "Anyone else wanna toss that damn heart monitor out the window? I swear that beeping lives on in my head for hours after we leave."

Foster nodded. "Every time I walk through those doors, I expect to see him hooked up to a ventilator.

How the hell are they sure he's not just going to stop breathing?"

Chase sighed. "His brain stem wasn't affected and so far, he can still regulate his breathing. That could change, though."

He didn't voice the obvious. That every day Rhett remained lost reduced his chances of ever making it back. Breaking through that veil. Not when they already knew.

Zain shook his head. "I thought he was responding to vocal commands? Isn't that what the doctor said?"

"There's been a bit of brain activity, and one of the nurses thought she saw him blink, but they haven't been able to replicate it." Chase squeezed Rhett's shoulder. "I know you're faking, Oliver. The jig's up so open your damn eyes before I get Nyx up here to lick your ugly-ass face."

Chase collapsed into the chair beside the bed, guilt clawing at his chest. He should have shielded the guy when Stein and Adams had opened fire. Should have given him more blood. Something that would have kept Rhett in the game long enough he would have still been conscious when Foster had landed back at base.

Kash booted Chase's foot. "Stop. It wasn't your fault."

Chase huffed. "You don't know what I was thinking."

"Yeah, I do, because it hasn't changed in the past year. You think you should have somehow pulled a miraculous save out of your ass, when you were hurting as much as everyone else and spread so damn thin, I'm surprised you didn't end up in a coma, too."

"That's not the point. I still owe him."

Zain scoffed. "For what?"

"That time in Eastern Europe, when he dragged my ass back to the chopper."

"You paid him back, brother. A few times over."

Chase crossed his arms. "Not nearly enough."

Foster coughed. "What about that time in Kandahar? Or that screwed up mission outside Caracas? Hell, that dive bar in Tennessee." He whistled. "Now *that* was above and beyond."

"They don't count when I let him down the one time he really needed me."

"Chase." Kash leaned back, giving Nyx a scratch. "You did everything you could that night short of magically changing places. You saved the three of us and Nyx. Stop beating yourself up."

Chase pushed back his chair as he raked a hand through his hair. "Remind me not to fall in love, because the three of you have gotten disturbingly Zen since you shacked up. It's annoying."

Foster laughed. "Too late, buddy."

Chase arched a brow. "Are you smoking something? Because the last time I checked, I was the only one still sane."

"Except where you're already hopelessly in love with Greer."

Chase groaned inwardly. He never should have steered the conversation in this direction. Given his buddies ammunition to fuel the fire. Obviously, the strain of walking that tightrope around Greer had finally gotten to him, and he'd snapped. Had started blurting out the first words that popped into his head instead of weighing them out, first. Looking for any opening his asshole teammates would take to bring Greer up. "Can we not do this?"

Foster arched a brow in challenge. "What's wrong? Afraid Rhett's gonna open his eyes and agree? Because even he knows how far gone you are."

Chase held up his hands in defense. "We're friends. Until she decides she wants more than that, it's a moot point."

Zain scoffed. "Have you even tried asking her out? Or are you just making assumptions because she hasn't shown up on your doorstep wearing only a smile."

Chase chuckled. "We both know she'd never go anywhere without her service weapon and her badge but nice visual."

Kash kicked Chase's boot, again. "What Zain means is that maybe she's not the problem."

Chase groaned, allowed his head to tilt back. Damn, he was tired. Exhausted, and not just from the long shifts and physical work. Or walking into the lodge three times a week, hoping for some glimmer of hope only to leave dejected. Disillusioned. This thing with Greer...

It had drained him to the point he had trouble remembering his own name most days, all his energy spent on holding his emotions in check. Ensuring they didn't spill out along with three words that looped endlessly through his head.

That somewhere over the past several months, he'd fallen hopelessly in love with her, just like Foster had claimed.

That insanity seemed like his only viable option.

"Chase." Foster waited until Chase forced himself to meet his gaze. "All we're suggesting is that maybe it's time to tell her how you feel. It's obvious she has feelings for you. Maybe you're both just waiting for the other to make the first move."

"She'd need to stand still long enough for me to get it out, which is damn near impossible." Chase shook his head. "She's running on empty and sooner or later, it's gonna bite her in the ass. Which isn't why we came here." He turned back to Rhett. "Unless you have something you want to add, buddy?"

He blew out a rough breath. "That's what I—"

A squeeze.

Not much. More of a flutter, really, than an actual grasp, but Chase snapped his gaze to the bed — leaned in close.

"Rhett?" Chase studied his face, searching for a hint of a reaction. "Brother, do that, again."

His buddies gathered close, breath held. Gazes focused on Rhett's face. Silence filled the room, just that numbing beep in the background, endlessly marking out time. Making Chase's left eye twitch until Rhett inhaled. Not all soft and slow like he'd been doing. This was raspy. Forceful, as if he needed more air to get everything working. He blinked a few times, his fingers closing around Chase's before he slivered open his eyes — stared up at them.

"Zain. Get the doctor." Chase inched closer, holding Rhett's gaze. "Easy, brother. You've had a hard go of it."

Rhett blinked, looking as if he'd passed out before he pried his eyelids open, again, shifting his gaze to Foster and Kash before sliding it back to Chase. Giving him a hint of a smile. "Hooyah."

Chase whooped. "Hell, yeah. I knew you were faking."

He moved so Kash could sneak in closer, put his palm over Rhett's dog tags. Kash's way of telling Rhett they were there — hadn't given up on him.

Chase squeezed Rhett's hand again. "Hold tight. The doctor's on his way."

Zain appeared a moment later, Dr. Tremblay in tow. The man stepped to the opposite side, flashing a small beam in Rhett's eyes as he studied the monitors.

He nodded. "Can you hear us, Mr. Oliver?"

Rhett grunted, fading for a few seconds before nodding. Mumbling a raw, "Yeah."

"Good." Tremblay grabbed his hand. "Can you squeeze my fingers?"

Rhett responded, then faded, eyes once again drifting shut.

Tremblay did a few more tests before straightening. "I'll be damned. Guess those bits of activity we saw weren't erroneous, after all. Though…" He pinned all of them with a firm stare. "This is just the first step, albeit a great one. But no one should be celebrating, just yet. Your teammate has a long way to go before he's out of the woods. However, I'm cautiously optimistic he might just beat the odds."

Foster grinned. "Oh, he'll beat them. Bastard never did know when to quit."

Tremblay laughed. "Well, he's going to need his rest. I realize you probably want to camp out and wait for another moment of consciousness, but he really needs to save his strength." The doctor walked to the door. "Go home. Get some rest and come back tomorrow. I'm betting you can rouse him, again. We'll call if anything changes or he comes fully out of it. You have my word."

Foster waited until the man left. "Does he seriously expect us to leave when we've been waiting a year for a sign Rhett's coming back?"

Chase sighed. "I know, but he's right. I can only imagine the toll it takes trying to shake all this loose. We should let him rest — grill the shit out of him tomorrow."

"It's your compassion that makes you such a great medic, buddy."

"I know."

Zain patted Rhett's thigh, then followed the others out, leaving Chase alone with the man.

Chase leaned over Rhett, glancing toward the door when a flash of movement caught his eye. A shadow played along the hallway, the silhouette of a man lingering across from the door for a few moments before he walked in front, hoodie covering most of his face, black boots peeking out from beneath a pair of tan cargo pants. Chase caught a glimpse of skin — what could be scars or burns — before the guy moved out of view, his footsteps tapping down the hallway. Steady. Confident.

Chase focused back on Rhett. "I knew you could

hear me. So, all that shit I confessed about Greer over the past few weeks is top secret. No spilling to the guys, you hear?"

Rhett managed to drag himself back for a moment — give Chase what looked like a wink. "Whiskey."

"You sly bastard. Still blackmailing us with Glenfiddich, huh? Fine. I'll bring you a bottle, but you'd better keep your end of the bargain."

Chase turned when Rhett's hand closed over his, drawing his focus back to his face.

Rhett slivered his eyes open — managed a sloppy smile. "We're… even."

"Tell me that again tomorrow, and maybe I'll believe it." He squeezed Rhett's hand one last time. "Damn, we've missed you, brother. It's great to have you back, so, no more laying on your ass. We've got a lot to catch up on."

He waited until Rhett drifted off, then headed for the door, staring down the hallway where that guy had disappeared. While he couldn't place it, something felt off. The way the man had lingered just out of sight, then rushed past with his face hidden as if he didn't want anyone to notice him. The echo of his footsteps along the corridor, the weight and pace seemed vaguely familiar. Nothing Chase could really pinpoint, but it had Chase's protective instincts on high alert.

He sighed and pushed the odd thoughts aside. Rhett was back. That's all that mattered, and Chase would ensure he didn't let his buddy down, again. He'd erase any red still hiding in his ledger, whether Rhett thought they were even or not.

Chase smiled to himself, the pressure on his chest finally lifting as he jogged to catch up to Foster and the others as they talked to the staff at the nursing station. If this wasn't a damn cosmic sign, then nothing was. Which meant, Chase was done waiting. Time to man up and make a move. Have that chat with Greer he'd been avoiding for the past month. How things had changed since she'd helped out Saylor a few weeks back. He just wasn't sure if the events had forced her to make a decision — one that might not go in his favor — or if she was drowning like him.

Either way, he'd take the leap of faith, tonight. See which side of the line he landed. Rhett wasn't the only one who needed to jump back into the land of the living. And it was high time Chase took his own advice.

CHAPTER TWO

She could do this.

It was just dinner. Another gathering with friends. The same setup she'd been part of for the past several months. All she needed to do was breathe.

Nothing fancy, just in, hold, out. Ignoring the nauseating lemon scent clinging to every surface. How one of the toilets behind the stall doors kept running, the constant trickling sound making her left eye twitch. Not as bad as how that damn sonar weapon had rattled her brains a few weeks ago, the tone still lingering in the back of her mind. Driving her to the brink without warning. But it seemed everything set her off these days.

Sheriff Greer Hudson stared at her reflection in the bathroom mirror. Dark circles rimmed her eyes, the lines around her mouth deeper than she remembered. A couple butterfly bandages secured a cut across her left temple, only a hint of the bruising bleeding through the thick foundation she'd dabbed over top. Fallout from an early morning encounter with a couple drunken, rowdy frat boys.

She smirked. They were still sweating it out in one of the cells.

But it wasn't the obvious exhaustion paling her skin that worried her. More the gleam in her eyes that broadcast how damn lovesick she was over one, irritatingly handsome medic. While she doubted his teammates would notice — look beyond the smudges and tape — *he* would.

Chase Remington.

Ex-pararescue turned SAR tech, and the man slowly driving her insane.

She groaned, splashing another handful of water on her face, careful not to remove more of the concealer. She'd arrived at the café ten minutes ago and had detoured into the washroom to freshen up. Decompress after another eighteen-hour shift. Until she'd caught a glimpse of herself in the mirror.

Seeing her feelings for him staring back at her had stopped her cold, and she'd been backpedaling ever since.

The handle on the old wooden door rattled, the hinges creaking in protest as the door swung inward, clattering against a metal stop. Mackenzie Parker swept into the two-stall bathroom, her long brown hair twisted up into a messy bun. She smiled when their gazes clashed, glancing over her shoulder before helping those rusty hinges close.

Mac ambled over to the counter, dabbing at the corner of her mouth. "Everything okay? You look... concerned."

Greer turned and braced her ass against the wall. "Are you checking up on me?"

Mac eyed her in the mirror.

Greer sighed. "Shit, you are."

"I saw you stroll in, then head in here, and..."

"And what? Did I reach some magical time limit that had you questioning my well-being?"

"It's been ten minutes. You never take more than five, tops. And that's only when you have to wash off blood or something from an altercation." Mac waved at the strips on Greer's temple. "And based on the bruising you're trying to hide, that's at least twelve hours old, so..."

"I think you missed your calling. You should have been a detective."

"Please, those few ground encounters I had with Striker were enough to remind me why I prefer to attack a situation from the sky. Facing tangos on the ground is creepy."

Greer laughed. "You're not wrong."

Mac turned, leaned her hip against the counter. A small bump pressed against her hoodie, her pregnancy just starting to show. "I'm not wrong about something bothering you, either."

Greer plastered on a fake smile. "I'm fine, just tired."

"I don't doubt the tired, but you're not fine. In fact, you've been off since that insane mission on the salvage ship with Zain, Saylor and Chase."

Greer's lips quirked as Chase's name echoed through the small room, rattling around in her head like that damn sonar weapon had. Lingering in the background like a benediction. She fisted her hands, searched for something to say, but nothing fit.

Mac sighed. "If you need to talk about Chase, but you're afraid what you have to say is going to hurt him—"

"He stepped in front of a bullet."

The words rushed out in a heated mess, jumbling together until Greer wasn't sure if she'd gotten more than just *bullet* out.

She huffed. "Three, actually. Meant for me. And he would have staggered to his feet and taken more if I hadn't dragged him into a storage room a second before that damn sonar went off. Dropped us both." She shook her head. "I know that's what he does. What they all do, but…"

How did she say that one selfless act had changed her without admitting she was floundering? That she couldn't look at him without hearing the pop of gunfire. Seeing him jerk from the hits, yet holding his ground.

That she couldn't picture any other man ever standing up for her the way he had.

Mac slipped her hands over Greer's. "Is that a bad thing?"

"It's insane."

"That's kind of the team's default position, and you're part of it. There's nothing any of them wouldn't do, but Chase…" Mac squeezed. "He's been all-in from the start."

Greer bowed her head in defeat, aware she needed to tell someone the truth before it spilled free over coffee. "I'm crazy about him."

Mac laughed. "You say that like we didn't already know."

"It's more than that, I..." Greer worried her bottom lip, all the words just tumbling free. "Do you think it's possible to fall in love without even kissing? Going on a date?"

"Pretty sure Foster had me hooked before he shoved me against his front door."

Greer looked up at her. "I don't know what to do. It's getting to the point I can't focus when he's around. Can barely breathe. But I don't know how..."

Mac let go of her hands, inched closer. "Whatever's holding you back, I promise it isn't the deal breaker you've concocted in your head. We all have demons — Chase included."

"I just can't be wrong, again. Not like my last few assignments with the bureau. With Thompson."

"First, Thompson's not on you. In fact, if you hadn't been willing to dig deeper, despite knowing he'd have your badge if he found out, we'd still be under his rule. Still have him running his drugs through town." Mac inched closer. "But more importantly, I don't think you're afraid of being wrong about Chase. I think you're afraid of being right."

"You read that in a fortune cookie?"

Mac merely smiled, then walked over to the door. "C'mon. Before Foster sends out a search and rescue team."

Greer sighed, took one last glance in the mirror, then headed out, following Mac over to the table. Chase and his teammates looked up, the lively conversation cutting off as the two of them approached the table.

Foster stood, holding out Mac's chair. "I thought I'd have to send Jordan in to do a recon. Find out if you'd somehow gotten trapped."

Mac rolled her eyes. "Men. Besides, look who I found."

Chase copied Foster's approach, grabbing the empty chair beside him and offering it to Greer. "Your shift should've ended an hour ago. You need to take better care of yourself." He leaned in as he helped her scoot the seat forward. "You look exhausted."

Greer smiled. "Aren't you the charmer."

"If you don't want me to call you out, then don't start working before five."

She arched a brow. "Are you stalking me?"

"Will you arrest me if I say yes?"

"Might give me an excuse to use my handcuffs."

Chase coughed, glanced at his buddies. "We got called in early, and we pass your office. You were already there."

Greer ignored the smug smiles staring back at her. "It's the start of Hell Week. Things should settle down once it's over."

Kash frowned, popping a fry in his mouth. "I thought all that fraternity hazing crap was outlawed?"

Greer glanced at Chase when he shoved some nachos her way. "Most universities and colleges claim they've cracked down on it, and it tends to be more stupid pranks than anything, but the fraternities really just shifted the stunts to smaller communities where they think local law won't care."

Zain motioned to her head. "Is that how you got that cut?"

"Nothing I couldn't handle."

Chase muttered something under his breath, shaking his head as the conversation drifted to safer topics, mainly their buddy Rhett Oliver. How he'd roused for the first time in a year. A sign they hoped meant he was finally rejoining the living.

Greer settled in, their combined buzz more than a bit infectious. The way they laughed, teasing each other and looking as if a weight had been lifted, drew her in. And just like that, all her reasons for keeping Chase at arm's length slowly crumbled amidst the press of his thigh against hers. The way he smiled whenever she risked a glance. Her heart rate had already tripled when Saylor leaned back in her chair.

She took a sip of pop. "Zain says you've got a new deputy starting tomorrow. Some guy they knew back in the service."

Greer nodded. "Elijah James. He did a few years as an Army Ranger until an injury pulled him from the field. He shifted to military police, then decided to go civilian. And the entire team swears the guy's solid—"

Zain groaned. "Trust me. Eli's solid. Guy was a beast until that IED pulverized his leg. He's lucky he didn't lose it."

Kash shifted forward as he rested his elbows on the table. "And he worked like hell to get most of the mobility back." He glanced at Chase. "Chase wouldn't let us recommend anyone we wouldn't trust with our lives let alone yours, right buddy?"

Chase sighed. "Eli's good people. We all did a number of joint task forces with the guy." He leaned in close to Greer, sucking out all the available oxygen with his smile. The way his gaze swept the length of her. "And yeah, I wouldn't let anyone back you up I wouldn't go into battle with. Period."

Greer swallowed, coughing when it didn't quite go down right. "Good to know. Besides, it's painfully evident my resources are already spread too thin across the county."

Saylor arched a brow. "Does this mean you might actually take a day off?"

"Let's not get too crazy, just yet." Greer grinned at Chase. "But I'm hopeful. I know I've been a bit *resistant* to giving up complete control, but I think it's time."

Chase pursed his lips, looking as if he wanted to add something before palming the table and standing. "Looks like my wallet slipped out on the drive over from the lodge." He nudged Greer. "You've got a Maglite, right?"

Greer arched a brow. "As do you."

Zain laughed. "Ask Chase what happened to his light earlier today?"

Chase flipped the man off. "Yeah, yeah, I didn't clip it in all the way, and it flew out of the chopper after that rescue." He looked at her, again. "Give me a hand?"

She glanced around the table, his teammate's

expectant gazes spiking her heart rate — from already elevated to marathon-level effort in a flash. Especially with the way he stared at her, his hazel eyes edging more toward green than usual. A slight flush on his cheeks. As if he wasn't quite as calm as he appeared, either.

She scraped back the chair. "If this means you're treating for dessert, then I'm all-in."

He froze for a second, then waved toward the entrance. "I think that's a given."

His hand landed on the small of her back as she headed for the door, the heat from his palm nearly dropping her to her knees. This was what she'd tried explaining to Mackenzie. The sheer effort it took Greer to keep her feet moving instead of turning and dragging his mouth to hers. Finally discovering if he tasted half as good as she'd imagined.

If he'd blow all her expectations out of the water the second his lips touched hers.

The chilly evening cooled some of the heat, the hint of rain lingering in the air accompanied by thick fog cloaking the landscape. Chase angled her over to his truck, rounding the grill to the driver's side. The lock clicked open, the hinges creaking as he cracked the door open, heavy shadows covering the interior.

Greer grabbed the light from her belt, switched it on, then danced the beam around the seat and down the sides. She glanced at him over her shoulder, gesturing toward the vehicle. "Are you sure your wallet fell out in here?"

Chase patted down his jacket, smiling at her as he

removed the leather billfold from his inside pocket. "My bad. Guess I forgot to put it in my back pocket."

"You forgot? That's what you're going with?"

He moved, snugging her against the truck as he stepped in front, effectively trapping her between him and his Chevy. He braced one hand on the roof, the other on the door frame as he leaned in, his face level with hers. "We need to talk."

Four words, the weight of them crashing through the last of her barriers. Whether it was the prospect of him admitting his feelings or confessing he was done waiting, she wasn't sure. Only that it was now, or never.

"We could…" She reached up and fisted his shirt, dragging him closer. "Or you could just kiss me. Your choice."

He froze, breath held, the pulse at the base of his neck fluttering wildly beneath his skin before his eyes widened, and he closed the distance. He stopped with his mouth barely touching hers as if waiting for some kind of sign. Maybe to see if she'd change her mind. Instead, she tugged him that last half an inch.

Explosive.

No other way to describe the instant punch of heat through her veins. How the world spun for a moment, everything speeding around her until it stopped. Anchored by the way he stepped into her, crushed her against the truck as he ate at her mouth, pausing just long enough for them to catch a breath before he returned. Harder. Tilting her head back as he deepened the kiss. Made everything around them disappear.

Cars passed in the distance, the eerie call of the

lighthouse echoing through town, as they stood there, completely entwined. He dipped lower, kissing his way down her neck, when a throat cleared beside them, the air swirling as someone settled off to their left.

Chase clenched his jaw as he eased back, closing his eyes before blowing out a harsh breath. He gave her a smile, then tore his gaze away. Looking less than amused. "Problem?"

Greer managed to shift her focus, cringing at Foster as the man shook his head, smiling as if he'd expected to find them like this.

He shoved his hands in his pockets. "Just wanted to make sure you hadn't gotten waylaid."

Chase huffed. "It's only been a couple minutes, *buddy*."

"Try over ten. Edging on twenty."

Chase sighed. "As you can see, we're fine."

"Better than fine." He chuckled. "We already settled up. Maybe you can grab Greer some dessert on the way home." He glanced behind them, footsteps tapping on the pavement. "We're heading back to the house for a cautiously optimistic mini celebration over Rhett's return to the living. You're obviously welcome to join us, though, I suspect you two might have other plans."

Kash stopped behind them, one arm wrapped around Jordan's waist, Nyx at his side, as Chase shifted, giving Greer enough room to breathe. "Find your wallet?"

Chase rolled his shoulders. "Are you all going to be asses for the rest of the night?"

Kash laughed. "No more than usual."

"Right. And I think—"

A blast of static drowned him out, Greer's radio crackling to life on her belt.

"Sheriff? You copy?"

Greer groaned, drooping her head forward as she sucked in a breath, then grabbed the unit. She tamped down the punch of disappointment and keyed up the mic. "Loud and clear. What's up, Shirley?"

"Looks like we've got another round of hazing. I just got an anonymous report of people prowling around that old psychiatric hospital off Cliffside. Our Good Samaritan was worried someone might be hurt. Fool kids probably got caught up on some barbed wire or broken glass. I'd send Bodie, but he's already dealing with another disturbance over at the old ranger station, and you asked me not to call Jordan after hours unless it's life or death."

Greer ignored Jordan's huff. "You made the right call. I'll go have a chat with our trespassers. Radio and cell service is pretty spotty up there, but I'll check back in once I've cleared the building."

"Roger." Shirley paused, another hiss sounding over the speaker. "You'd better call me back within an hour or I'm sending in Raven's Watch. And it'll be Foster's team so, don't think they won't storm the place."

"Glad you're not one to overreact." She shoved the radio back on the clip and clenched her hands, cursing under her breath before facing the others, her heart still tapping wildly in her chest, the ground still slightly off-kilter. "Looks like I'm going to have to pass on the celebration for now."

Jordan crossed her arms. "This is crazy. I can go. You've already worked a double—"

"Oh no. We have an agreement. I won't make you ride a desk until you're ready, and you don't work overtime while you're making a whole new human."

Jordan grunted, then turned, walking off a way, back rigid. Hands fisted at her side.

Kash sighed. "She's still adjusting to not being in the fray every other second."

Chase tsked, then tossed Kash his keys. "Hold those for a moment."

Greer frowned as Chase headed to the rear of his truck, rummaging around in the flatbed before walking back, tactical vest strapped around his torso with enough weapons he could take on a small invasion. He had his medic bag slung over one shoulder, the sheer size of it making her back ache. How he moved like a wraith with all that weight still amazed her.

She hitched out one hip. "What's all this?"

Chase shrugged. "I can't have your back without proper gear. You've got a vest in your Bronco, right? Or do I need to bring my spare?"

"Who said anything about needing backup?"

He pointed at her radio. "You heard Shirley. Possible injuries, which translates into you needing a medic. Fortunately, I'm a registered first responder, so no worries about legalities."

"And if bullets start flying?"

"Then, you're lucky I'm familiar with both ends of a rifle."

Another blast of heat punched through her gut. The

guy was going to be the reason she ended up in a straightjacket. "While I appreciate the gesture and would love the company, you've already worked overtime, too. You really don't have to—"

"Yeah. I do." He moved in close, again, quickening her pulse. Making all those butterflies flutter to life, again. "Don't take this wrong, but you really do look exhausted. And I know today's not your first double shift. Having Shirley on standby's a good safety measure. Taking a partner… Even better."

She arched a brow, all that heat simmering beneath her skin, threatening to spontaneously combust at any given moment. "Are you going to insist on driving, too?"

"We can split it." Chase motioned to his truck as he looked at Kash. "Go easy on the clutch."

Kash scrunched up his face. "When don't I?" He whistled, and Nyx jumped into the cab. "We expect you both at the house in an hour, or we'll come looking whether Shirley calls us or not."

Chase offered her his hand, smiling when she slid her palm over his as they walked to her SUV. Foster slowed as he drove past, motioning for Chase to call him before pulling onto the road, then turning right at the lights.

She unlocked her vehicle, grinning when Chase circled around to the passenger side. He tossed his bag in the back, jumped in and buckled up without saying a word. She joined him, bringing the area up on her nav. "You know it's likely just more frat kids, right?"

"Probably. Doesn't mean you don't need someone to watch your six."

He leaned over, claimed her mouth in a kiss that she swore lit her hair on fire. Had tiny arcs of electricity jumping from her skin to his. He brushed his thumb across her lips. "Just a reminder that we're not close to finishing our conversation. Now, drive. Before I forget about duty and spend the next hour making up for lost time."

CHAPTER THREE

Chase sat in Greer's Bronco, watching the scenery blur past as she headed north out of town. The main square gave way to larger farms, everything eventually turning into endless forest on one side, the ragged coastline on the other. The rising moon set off the fog in a warm glow, a hint of it painting the tops of the waves.

He glanced over at Greer, her face occasionally lit by the odd streetlight. There weren't many, the majority of the road shrouded in darkness, the headlights cutting twin beams through the misty shadows. But he enjoyed the way the sparse lamplight highlighted the hint of blush on her cheeks. The strands of cooper in her auburn hair that practically glowed with each passing flash.

Greer obviously felt him staring because she grinned as she slid him a quick side eye. "Everything okay?"

He smiled as he reached out and brushed some strands off her shoulder. The ones that had pulled free from her clip when he'd stabbed his fingers through her hair as he'd ravaged her mouth. "Just enjoying the view."

She snorted, the adorable sound going straight to his groin. "I'm glad you're not making this awkward."

"I've been waiting several months to kiss you. If anything's awkward, it's because I can't help but wonder what changed." He held up one hand. "Full disclosure, I was going to put it all on the line tonight until you turned the tables on me. Nice, by the way."

"It's not as if I planned that to happen."

"I'm not complaining."

She sighed, the wisps around her face fluttering. "I know I've been... *resistant*. Standoffish, I guess. But it's not because I haven't wanted to kiss you all this time, either. It's just..." She blew out an exasperated breath. "Between some shit that went down with the bureau and freaking Thompson turning out to be a drug runner, I guess I've been questioning my ability to read people. Not that you've been anything but transparent and impressive since we met, it's just..."

He reached up and tucked that hair behind her ear. "You weren't sure."

Another sigh, only it sounded different. Heavier, maybe. As if this one held more weight. "I knew you were different from the start. That this had the potential to be... more. And I guess I wasn't sure if I was ready for that." She gestured between them. "For all of this."

"You know we can take it as slow as you need, right? That I'd never push you."

"I think the fact you've waited months for me to get my head out of my ass is proof of that. And it's not you I didn't trust."

She brushed some stray hairs off her forehead, turning onto a long winding road, a massive silhouette looming at the top of the cliff. The building emerged out of the night as she pulled up to the chain link fence surrounding it, the gate noticeably shoved open.

Her Bronco lit up the front of the abandoned facility, highlighting broken windows and vine-covered walls. It looked like the setting for a low-budget slasher flick. All it needed was mood lighting and eerie music. But the ominous vibe was far too real.

She shoved her vehicle into first and yanked on the parking brake before spinning to face him. "Real talk time."

She took a breath, and Chase knew everything was about to change. "I'm crazy about you. Have been for months. I just have a really crappy track record with relationships and this..." She motioned between them, again. "This is unlike anything I've ever felt. You..."

All those doubts swirling in his head eased, the truth shining in her eyes. In the nervous way she darted her tongue out to wet her lips.

She pushed out another rough breath. "I just can't fight this, anymore. Not without losing my damn mind. You get close, and I can't breathe, can't think, I—"

He kissed her. No hesitation, no waiting to see if she really wanted it, just his hand sliding across her cheek to the back of her head as he leaned in — claimed her mouth. And damn if it wasn't better than before. Hotter.

Deeper. Her confession shattering the last of the walls he'd been trying to scale.

He didn't drag it out too long, aware this wasn't the time or the place to get completely lost in her mouth. To let their guard down and finally act on all the heat they'd been building between them. But enough she knew, without him saying a word, that he was just as invested — just as far gone as she was.

Greer closed her eyes as he rested his forehead on hers, the intimacy of the moment humbling him. "I knew you were trouble the moment I met you."

He chuckled. "It's not like you're the only one who's stumbling here. But I think you know that I haven't been hanging around all this time hoping for a quick fling." He cupped her chin in his palm. "I'm crazy about you, too. Well past crazy, actually. So, stop worrying if I'm suddenly going to grow another head or worse, change my mind that you're not the most incredible person I've ever met, and enjoy the ride. Because I have a feeling it's going to be one hell of a rollercoaster. You ready?"

She stared at him for a while, as if she wasn't quite sure of the answer, then nodded. He opened the door and stepped out, grabbing his medic bag from the back while Greer rounded her Bronco and retrieved her vest.

She shook her head as she secured the straps. "Not sure this is ballistic vest worthy, but I'd hate for things to go sideways and you have that to hold over me."

"Right, because gloating would be my biggest concern if you got hit."

"Just don't step in front of any bullets, this time. I'm still reeling from the last three."

Chase hooked her arm when she went to dart past him. "I'm always going to step in front. You know that, right? I'd do it for strangers. For you…"

He rolled his shoulders, pushing down all those protective instincts. Reminding himself how skilled she was. That she'd been in the bureau for a dozen years before coming here. And he bet his ass she hadn't sat behind a desk.

Greer sighed. "As long as you acknowledge that I'm entitled to do the same damn thing."

"You're trying to give me an aneurism, aren't you?" He moved in beside her as they slipped through the gate and headed for the main door. "You know, in all the time we've known each other, you've never mentioned what you used to do for the bureau."

She tensed, the muscle in her jaw jumping a few times before she blew out a harsh breath, as if she wasn't sure if she wanted to tell him. Hell, maybe if she could tell him. "I started in counterintelligence. Worked a number of fugitive recovery task forces to gain more tactical experience, until one went…"

She drifted off for a moment — what was obviously a story she wasn't quite willing to share yet — then glanced at him, her green eyes slightly shadowed, what looked like a world of weight on her shoulders. "I shifted to counterterrorism focusing on behavior analysis of extremist groups. Spent most of my time in various JSOC units, a lot of that in the field."

Chase stopped, staring at her when she turned to look back at him. "Christ."

"What did you think I did?"

"I don't know, but that…" He whistled. "Maybe I *should* let you jump in front, next time."

She rolled her eyes, then jogged up the short set of stairs to the main entrance. The glass on the doors had holes punched through them, spiderweb cracks running the length of the panes. A thick chain hung off one handle, a broken lock kicked to the side.

Greer reached for the right side, then froze. Hand almost touching the chrome handle, gaze focused on the matching silver panel above it. "Chase."

He moved in beside her, his senses kicking into overdrive at the bloody print smeared across the surface, the marks trailing toward the edge. "Still think this is frat kids?"

She removed her weapon, holding her flashlight beneath it in her other hand as she entered the abandoned building, the door creaking shut behind them. Chase stayed at her side, gun at the ready, constantly scanning every corner, every recess. Memories scratched at the back of his mind, images of missions gone wrong. That he couldn't afford to miss anything with Greer's life potentially in the balance.

Scraps of garbage littered the floor, years' worth of dust and grime smeared across windows and walls. Thread-worn furniture emerged in the circular beams, like soldiers standing watch over the resident ghosts. Old books filled a few shelves, the air thick with decades of decay.

They moved down the hallway, clearing each room before heading to the next. Branching corridors snaked out in every direction, the hallways bleeding into black.

A scuff.

Not much. More like a hint of a step. How his footsteps sounded. Like someone accustomed to moving silently. Someone trained.

Greer obviously heard it too, because she picked up her pace, muscles primed, ready to bolt at a moment's notice. They moved in unison, narrowing in on the sound when the hairs on the back of Chase's neck prickled. An eerie déjà vu playing in the back of his mind.

He stuck out his arm, stopping Greer as they reached a junction. Something about the way the room opened up on one side while the hallway continued into darkness had him on edge. As if he'd already lived this scenario and knew it ended poorly. He crowded her over to one side, motioning for her to wait as he inched forward, gaze focused on the shadows at the end of the corridor.

A tread.

Not even as loud as that scuff. A whisper of sound that barely reached him. What could be his heightened senses playing tricks on him. The building simply settling. He held firm, feeling the way the air moved, how the shadows played in the beam when a boot shifted into view.

Black.

Battle worn.

He reacted. Turned, grabbed Greer and took her to

the ground a heartbeat before three sharp pops shattered the silence, slicing through the wall above their heads, raining bits of plaster over them.

Chase rolled, Greer firing off a few cover rounds until he got them clear of any obvious sightline before springing up, backs pressed into the wall, weapons raised at their shoulders. He inched forward, ready to dive out, when more bullets filled the hallway.

Greer tapped his shoulder, nodding toward the far side. She mouthed the countdown, slipping out when she reached one — going through half her mag while Chase dove across the open space, getting off a couple shots before the asshole returned fire. Bullets punched through the plaster, casings clattering to the floor in the background, the constant rattling sound sparking more memories. All the missions that had gone sideways — brothers he'd lost in the fallout.

Greer waited for a lull, then popped out, again, sliding back when she needed to reload. Chase took point, listening for any indication the bastard was heading their way — thought he could flank them — when a canister skipped down the corridor, bouncing past them, then spinning to a halt by the wall.

Chase lunged across the opening, catching a round in his vest before he tackled Greer — covered her head as he braced for impact. Everything froze, that eerie calm choking out all the air, before the grenade exploded, filling the space with sound and smoke — the kind of ear-piercing shrill that made the room spin. Had everything shifting left and right.

The voice inside Chase's head had him fighting

through the pain, rolling partway off her as he covered their six. His Sig shaking in his hands, the smoke blurring in and out of focus as his stomach threatened to heave. He blinked, nearly tumbling onto his ass, but he maintained his vigil, waiting for some asshole to materialize out of the white cloud.

Greer groaned beneath him, then gave him a light shove, stumbling to her feet when he jumped off. She tripped against the wall, staggering with him as he backed them up to the next corridor. Scanning it with his flashlight before turning and focusing on the junction.

He counted the time in his head, looking for a swirl or shift — something that gave their tango away. Constantly checking that adjoining hallway, when Greer inhaled, tossed him sideways as she twisted and fired toward the entrance. He took a couple stumbling steps, the flash bang still messing with his equilibrium before regaining his balance as heavy taps raced down the corridor.

One step, and he was zeroed in. Had that asshole's silhouette in his sights, Greer watching his six. He hauled ass down the hallway, bouncing off the wall a few times when the floor tilted, but he kept running, slowing enough to clear those other corridors — sneak a quick glance in any open room — as they raced through the building, following the guy through one branching wing after another.

A lone door loomed in the distance, dull moonlight brightening that one panel of glass. The guy's silhouette appeared against the backlight as he hit the door at a full sprint, disappearing into the fog as the heavy door inched closed behind him.

Chase stopped at the exit, grabbing the handle as he nodded to Greer. She took a breath, then swept out, covering every angle as he stepped behind her, ready to tackle her, again, if he saw so much as a hint of a weapon directed their way. A dark figure shifted in and out of view amidst the fog a hundred meters off, heading toward the fence.

The bastard didn't even pause, just vaulted over the barrier before continuing on with the kind of easy precision Chase had only ever witnessed in the military. Disappearing into the mist — on what Chase assumed was a path leading into the thick forest bordering the property.

Greer reined him in as they hit the fence line, shaking her head when they reached the spot where the asshole had vanished. "This place butts up against a state park. Nothing but forest and rugged coastline for miles. I'm not saying you couldn't track him. In fact, I know you could. Would probably have to slow down so I could keep up, but I'm more concerned about that blood. If we interrupted something, and he left someone behind because that…" She shook her head. "That sounded like an AK-47, and who the hell packs flash bangs?"

"No one who hasn't trained with them."

Chase stared at the path, something about the way the guy had moved nagging at him. A limp or maybe a slight familiarity. Something that settled hard in his gut. Made Greer's words slither down his spine. A foreboding he hadn't sensed since a second before Stein and Adam's had opened fire inside the helicopter that fateful night.

He snagged her arm when she turned to double back, pain pulsing through his side where he'd caught that round. What he knew would be an impressive bruise by morning. "Before we go, are you okay?" He swept his gaze the length of her. "Did you get hit?"

"How could I with you as my human shield?" She glanced at his side. "And you're the one with a slug in their vest."

She took off, heading toward the building in long measured strides. Chase wasn't sure if she was pissed or impressed, but he could worry about that later. He hadn't been lying. He was protective by nature. Throwing her into the mix...

It blurred the lines. Reduced her safety to simply black and white. He either kept her safe or died trying.

He moved in behind her, scanning every direction, using all those years in the service to maintain a vigil. They closed in on the rear door, when a hint of a glow caught his attention. He snagged her arm, still scouring the grounds as he stepped in close. "You see that?"

She squinted, then inhaled. "Shit. It looks like that might be a flare or something."

"I've got a very bad feeling about this."

Greer angled toward the side of the building, sticking close to the wall and reducing any possible sightline. Chase's phone buzzed, an incoming text he'd worry about later. Though, knowing they might be able to get off an SOS if needed eased the jumpy feeling in his gut.

The fog took on an ominous red glow as they neared what looked like a courtyard, the flare appearing out of the mist in a burst of light. His phone buzzed, again, as boots ghosted into view — black, scuffs marking the toes.

Chase tapped her shoulder. "I know we both want to rush in, but after the AKs and the flash bangs, we'll take the extra few seconds and check for wires."

She nodded, circling the man propped against the wall, head slumped forward, hands resting in his lap. IV tubing wrapped under his arms, the ends spiked into the building's siding above his head. Reminiscent of a rescue harness. Blood stained a spot on the guy's chest, more oozing from a wound to his shoulder — bullet or maybe a knife — a few drops still dripping onto the cracked concrete. Leaving perfect dark circles against the weathered gray.

Chase's phone buzzed a third time, something about the urgency of it sent more shivers down his spine.

Greer crouched low, her radio crackling a few times as she skimmed her fingers along the man's legs and torso. "I can't check fully beneath him, but I don't see—"

More static, then a few broken words. *Foster... Rhett... missing...*

Chase froze, his gaze flying to the man's head. What looked like camo paint covering the swath of skin visible beneath hair and shadows. He rushed forward, sliding his medic bag off his shoulder as he went. He felt for a pulse. Thready. The guy's skin clammy. He took a breath, held it, as he tipped the man's head back, noting the familiar curve of his jaw. The shape of his eyes. The overwhelming sense of dread that clamped Chase's throat shut. Held him prisoner for one agonizing moment.

Greer released a harsh breath. "Chase?"

He clenched his jaw, then uttered the two words he knew would forever change him. "It's Rhett."

CHAPTER FOUR

One breath.

That was all Chase allowed himself to process the scene. To stare at Rhett's face, his heart lodged in his throat, his hands shaking from the cold slide of fear down his spine.

One defining breath.

Then, he moved, got Rhett onto his back, bandages and clotting powder tossed onto his legs. Chase took vitals, cursed, then ripped open Rhett's shirt.

He froze.

Stared at the number carved into Rhett's skin — forty-two. Deep. Precise. The edges too smooth to be unpracticed.

He glanced at Greer when she inhaled, then shoved it all down — went to work.

Pressure on the wounds.

Quick body scan for other injuries.

IV for fluids and meds.

Greer barked out orders over her radio and cell,

guarding his six. Allowing him to completely focus on pulling some kind of miracle out of his ass. A damn repeat of that night in the chopper, only this time, Chase could alter the outcome. Be the man Rhett needed him to be.

He got Rhett bandaged, then heaved him onto his shoulder. Greer didn't wait for instructions, just took off, clearing the way, dancing around him in an effort to block any possible attack as they raced for her Bronco. She had that wire gate shoved all the way open, her back seats collapsed forward with the tailgate and window wide open by the time he reached her. Jumping inside, he laid Rhett down, as Greer slammed the tailgate shut behind him.

A chime sounded as she hopped behind the wheel, then the engine growled as the SUV lurched backwards. Rocks and dirt pinged off the chassis as she spun the vehicle, punched the gas.

The tires screeched, a plume of smoke billowing out behind them as she swerved onto the winding road, taking the turns with laser precision. Far smoother than he thought possible as she continued talking into her radio.

Chase gave Rhett a firm shake. "Rhett! Brother, can you hear me?"

Nothing.

No blinking, no twitching. Chest barely moving.

Chase rubbed his knuckles along Rhett's sternum, counting it off in his head. He'd give it a good thirty seconds — the length some patients needed to respond.

Outliers, true, but he'd afford Rhett every chance to react.

Chase got to twenty-five when Rhett's eyelids fluttered, a fleeting glimpse of brown as the man stared up at him. "I've got you, just stay with me."

Rhett's mouth moved, what looked like Chase's name forming in silence, his hand fisting Chase's shirt before he drifted off, head lolling off to one side, that arm falling to the floor with a thud.

Chase checked his pulse, again. Weak. Slow. Pressure reading eighty over forty and dropping. "Damn it, I need more supplies. Blood. Monitors. A fucking defibrillator. I need the equipment in the chopper."

Greer spared him a quick glance. "Foster's on his way. I'll pull over wherever he can land."

He pushed down the surge of panic until everything burned into ice-cold determination. No emotions. No hint of the man beneath the medic. Just his gear and the experience of twenty years' worth of battles. Of bringing soldiers back from the brink. Carrying them for miles. Treating amidst skirmishes and incursions. Whatever it took. Whatever the means.

Greer hit the main road, then abruptly swerved to the side, a distinct whop whop whop sounding above the weight of Rhett's weak pulse. Dust and dried leaves swirled around the Bronco as the trees shook, the entire SUV rattling as Foster roared overhead, insanely low before flaring off the speed, squeezing the damn helicopter across the pavement, somehow planting the machine between towering pines and electrical lines.

Greer opened the back, shielded some of the

downwash swirling the fog as Chase heaved Rhett onto his shoulders — booked it for the chopper.

Kash, Nyx and Jordan jumped out, talking to Greer as Zain held open the doors. He gave Chase a boost, shutting the doors after Greer hopped in, staying close without crowding Chase. Zain grunted, what Chase assumed was the result of that bloody number glaring up at them, then settled.

Saylor sat on the far end, sleeve already rolled up. "I'm O neg. And before you ask, I'm not pregnant. Nothing to compromise his health. Promise."

"Give me a minute."

Chase grabbed leads and tubes, hooking up oxygen and monitors. Readying the defibrillator for the inevitable cardiac arrest he knew lingered. Waiting to strike. The scenario he feared would be the true beginning of the end as he fought to keep Rhett alive until they reached the hospital.

Chase swabbed Rhett's arm — readied a line before checking his heart rate. The man's jagged rhythm looking like a damn seismograph jumping across the screen.

"Shit. He's got bradycardia, runs of V-tach. He needs more than I can give him, Beckett."

The helicopter shook as Foster pushed the nose forward, gaining more speed. What Chase suspected bordered on mechanical damage. That razor-sharp line Foster often rode when a soldier's life was on the line.

And Rhett was far more than that.

Chase started the direct transfusion, setting a timer to prevent taking too much. Putting Saylor at risk, too.

A tone.

Steady.

Unforgiving.

"Damn it, no pulse. Starting compressions." Chase drove down hard on Rhett's sternum, hands locked, arms stiff. Hoping he didn't crack too many ribs in the process. "Zain, remove his mask and grab the bag. Every thirty, brother."

Chase rattled off the count, Zain following along. Repeating the procedure, that damn monotone sound mocking Chase in the background, only a hint of a wave registering through the sticky pads on Rhett's chest."

"Greer, grab the paddles for me."

He paused after she'd added some gel, had the paddles positioned in front of him.

"Charging to two hundred. Clear!"

The defibrillator paddles hummed, then discharged with a violent thump that jerked Rhett's body. The screen went black, then snapped back — still chaotic, the heart quivering uselessly.

Chase cursed. "Still V-fib. Charging to three hundred. Clear!"

More humming followed by another shock. Rhett jerked, again, the damn monitor still mocking Chase.

"Charging to four hundred. Clear!"

Nothing.

No P-waves. No QRS intervals.

"Pushing one milligram epi."

He plunged the syringe into the IV port. Waited, cursed the lack of response.

More compressions.

Another shock.

Still nothing.

Just that faint squiggly line. A dwindling glimmer of hope.

Chase restarted CPR, sweat beading his brow, arms cramping, but he kept pumping, alternating his focus between Rhett and that monitor — the increasing bloody patch on his shoulder. The gunshot wound Chase couldn't worry about with Rhett barely holding on. "Come on, Rhett. Don't fucking quit on me, now."

Minutes bled into each other, Foster talking over the radio. Readying the trauma team. As if their combined will might bend biology — reverse the damage. Chase stopped the transfusion, muttering a quick thanks — that Saylor needed to stay seated, keep pressure on the needle site and grab some food — shocking Rhett one last time.

The helicopter flared over the helipad, Foster plowing the damn thing on without jostling them. The exact opposite of what his aggressive approach suggested. The doors opened, a team gathered around the machine.

Chase kept up compressions, rattling off vitals and procedures, meds and methods, as they lifted the stretcher onto a gurney, then raced into the building, the large, double doors whooshing closed behind them. They headed for a trauma room, taking over Rhett's care once they had the gurney secured — doctors and nurses swarming the room.

Chase held firm, shaking his head when one of the

nurses asked him to leave. "No. Not until I know he's okay."

Foster's hand landed on his shoulder, the weight nearly taking Chase to his knees. Not comforting, like his best friend had done a thousand times before. This was different.

Resolute.

A finality Chase wasn't willing to accept.

Foster's fingers curled around his arm a moment later. "You've done all you can. We need to let them work."

Chase shook his head. "No. Not, yet, I can't—"

He swallowed, wanted to puke. He couldn't leave. Couldn't abandon Rhett with his life on the line. The damn monitor still calling out that eerie tone. What had been an annoying beep just a few hours ago.

Crushed beneath the truth that, despite everything — the blood, the meds, the damn race against time — they'd already lost him.

Foster sighed. "Chase."

His tone spoke volumes. No upbeat pep talk. How strong Rhett was. That he'd conquered worse. Just Chase's name slapping him in face. The final blow before it all collapsed.

Chase looked down at his hands. The blood. The sweat. A smear of gel across his knuckles. Remnants of a life's worth of training and skill reduced to elements he knew hadn't been enough.

He hadn't been enough.

He turned, walked out, each step harder than the last. Bleeding what was left of his sanity onto the floor.

Just another mess the hospital staff would mop up — wash away along with his soul.

Voices echoed in the background, people rushing past in a hazy blur as he planted his ass on a chair. The air settled heavily around him, the lights casting his shadow on the floor.

No comfort.

No more chances.

Just the voice in his head screaming out in anguish. The blood on his hands silently mocking him.

No other choice but to wait.

* * *

Greer stood in the hallway, everything blending into flashes of white coats and blood-soaked gauze. Voices shouted out vitals and procedures, instruments clattered onto trays. Someone clipped her in the shoulder, but she barely registered it, her gaze focused on Chase — ass in a chair, head bowed in defeat as he stared at his hands. Blood coated his skin, more soaked into his clothes.

She closed her eyes, forced it all down. How she'd been in this situation before. Been the one sitting in the hard, vinyl chair, waiting for someone in scrubs to crush her heart. Take away what she valued most.

That like her brother, Troy, Rhett wasn't going to make it.

She scrubbed a hand down her face, rerunning the sequence of events. The call, the attack… Had it all been a coincidence? Or a ruse to cover up some shadow ops agent tying up loose ends? Something Rhett had been involved in before that mission had left him in a coma. That the mere thought of Rhett regaining consciousness had started a chain of events designed to throw her off the scent. Have her chasing red herrings when Rhett's death had been the end goal.

Or was it the start of something bigger? Darker.

Forty-two.

It could mean anything. Just like the flare and the staging — how the tubing had been wrapped around him, holding him up. Elements that sent shivers down her spine.

She'd spent too many years getting into the heads of monsters. Learning how to conjure their dark thoughts. Planning for every contingency.

Now, she couldn't crush the voice in her head whispering that Rhett's survival had never been up for debate. Had been sealed before she and Chase had gotten out of her Bronco, and that nothing Chase tried — the heroic measures he'd executed in and out of the chopper — could have stopped it.

That they'd been given just enough hope to lure them in — make them believe they could alter reality.

She snagged one of the nurses standing on the periphery. "I need all of Mr. Oliver's clothes. Anything on him you removed, no matter how insignificant it seems. Bagged and ready once…"

She didn't finish, the nurse simply nodding in reply. Greer retreated into an empty room, grabbed her radio. "Bodie. Jordan. I need an update."

The radio crackled, the static blast scratching at her last nerve before Bodie sounded over the speaker.

"Scene's secure. Jordan's with Kash. They're scouting the area. Nyx caught a scent, but they're keeping the search contained. Jordan's checking in every fifteen minutes, so any chatter doesn't give away their position. I did as you asked and called Eli in early."

Bodie paused, voices sounded in the background. "The guy didn't hesitate. He's already here. Crime techs should arrive within the hour. We'll stay until they're done, though, with the entire building to scour, it'll likely take some time. I've got my buddies on standby to help spell peripheral security if needed."

Greer ran through the checklists in her head. Acutely aware neither of them had dared voice the word murder, yet. "I called Lieutenant Morgan up in Warrenton. He's got another CSI crew gearing up. They can process Raven's Lodge. See how our perp grabbed Rhett out of his damn bed without anyone noticing. Morgan knows to send you all the video evidence along with copies of the forensics. But we'll need the state police's help if we want to contain this quickly."

"Roger, that."

She pushed out a rough breath. "Just remember, nothing heroic until daybreak. This guy…"

"I saw the damage inside — what's easily several dozen casings. Kash knows the score." Bodie paused, the unspoken question hanging heavy in the air. "How's…"

Greer swallowed, closing her eyes against the strain. "Doesn't look good."

"Shit."

Silence stretched along the airways, the pressure of it stealing her breath.

Bodie sighed. "This doesn't feel isolated."

"The beginning rarely does."

"You're thinking there's more to come." He hadn't asked, and she simply blew out a rough breath.

"I really hope that's not the case, but…" She wasn't convinced, and they both knew it. "I want regular check-ins. I'll be there as soon as I can."

"Screw that."

"Excuse me?"

Bodie grunted. "Greer. You've been up for twenty-four hours straight. We've got this covered. Besides, you're needed there. Stay with Chase. Get a few hours of sleep if you can. I'll keep you updated, but you need to be focused, and you can't do that if you can't see straight."

"Have you always been this bossy?"

"Only when you're being incredibly stubborn. I know this is personal… For all of us. I won't let you down."

"Never thought you would. I'll check-in once we're out of here. Just, watch your damn six."

Greer signed off, giving herself one moment to suck in a breath — tamp everything down. Puzzle out how to be the sheriff and a friend at the same time.

How to pretend this wasn't another epic failure on her watch.

The fluorescent lights seemed overly bright as she slipped back into the hallway, blinking a few times until her vision adjusted. She turned, inhaled at the scene — a doctor standing with Chase and his teammates. Head bowed. Motioning with his hands. She didn't need to hear the conversation to know how it had ended.

The tight lips. The furrowed brows. The slashes of red across their cheeks a harsh contrast to the ashen hue of their skin. How Zain palmed the wall as if he wanted to punch his fist through it. It all spelled out the same conclusion…

Rhett Oliver hadn't made it.

CHAPTER FIVE

Silence.

The kind that lingered in the dark. Hovered in the empty spaces where hope died.

The kind only time lifted.

It followed them back to the hangar, no one uttering a word until they landed, and she corralled Zain and Saylor. Asked them to take one of Saylor's Zodiac's in the hope of scouring the coastline. Looking for any hint their perp had taken refuge in a cave or tunnel. Maybe waiting for daybreak to make a run for international waters.

While Greer doubted it — couldn't shake the feeling this was only the first in what she feared would be a parade of bodies — she needed to consider every option, every scenario. No stone unturned as the saying went. Maybe then, she'd be able to meet the gaze in her reflection.

Feel some semblance of redemption.

She sighed. Redemption had a funny way of staying

just out of reach. A brass ring that slipped away as soon as her fingers brushed the surface. But she'd try. Pray she'd eventually make peace with the ghosts.

Zain had muttered a simple, "Yeah," then taken off with Saylor, his fierce strides speaking louder than words. The unresolved anger. The restless energy. All mirrored in the loud taps. The way the truck shook as he gave her a boost, then slammed the door — peeled out.

Arriving at Foster's hadn't lifted the oppressive weight. The lights on his porch were duller than she remembered. Grayer. As if the night's events had sucked the life out of everything.

Mac squeezed Greer's hand, claiming Foster's once he'd rounded the truck. He dropped a kiss on her forehead, palming her belly as if he needed something to anchor him. A reason to walk into the house instead of running into the forest — screaming at the moon.

Foster turned and stared at Chase, frowning as his best friend stood in front of the grill, back rigid, hands fisted at his side. He'd washed off the blood, but Greer knew it hadn't vanished. That it clung like an invisible cloak.

She'd been there. Had lived for months with the stains lurking beneath her skin. Waiting for a moment of weakness — of hope — to reappear. And she vowed she'd do whatever it took to help Chase claw his way back. Escape the abyss she knew he'd fallen into.

Foster glanced at her, then back to Chase. He took a step, one hand shoved in his pocket, the other gripping Mackenzie's like a damn lifeline. "Chase."

Chase tensed as Foster's voice shattered the silence, the pieces falling around them like glass. Chase glanced over his shoulder, not quite looking at any of them before turning away. Shoulders so stiff Greer feared any slight movement would break them.

Foster rolled his right shoulder. "Brother, I know you don't want to hear this, that you're not ready for forgiveness, but this wasn't your fault."

Chase's head tilted forward as he kicked at the ground. "The hell it wasn't."

"Chase—"

"One job." Chase turned, eyes narrowed, mouth pressed into a firm line as he clenched his jaw, the muscle in his temple jumping from the strain. "Save him. That's all I had to do."

Foster matched Chase's stance, drawing himself up. Using his massive physique to command the space. He had three inches and about twenty pounds of muscle over Chase, and yet Chase seemed infinitely larger. An immovable force exerting his will over everyone else.

Foster shook his head. "Rhett was already compromised. Had been circling the grave for the past year. Hell, he'd only just roused. Any trauma was bound to be more than he could take. The fact he made it to the hospital…"

"But he did." Chase tapped his chest. "*I'm* the one who let him down. Who didn't fight hard enough. Long enough. All those minutes I wasted worrying about snipers and IEDs was time I *could* have been working on him. *Could* have been stabilizing him. Instead, he died because *I* wasn't good enough."

A snarl twitched at the corners of Chase's mouth. "He'd dragged his ass back. Twelve months of nothing, but he'd kept battling until he'd beaten the odds." He grunted as he booted a rock across the gravel drive. "Rhett deserved better than what I gave him."

"What the hell do you think you could have done better? You administered blood, meds, performed fucking CPR for over twenty minutes straight." Foster took another step, and she swore it echoed like thunder around them. "You did everything short of changing places. No one can ask for more than that."

Chase snorted, the sound raw. Slightly unhinged. "Yeah, well, it didn't matter in the end, did it." He turned, started walking.

Foster pounded his fist against his thigh, looking back at Greer. "I can't leave him like this."

Greer sighed. "I've got his back, tonight." She cut off any reply with a calculated step. "He's not the only one who's lost a brother. Who harbors that guilt. I've got this. You two try to get some rest. We'll meet in your kitchen in a few hours. Hit the ground running."

Foster glanced at Mac, frowned when she shrugged, then stared at Chase's silhouette one more time before heading for their house. Greer was almost surprised to see it still standing. She half-expected the roof to crash down or the windows to blow out — a tangible display of their fractured hearts.

She waited until they'd closed the door before following Chase, still checking her six every other step. Fog curled through the trees and between the houses, cloaking the property in a heavy gray pall, the sheer pressure of it dulling every sound until only her pulse thundered in her head.

Head still low, Chase paused at his door before he slipped inside, leaving it ajar. Proof he'd known she'd follow. Or maybe she'd made more noise than she'd thought, her footsteps as heavy as the air, because he hadn't looked back.

Greer made one last visual sweep of the area, staring at the trees, waiting to see a hint of that black boot emerging from the dark before following him inside. Deep shadows engulfed the room, a lone light burning down a hallway.

She kicked off her boots, armed the security system, then walked into the main living area. While they usually gathered at Foster's place, she'd spent a few evenings at Chase's over a game of poker. Chase referred to it as his cabin, with its warm wood and river rock accents. She'd always thought it felt like a favorite sweater. Inviting. Comforting. Nothing like the sterile vibe of her apartment. But tonight, the plush couch and reclaimed wood table and chairs seemed isolating.

Cold.

Chase stood in front of the large picture window, staring out into the forest beyond. Looking as if he'd shatter like the silence if she made the wrong move. Spoke too loudly or even brushed his arm.

He tensed further when she stopped at the edge of the couch, his hands fisting and releasing at his sides. "I don't want to talk."

She nodded, despite the fact he hadn't budged,

hadn't so much as glanced her way. "I wasn't going to ask you to."

His head tilted. Not enough that he looked back at her, but she caught a glimpse of his chin. How he'd squared it as if bracing for a fight. "I don't need a fucking pep talk, either."

She snorted. "I'm not Foster. I don't have any of those handy."

Heading for the small wet bar on the far side of the room, she grabbed a glass and the bottle of Cuervo. She didn't drink shots too often, but if she was going to open up about her past, she needed the liquid courage.

She poured a generous amount, took a deep breath, then knocked it back, closing her eyes as the tequila burned a path down her throat, hitting her stomach like a fireball.

It lasted about a minute, then started to ease, slowly fading into a comforting warmth. The kind she'd relied on for far too long after Troy had died. She poured two more, socked them back, then filled it one last time.

"Jesus, Greer. You might want to slow down." Chase's footsteps sounded behind her, stopping partway across the room.

She took a couple soothing breaths, the alcohol slowly lowering the walls she'd built around her. The ones Chase had scaled or maybe punched through over the past several months. Barriers the past couple hours had instantly reinforced.

She held up the fourth glass, only drinking a third as she closed her eyes — allowed the story she hadn't shared with anyone short of her mandatory meetings with the bureau shrink to slip free. "I had a brother."

The truth of those four words hit her hard, and she placed the glass on the bar, using the counter to steady herself. She hadn't talked about Troy in years. Hadn't trusted herself to get through the memories without breaking. A mistake, she realized. Not honoring his sacrifice. But she'd never been around people she truly believed in.

Not until Chase and his teammates had moved to Raven's Cliff.

Until he'd made her care.

Chase huffed, sounding as if he wanted to say something else, but he just stood there, watching her as if she might suddenly combust.

She took another breath, a slight buzz easing the rest of the words free. "We weren't even two years apart. Thick as thieves, my parents used to say. My dad was military, so we moved a lot. Every couple years, a new base, a new school. A new... everything. We learned pretty quickly that the only people we could really count on were each other."

She toed at the floor, watching the reflection of the wood ceiling in the surface of the tequila. "Troy was... perfect." She laughed. "The stupid jerk was great at everything. He rarely studied and still got straight A's. Was a star athlete. Could shoot the balls of a mosquito at fifty yards. The kind of guy you really wanted to hate but couldn't because he was just so... sweet. Compassionate. Never let his insane abilities go to his head."

The words tasted bitter on her tongue, but she continued, unable to stop the tale from pouring out. "He joined the Marshal Service right out of college. Graduated top of his class at Glynco, the ass, then settled in Seattle. Being his annoying little sister, I followed in a way. Went to Quanitco, then got transferred to Seattle a year later. By then, he'd worked his way onto the Pacific Northwest Fugitive Apprehension Task Force. Hunted high-priority fugitives across Washington as part of a multi-agency team. No surprise, he excelled at it."

Images flashed in her head. Not just that fateful night, but it overshadowed everything else. Tainted the good memories with pain and guilt.

Chase inched closer, his sheer presence warping the air, drawing her in. "He's why you applied for the bureau's joint fugitive task forces. You wanted to work with him."

She held her ground, aware she'd never finish if he touched her. "It wasn't always a given, but it happened more often than I'd thought. Watching him work… It never got old."

Gunshots echoed in her head, each report like a punch to her gut. The blood. The utter helplessness. It drowned out the room, the light, the damn air until nothing remained but the crushing weight of her failure.

"Greer."

She shook her head, downing another third of that shot as she shifted out of reach. Not that he'd tried to touch her, but she couldn't take the risk. Accept any form of softness when she knew he was still lost in the angles. The areas light never quite reached.

The hit of tequila got the words flowing, again. "We were working a recovery op. Prison transfer van had been hijacked. Bodies in the ditch. Their weapons missing. Troy had tracked the fugitives to this chop shop in the warehouse district. Had them cornered in the garage."

She swirled the last of the liquid around the glass. "Looking back, it had been too easy. Too quick. But at the time…"

She stared at the alcohol, wishing it held the forgiveness she still needed. "They were waiting. Gang-level resistance. We managed to secure a location — reduce their numbers as we waited for backup — when this guy just… appeared. I don't know if he jumped off a perch near the roof or popped out of a trap door because there'd been nothing, then he was standing there, semi-automatic aimed our way. Finger already inside the guard. He fired, and Troy did what he'd always done… Protected me."

She closed her eyes against the rush of memories. More ghostly shots. More darkness. All crushing in on her. "Backup arrived, but two of the bullets had punched right through his vest. I tried…"

She steeled her resolve, then turned, finally meeting his gaze. "Seeing you work tonight, I couldn't help but wonder that if he'd had someone like you. If I'd been able to give him half the chance you gave Rhett… Maybe…"

The last of the tequila burned down her throat, and

she placed the glass on the counter before motioning to him. "What I'm trying to say is, you can rage. Cry. Punch your fist through the wall. Whatever it takes to work through this, but I'm not going to let you run from it. Hide in that place that draws you down until there's so little light, you can't find your way back."

She took a single step. "Until there's nothing left worth saving."

She pushed past him, claiming the last cushion on the sofa. "So, I'm going to plant my ass on your couch. Close my eyes for a few hours, then make it my sole mission to track this bastard down. I'd appreciate it if you didn't make me bust your ass for trying to ditch me. But I will. And don't think I won't catch you just because you're ex-special forces."

The room fell silent, the intensity of Chase's gaze fluttering her stomach as she leaned against the cushions — closed her eyes. The evening's events lingered in the background, mixing with echoes of that night — Troy wrapped in her arms. Blood seeping through her fingers. How she'd tried everything, but it hadn't been enough. Witnessing Chase work on Rhett had only showcased how unprepared she'd been. How little she'd had to offer Troy.

That she wasn't half the force she'd once imagined.

Time ticked over in her mind, some of the tension easing against the give of the couch. The familiar scent of citrus and evergreen that clung to every surface. The aroma she equated with Chase.

The floor creaked a second before the couch shifted against Chase's weight, the cushion next to her compressing. She blinked, staring up at those hazel eyes, wondering if she'd ever cared this much about anyone other than Troy.

Chase tsked, all but lifting and repositioning her until her back was snugged against his chest, her head on his arm. He didn't say a word, just held her tight, squeezing whenever an errant tear burned a path down her cheek — landed on his skin.

She'd give herself tonight to wallow in the pain. The loss. Then, she'd pick herself up and work the case. Whatever it took, even if it meant swallowing her pride — calling the bureau. Every resource. Every marker.

CHAPTER SIX

Greer stared at the whiteboard pushed up against the far wall of the station, hoping the answers would suddenly materialize out of the words and lines she'd scribbled across the surface. A throwback to her federal days. Overkill, maybe, but she needed to see everything spread out — tabulated and organized until that one hidden clue appeared amidst the useless drivel.

The one lead that would break the case wide open.

The door to the station creaked as Bodie and Eli walked in, rain beading on their jackets, fatigue lining their faces. They hadn't stopped since she'd called them to the scene late last night, and she knew they'd keep going until they either dropped from exhaustion or caught the guy.

Not that she'd taken any down time. Other than the four hours' sleep she'd gotten last night wrapped in Chase's arms, she'd been running from one crime scene to the next, tracking down possible witnesses, wasting hours on the phone trying to cut through military red tape — get Rhett's service file sent over. But even after twelve hours of digging and collecting, all she had to go on was a bunch of unanswered questions.

Bodie stopped next to her, nodding at Foster's crew milling in the background before motioning to the board. "Someone's been busy."

She shrugged. "I think better when it's all laid out."

"Any luck with Rhett's file?"

She shifted her gaze to Bodie for a moment. "Foster's pulling some strings. I hope to have something by morning." She raked her hand through her hair. "Any luck with those CCTV files Morgan's team sent you?"

Bodie pointed at the grainy image she'd taped to the board. "Other than that one crappy photo? Nothing, yet. But I'm still waiting on traffic cam and ATM footage. I should have everything on my server by tomorrow. And Judge Palmer finally signed the paperwork to access medical, phone and financial records. I've contacted the Lodge — put them on notice. They'll have everything on your desk by morning."

Greer nodded, staring at the meager intel until everything swirled together, the resulting spin increasing the throbbing pain behind her eyes. God, she was tired. Not just physically. Baring her soul to Chase had drained her in a way she hadn't expected. Left her vulnerable. Off-kilter. And she had a bad feeling she wouldn't regain her equilibrium until the case was over.

Or she broke down and acted on all the heat still simmering between them.

He'd been distant. Quiet. But functioning. Which

seemed about as much as she could ask for considering the circumstances. And he'd still shoved coffee and a bagel her way — proof he hadn't fully disconnected. That his protective instincts hadn't completely shut down.

If anything, he was edgier than ever — hypervigilant, really — constantly checking his six. Looking as if he'd tackle her to the ground if he got even a whiff of trouble. She'd nearly bumped into him a dozen times throughout the day because he'd been hovering. Tailing her in case he needed to react. Which she would have found endearing if the rest of him wasn't a million miles away.

If he looked at her the way she knew she still stared at him.

She groaned inwardly. Now wasn't the time to think about Chase and how badly she wanted to hold him. Sink into that safety net until all the darkness looming in the background faded.

Until she believed this was nothing more than a one-off.

She startled when Eli nudged her, a steaming mug in his hands. He held it out, smiling when she offered her thanks. She took a sip, coughed when the sheer strength of it stole her breath, before focusing on him. "I haven't had a chance to thank you for jumping into the fray. Hell of a first day."

Eli glanced at the men leaning against the opposite wall, then back to her. "I just wish it hadn't been because…" He let the words fade, but she knew what he meant.

He motioned to the bits of information she'd written across the board. "So, is this how you worked cases in the bureau?"

She sighed. "Everyone has their own method."

"Call me crazy, Sheriff, but it looks as if you're expecting more casualties."

Greer tensed, Eli's observation echoing through the space. The elephant in the room she hadn't addressed yet. Not because her thoughts hadn't strayed in that direction, but because she didn't have anything to back up her suspicions other than a shiver down her spine and over a decade of hunting monsters through the shadows.

She glanced at Chase and his buddies, releasing a rough breath as she walked over to the board — stared at the large empty space off to one side. "As of right now, this is an isolated incident. While I'm keeping all avenues of this investigation open to various options, I don't have any evidence this was more than someone targeting Rhett Oliver."

Eli nodded. "But it's crossed your mind."

"It crosses my mind every time I investigate a murder. But I'm not going to dive down some rabbit hole before there's a reason to start digging. We stick with the facts and follow the evidence. Leave my internal voices out of it. Though, the possibility raises a concern we need to discuss."

Foster stepped forward, ever the leader. "We know where you're heading with this. If someone was targeting all of us, why wait until now to start picking us off? We've been here for nearly a year."

"True. Since nothing happened until Rhett started regaining consciousness, this is likely something he was involved in before he landed in that coma. But until we're sure, I think erring on the side of caution would be prudent." She hitched out a hip. "I'm not saying it's time to circle the wagons. To ask any of you not to do your job. Just try not to isolate yourselves for the next few days while I'm waiting on ME reports and toxicology. That goes for Mac, Jordan and Saylor. Anyone you consider a teammate."

Chase grunted, one of the few sounds he'd made all day. "You realize that includes you, right? And Bodie."

Greer glanced at Bodie, then back to Chase. "In a perfect world, no officer would patrol alone." She sighed as she leaned against the wall to her office, fatigue settling heavy on her shoulders. "We're a small county with an even smaller budget. I'm already stretched thin. It's the unfortunate reality we face. But... we'll be vigilant. Double up when possible."

Chase crossed his arms, stretching his jacket across his muscular form. "Then, it's a good thing you've got four other trained personnel to help out. Five if we count Nyx, and she'd be hurt if we didn't."

"Chase..."

"We're registered first responders."

"Which allows me to push the gray areas. Skirt the lines without completely obliterating them. But I can't hand you all service weapons and send you out to patrol, even if I want to."

Zain coughed. "We don't need weapons, and we're willing to face whatever consequences arise."

Greer let her head tilt back as she scrubbed her hand across her face. "If I receive any calls with even a suggestion of something search and rescue related. If there's a hint that someone's hurt or a question of their whereabouts, you'll be the first people I task. But I can't send you on traffic stops or suspected break-ins without just cause. The town needs you. Needs Raven's Watch. I have to consider every soul under my protection."

Greer raised a brow when Foster stepped forward, looking as if he was going to argue. "I'll bend the rules as much as I can. I promised I'd keep you all up-to-date. That I wouldn't hide behind my badge or the facts, even if they're going to hurt. I'm just asking you to walk that fine line with me."

Footsteps clicked across the linoleum floor, Shirley's wiry frame appearing around the corner. "Sheriff?"

Greer glanced over at the woman. "What's up, Shirley?"

"I've got Shaun Faraday over at Raven's Lodge on the line. He's asking if he can have the room sanitized, now?"

"Of course, he is." Greer stretched her neck from side to side. "Tell him I'll be over shortly. That I'm going to do one more sweep. And if I see so much as a dust line from a broom when I get there, I'll arrest his ass for obstruction."

Shirley grinned. "I'll take great pleasure in letting him know. The guy's an ass."

Bodie chuckled. "We'll go clear the scene."

Greer tsked. "Oh no. You've both been on duty for

far too long. Go home, and get some sleep. I'll stand watch tonight."

Bodie simply crossed his arms. "Seriously? You've been pulling double shifts all week. Hell, for months. I agree we all need a break, so we'll head home but only for a few hours. We'll be back here at eleven sharp. I expect you to take the rest of the night off."

"And here I thought it said sheriff after my name?"

"I think you've mistaken that 'S' for stubborn." Bodie inched closer. "You're just cranky because you know I'm right. I know you want to wrap this up quickly. Put this bastard behind bars, but things move a bit slower in small towns. Get some sleep, and you can attack it head-on tomorrow." He tapped Eli on the shoulder, then headed for the door, glancing back at her as he held it open. "I expect you to take your own damn advice and go back to Chase's or Foster's since Eli's bunking in my guest suite."

Greer shook her head. Bodie was as protective as the rest of them and just as loyal.

Foster stepped up beside her, hands shoved into his pockets. "He's right. You take care of everyone else but rarely consider your own safety."

"I'll be careful."

"You'll take backup." Foster cut her off with a harsh breath. "You think we haven't noticed how you've allowed Kash and Nyx to shadow Jordan all day?"

"They were scouring that wooded area. It was appropriate."

"And tomorrow? The next day?"

Greer pursed her lips, holding her head high.

"Jordan's pregnant. While I don't have enough resources to sideline her, especially this early in her pregnancy and with everything that's gone down, I'm not immune to the situation. If I lose my job for ensuring she's safe, then so be it."

Foster's muscles eased, a slight smile curving his lips. "No one's going to fault you for that. Just like they won't fault you for having Chase ride shotgun whenever possible." Foster cut her off before she could protest. "He's a medic. You can push those lines a bit farther where he's concerned."

Greer snorted. "You guys really are a giant pain in my ass."

"We love you, too."

"Go home. Shirley's working the night shift. She knows to call if anything pops up, so keep your phones handy. I'll be along once Bodie and Eli are back."

Foster glanced at Chase, one of those annoying silent conversations passing between them before he and Zain headed out, giving her one more look as the door closed behind them.

Chase rolled his shoulders before moving in beside her. Close, but still removed. She checked her weapon and ammo, stopped to update Shirley, then headed out, constantly scanning the area as she walked toward her Bronco. Clouds blocked out the star shine, and rain splattered against the pavement, puddles slowly forming along the street.

Chase tapped her arm. "Give me a sec. I need to grab my bag."

She sighed. While she didn't anticipate any issues,

she knew Chase rarely went anywhere without his medic bag. And after losing Rhett last night...

She slipped behind the wheel, the hairs on the back of her neck prickling when she caught a glimpse of the backseats in her rearview — still tipped forward and bloodstained. A reminder of all they'd lost.

She pushed down the resulting hurt as Chase jumped in the other side, then joined the evening traffic, heading for the west side. Chase sat in the passenger seat, gaze focused out the side window, that scent of citrus and pine surrounding her like a damn promise. His mere presence made the interior seem small — her arm brushing his whenever she shifted gears.

Chase waited until she'd turned onto the long winding driveway — the lodge rising out of the ground like an omen — before giving her a quick glance. "Do you really think this is about us? That it's not over?"

She bit back the punch of disappointment. She'd hoped he might want to talk about something else. Anything else. Like the obvious rift separating their seats. "Foster has a point. You've all been viable targets for months. And the timing definitely points toward Rhett being the prime target. I'm just keeping my options open."

He grunted, turning to face her. "I'm not the mayor or the press. I don't need you to dance around the subject."

She clenched her jaw as she parked in front of the main entrance. "I'm not dancing. I'm sticking with the facts."

"You're walking the line."

"Is that what you think?" She twisted to face him. "That I'm playing it safe?"

"I think you've got some pretty strong opinions you're not sharing, that empty space on your board proof enough."

"Whoever did this lured us there, launched a military-worthy attack, then led us on a damn gauntlet run through the facility so we'd eventually find Rhett. Posed, with a damn number carved into his skin."

She unbuckled, stepped out and slammed the door, staring at him over the hood of her Bronco. "So yeah, Chase, that voice inside my head's screaming there's more to this than someone hiding a hired hit amidst a bunch of ritualistic trappings. But until I can prove any of that, I'm treating this like any other murder case, because that's what it is. And crying wolf isn't going to garner me any favors."

Chase snagged her arm as she headed for the entrance, spinning her to face him." Greer…"

"I get it. You're hurt. Angry. You want all of this to mean something. I want that, too. For it to be something I couldn't possibly have seen coming because when it's all said and done, Rhett was killed on my watch." She pulled free of his hold. "That's something I'll have to live with."

She struck off, her footsteps echoing in the night air, each step harder than the last. Like running through sand — moving without gaining any traction. Chase shadowed her, head on a swivel, every step orchestrated. Calculated down to the second it would take to tackle her to the ground — block a shot. That hyper-vigilance he'd been displaying all day.

She reached the door, paused long enough to take a breath — push down everything soft — then walked inside, Chase still guarding her six. She shouldn't have gotten terse. She was supposed to be lifting him up, not allowing her own frustrations to color her words. But standing there, nothing but pain between them, had rattled her, and she'd reacted without thinking.

Shaun Faraday met her before she'd gotten more than a few feet inside, his hands fisted at his sides, his thinning hair combed over the left side of his head. He huffed when she stopped, staring at her as if she'd launched a personal attack on his facility. "Sheriff Hudson."

"Mr. Faraday. I understand you're eager to repurpose Mr. Oliver's room."

Faraday snorted. "The man's gone, we have…"

His voice trailed off as Chase moved in beside her, head high, that death vibe his entire team embodied in full force.

Faraday cleared his throat as he adjusted his tie. "Obviously, we're immensely saddened by last night's events, but I'm sure you understand we have a long list of clients in need of our brand of care."

Greer shifted on her feet, staring the man down. "Which brand is that? The nurses and meds or the complete lack of security that allowed one of your *clients* to be kidnapped and murdered with nothing more than one grainy image to show for it?"

Faraday bristled, slashes of red creeping across his cheeks. "Our facility is designed to keep our clients from wandering off, not to prevent people from visiting."

"Except it was after hours, and no one seemed to notice for…" She withdrew a notepad from her inside pocket and flipped through some pages. "Ninety minutes. Is that typical of the length of time between check-ins?"

"The patients in that wing are comatose—"

"It's my understanding that Mr. Oliver had returned to the land of the living."

Faraday tugged on his suit jacket. "He'd had a few moments of clarity, hardly enough to confirm he'd fully regained consciousness."

Chase took a heavy step forward. "He woke on the race to the hospital before he died, you son of a—"

"Chase." Greer waited until Chase inched back. "I need to do one final sweep of the room and the facility before I can clear the scene."

Faraday glared at Chase, then motioned to the hallway off to his right. "This way."

Greer glanced at Chase, waiting until he'd pushed out a calming breath before following Faraday down the hall, through a couple of other wings, then into Rhett's room. Remnants of fingerprint dust clung to every surface, a slight chemical scent still lingering in the air. The blankets on the bed had been carefully pulled back on one side, the sheets wrinkled where Rhett had been sleeping the previous night.

She stopped a few feet back from the bed as she

peered at Chase. Arms crossed, back rigid, he looked like a man on the edge.

Faraday motioned to the room. "As you can see, your crime techs swabbed, sprayed and dusted every inch."

"If only your security had been as thorough." She made a circuit of the room, checking places the crime techs could have been missed, but the crew had been as meticulous as Faraday had mentioned. "You can reallocate the room. Just see that any of Mr. Oliver's belongings that weren't taken to the crime lab are returned to his teammates. And I expect all the information my deputy requested to be at the station come morning, or I'll have every department I can think of scouring your facility looking for even a hint of an infraction. And I doubt you want that kind of bad press."

Faraday glanced at Chase, then back to her. "Of course. Is there anything else?"

"Just that sweep of—"

The lights flickered, giving the room a strobe effect, then cut out.

Greer cocked her head toward the door as Chase stepped in close, his chest pressing against her back. Muscles tensed and primed for whatever might suddenly burst through the door. She didn't move, waiting for a generator to kick in.

Nothing.

No buzzing. No humming vents or mechanical sounds, just that foreboding silence.

"Faraday?"

Faraday coughed. "The automatic transfer switch should have engaged the backup generators by now."

"Any reason it wouldn't kick in?"

"Only if the system was down for maintenance or we'd run out of diesel. We do monthly checks and had the tanks filled after those epic storms last month knocked the power out for several hours. Regardless, I should get a push notification if—" His cell chirped, an alert flashing on the screen. "This isn't right. Someone has to physically disconnect the system, and no one other than myself and my co-director have the authority to do that."

"How long will the batteries last on your essential equipment?"

"A couple hours, tops."

Footsteps.

Tapping along the hallway. Steady. Strong.

Greer removed her flashlight and weapon, just like at the psychiatric hospital. Chase moved with her as she edged toward the doorway, aware it could be a nurse or resident. She reached the threshold, counted to three then popped out, clearing the left side as Chase dodged right.

A small glow brightened the far end off to the left. What looked like a cigarette or match, the light flaring for a moment before winking out, those taps fading into the distance.

Greer called Faraday up beside them. "What's down the left side?"

He pursed his lips, his face ashen. "More rooms,

then a service elevator and a set of stairs that lead down to the utility area then onto the rear exit. We use it to wheel out…"

He didn't continue, but Greer knew what he'd meant.

"Get this place on lockdown. I want your clients secured in their rooms. Staff huddled together. And call my office, have Shirley send Jordan and Kash over ASAP. Tell him to bring Nyx. We'll clear everyone to the left and continue down. No one other than my people enter or leave until I've got a handle on what this is. Got it?"

"I need to get maintenance in here before we run out of time."

"It won't take too long for us to clear the facility. You can have them on standby, but my orders stand. No one in or out until I know it's safe."

He nodded, eyes wide, overly white in the flashlight's glow. He glanced down the hallway, swallowed, then rushed off, his shadowy figure disappearing into the dark.

Greer stared up at Chase, noting the firm line of his jaw. How the muscle in his temple jumped. "You okay with the plan?"

Chase glanced at her from the corner of his eye. "Completely focused."

"Point or sweep?"

He froze, finally shifting his gaze fully to her. "You're asking?"

"I'm no slouch, but we both know your expertise outweighs mine. So, do you want to take point or guard my ass?"

"I'll always have your six, but..." He inched forward, his own flashlight cutting through the shadows. "I'll take point. Assuming you're not planning on putting a slug in my ass."

"Maybe later. For now, I've got your back."

CHAPTER SEVEN

He couldn't lose her.

That was the only thing going through Chase's mind as he stared at Greer, her green eyes shining in the yellowed light.

Point or sweep...

He still couldn't believe she'd asked. Given him the choice. Hell, that she'd allowed him to come at all. Especially after the distance he'd put between them — physically there and yet completely removed. Then he'd suggested she'd knowingly kept them in the dark because she hadn't wanted to share any theory where Rhett's death wasn't the only objective.

He'd been wrong, and that one mistake had cost him the fragile hold he'd had on her heart. She hadn't said those words, but he'd noticed the way she'd looked at him. As if she wasn't sure if he cared.

He wasn't proud of his behavior but...

Losing Rhett...

It had scarred him in a way even Sean's death hadn't.

Left him questioning his skill. His damn worth. Aware that if he didn't deserve happiness, he sure as shit didn't deserve Greer. Not until he found some semblance of redemption.

If he found it.

Chase pushed the thoughts out of his head. He could worry about a future if they still had one after clearing the nursing home. If he didn't let her down the way he'd let down Rhett.

He started down the hallway, pausing at each half-open door. The faint glow from the various monitors highlighted the mounded bodies hidden beneath sheets and blankets, the machines' batteries still pumping oxygen and marking out heart rates, each beep reverberating in the stillness. Greer shadowed his every move, constantly checking their six — watching both directions whenever he darted into a room to clear recesses not visible from the doorway.

A voice murmured farther down the hallway, wheelchairs and IV stands slowly materializing out of the dark, the flashlights casting distorted shadows across the floor. Her soft treads sounded in the stillness, lingering in the thick air.

Chase stopped at the last room, that voice sounding from inside. Greer nodded when he showed the countdown, busting through the door once he'd reached one. The man on the bed twitched, muttering a few words without opening his eyes before drifting back off. A spiderweb of lines and tubes wove across the headboard trailing to the monitors beyond. A single tray lay upside down on the floor.

Comatose ward his ass.

A creak.

Close.

What sounded like hinges groaning in protest, a soft whoosh following a few seconds later. They backtracked to the hallway, bouncing the beam along the far wall until they found the elevator and stairwell Faraday had mentioned.

Chase ran the beam across the silver doors, then across the exit to the stairwell before glancing at Greer. "Not that I'd take the elevator if it was even an option, but... you still good with clearing the lower level?"

"There's no way I'm leaving here until I know we've checked for any possible threat, so crack that emergency door open."

He studied her for a moment, admiring the determined line of her back. How she stood there, weapon ready, muscles primed, prepared for whatever waited behind the thick metal door. The woman was incredible.

He took a breath, counted to three, then shoved the door open. Greer swept onto the platform, clearing the immediate area before scanning the steps below. He darted in beside her, covering the door as it whooshed shut before scouring the stairs.

Movement.

Not much. More a shifting of the shadows at the bottom. Just like in the abandoned hospital. That ominous prickling along the back of his neck in full force. He traced the railing. Waited.

A scuffed black boot crept into the light, same one

he'd spied last night right before the bastard had launched that attack.

Chase grabbed Greer and yanked her back, hitting the far wall a second before bullets sprayed up the stairwell, ricocheting off the railing and into the walls. He covered her head against his chest, darting out to fire down the stairwell after the first wave. More footsteps tapped below him, the lower door opened and closed.

Greer shoved him, and they took off, racing down the stairs two at a time. He paused at the bottom, checked behind the stairs, then moved to the door.

He motioned for her to open it, arching his brow when she narrowed her eyes. "You got to go first upstairs."

"Only because you knew the bastard wouldn't be hiding behind it."

"We're not wearing our vests."

"Who thought this would turn into another damn gauntlet run." She grabbed the handle. "Don't get shot."

She reefed it open, and he dove out, rolling to his feet with his Sig already zeroed in on the far end of the corridor, ready to strike at the slightest hint of aggression. Something clattered in the distance as a shadow moved off to the left.

Chase pointed in the direction, then took off, sprinting down the hallway. He vaulted over a toppled gurney, dodging a large bin as he wove his way through the utility room, ducking behind some machinery when a figure crossed the hallway in front of him.

Greer darted in behind him, not missing a beat, as

she motioned to the corridor, then jumped out. He stayed with her, moving slowly — giving himself plenty of time to react. Muffled grunts sounded off to their left, a metallic rattling noise cutting through the quiet.

Chase covered Greer as she shuffled ahead, weapon aimed at a figure mostly hidden in the shadows before Chase pegged the silhouette with his flashlight.

She stopped. "What the..." She inched closer, her flashlight reflecting off a swath of plastic peeking out from beneath a set of scrubs, the dummy's wig tilted off to one side. "Is that a mannequin?"

Chase had Greer by the arm and pressed between him and a piece of machinery a heartbeat later, using his body to block any possible hit. "Someone walked across the hallway. Made those sounds."

"I know, but—"

A series of grunts drowned her out, the rough sound mixing with the hints of diesel in the air. Echoing off the shiny surfaces.

Chase scanned the mannequin, frowning at the cable knotted around its neck — a small speaker hanging off the end. "I've got an incredibly bad feeling about this..."

A blast of static crackled the air followed by a scream, then scuffling, something thudding to the ground. A wet gurgling noise echoed around them, reminiscent of that night in the chopper. The way Sean had sounded before he'd died.

How Chase imagined Rhett had been when he'd been lying there, praying his brothers would find him in time.

That *Chase* would find him.

Greer raised one hand to her mouth. "Oh, god." She moved out from behind him, her flashlight centered on the speaker. "Where... Wait. Do you hear what's in the background?"

Chase frowned, then inhaled. "Fuck, the foghorn."

He cleared the immediate area, then took off, dodging through the machines and extra supplies, jumping over boxes and crates. Heading for the service exit somewhere on the other side.

Light.

Not much.

Just a shade brighter than the room, but Chase angled toward it, aiming his weapon at the twin doors as they appeared in the circular beam. He barely stopped long enough to glance through the windows before bursting through the doors — racing into the night.

Fog crawled across the pavement, clinging to the hanging branches as rain drizzled from the sky. Hints of moonlight brightened the clouds low on the horizon, that mournful horn drifting on the light breeze.

Greer followed him out, running toward the edge of the rear driveway. Grass stretched out on either side, a few benches resting beneath towering maples dotting the landscape.

Chase moved in beside her, holding her back as he studied the lawn along the driveway. Looking for some kind of impression. A footprint or depression. Something to narrow the search.

Mud.

Caked along the grass in distinct lines.

The kind combat boot treads left behind. Heading toward the rear of the property.

Greer covered his six, trailing after him as he followed the marks, pausing at the corner. An engine growled to life in the distance, the telltale revs rising above the foghorn before fading into the patter of rain.

Chase peeked around the corner, searching for a sniper beam glowing in the fog — something to suggest their perp hadn't escaped in whatever vehicle had just taken off — then rounded the building, quickstepping over to an open courtyard. Tables stacked with chairs occupied half the space, decorative planters lining the sides.

Shoes.

Sticking out from behind one of the wooden boxes.

Overly white in the harsh beam.

Chase ran the last several feet, dropping to his knees once he'd reached the woman. Blonde. Slim build wearing scrubs and a name tag.

Stacey Bradford.

He swallowed, noting the familiar curve of her face. She'd been Rhett's nurse. Had always gone that extra mile to keep him comfortable, often allowing Chase and his buddies to visit after hours.

He checked a pulse. Weak but there.

Greer stopped behind him, her flashlight dancing over Stacey. "Christ."

He nodded, staring at the IV tubing twisted around her neck, a knot centered in front. Just like the mannequin inside. Her head tilted off to one side, streaks of mascara staining her cheeks.

He looked up at Greer. "I have to remove the tubing. Reposition her."

"Whatever you need. Lives, first. Evidence later."

He went to work, easing the line free before checking her vitals. "She's not breathing. Call Kash. I need to know if he's here yet."

Chase started rescue breathing, mentally keeping time, as Greer grabbed her cell — had Kash's line ringing in the distance as she shifted around him, looking as if she wanted to cover every angle while still keeping the woman encased in that circular beam.

Kash answered on the first ring. "Talk to me Greer."

"Hold for Chase…" She placed the cell next to Chase's head.

Chase grunted, pausing for only a second. "Where are you?"

"Just pulling up beside Greer's Bronco."

"My bag's in the back. Grab it and haul ass to the rear courtyard. Stick together and make sure Nyx is on high alert."

Kash ended the call, the emptiness a stark reminder of how the previous night had ended. Greer had Shirley on the line next, calling in backup, emergency services. Hell, everyone.

Kash rounded the facility a minute later, Nyx practically frothing at the mouth, hackles raised. She'd obviously picked up a scent based on the way she dug in with every stride, tugging against Kash's hold. Jordan kept pace, flashlight in one hand, KaBar in the other. Looking every inch the seasoned Shadow Ops agent she'd once been.

Kash handed off Nyx to Jordan, then dropped down on the other side, opening Chase's bag. "Tell me what you need, buddy."

"Nothing's getting through. Her throat must be too damaged from the trauma. I need that seven-millimeter endotracheal tube and laryngoscope."

Kash didn't miss a beat, handing him the instrument and supplies. Helping position Stacey as Chase attempted to intubate.

He cursed, trying several times before shifting back over. "Airway's obstructed and we're already two minutes in. She won't last much longer without oxygen. Cric kit."

Kash handed it over, then swabbed her skin. Chase focused on the woman's neck, slicing through flesh and membranes before inserting the large-bore tube.

He secured everything, then wiggled his fingers. "Bag."

Kash took over bagging her once Chase had it in place, freeing him to get the IV going, meds on standby as he did a quick body scan. He checked her pulse. Weaker. Pressure ninety over sixty and dropping.

Chase shook his head. "She's crashing."

Greer gripped his shoulder. "I've notified everyone, but there's been multiple calls for ambulances, and your night crew's aiding a water rescue."

"She's not going to last long enough for them to get here." He cursed when nothing moved beneath his fingertips. "Damn it. Starting compressions. C'mon, Stacey. Don't give up on me, now."

Jordan raced back from the facility a moment later

carrying a portable defibrillator, Nyx at her side. "I thought this might help."

"Thanks." Chase nodded to the spot beside him. "Do you know how to work one?"

"I've had some training."

"Of course, you have." He kept pumping, his arms already starting to cramp. "Get it juiced up, and we'll see if she's got a shockable rhythm."

Sweat beaded his brow, his chest heaving from the strain, but he kept going, pausing once Jordan and Kash had positioned the pads.

The machine started talking, going through the motions. Taking so damn long Chase had to physically stop himself from ripping off the leads and resuming compressions. It took a good thirty seconds before it finally sent out a charge, jerking Stacey's body before telling Chase to resume CPR.

He muttered under his breath. Stacey was young. Healthy. With her airway restored, he'd thought she'd rally. Sure, she likely had some internal bleeding on top of additional side effects from the hypoxia, but he'd believed she'd make it to the hospital. Would eventually pull through. Having her code so quickly after being attacked...

"Kash. Buddy, grab me one milligram of epi."

Kash snagged a syringe, measured out the meds then handed it to Chase. Chase stopped long enough to inject it into the IV port, then started up again when nothing happened.

Just his pulse thundering in his head.

Her limp body shaking with every compression.

Time ticked in the background as a siren sounded in the distance. Faint. What Chase guessed was still minutes away.

He tried shocking her, again, got the same non-response, then went back to work. He could spell off. Kash was highly qualified. Had saved Chase's ass a few times when he'd been the one to fall. But every time he opened his mouth to ask Kash to switch, her sightless gaze transformed into Rhett's wide eyes. As if he'd known it was the last time he'd see Chase.

Footsteps.

Not like before.

These were lighter. Faster.

Jordan took point, that freaking knife clasped in her hand, glinting whenever her flashlight caught the edge. She waited, relaxing a bit when a man rushed around the side of the building, glasses half-fogged from the weather, a small medical bag grasped in one hand.

Dr. Tremblay. Who Chase suspected had been on call.

The doctor headed straight for them, settling in beside Chase. "Jesus, Remington, what the hell?"

Chase hissed out a breath. "It's every bit as bad as it looks."

Tremblay ran through her vitals, shaking his head when another shock attempt failed. "How long has she been down?"

Chase kept working, his arms twice as heavy as when he'd started. "It's been ten minutes since I started compressions."

"Damn." He pushed another round of epi, constantly assessing the situation before sighing. "She's gone."

Chase grunted and kept pumping, glaring at Tremblay. "She's still got time. If we had more sophisticated equipment—"

"It's a twenty-minute drive to Providence. And the ambulance isn't even here, yet." Tremblay shook his head. "You did everything you could. It's time to call it."

"No."

"Remington…"

"We don't give up until there's not a ghost of a chance. No one left behind."

"This isn't the field, and she's not a soldier." Tremblay placed his hand over Chase's. "I know it's hard, but you can't save everyone."

Chase panted out a few breaths, slowly stopping his efforts until he simply hovered over Stacey, fingers still laced together, sweat running down his cheek. He glanced at her face, saw Rhett's eyes staring up at him again, before he rocked onto his heels. Closed his eyes. All that weight from the previous night closing in around him. Pushing down on his shoulders until he scrambled to his feet — backed up until his ass hit the building.

The rain picked up, the foghorn still sounding in the background as he stared at her, hands fisted at his side, defeat burning a hole in his gut.

A couple orderlies appeared around the corner, talking with Greer before erecting a makeshift tent around the body. Saving what evidence they could from washing away. Unlike his mental health. The wind shifted, and it slipped away on a surge of rainwater, his last shred of sanity drifting further away with every drop. Drowning in the puddles. Swirling away with the runoff.

Kash shouldered up beside him, face grim, his hands shoved into his jacket pockets. He didn't talk, just leaned against the wall, staring at the water running in rivulets along the courtyard.

Chase kicked at the muddy grass. "I should've been able to bring her back."

Kash sighed. "Losing people sucks, but it's part of the job. You did everything you could."

"I'm sure that's a comfort to Rhett and Stacey."

"Je*sus*, Chase, cut yourself some slack. You're not God."

"No, just cursed. It just took a bit longer to manifest than with my dad."

"You're not cursed, and you're not your father." Kash pushed off the wall and turned to face him. "I realize losing Rhett broke something inside you. That you saw last night as your second chance. That forgiveness you've been looking for since retiring. That all of this is somehow your fault. And I'm the last person who'd ever tell you to get over it. Hell, we're all to blame for Rhett's death because we were all in that fucking helicopter." He took a step closer. "What I will say, is that if you couldn't bring either of them back, then they were never going to survive. You're hands down the best damn medic I've ever seen."

Chase whipped his head down when Nyx nosed his thigh before sitting next to him. Nothing overt, just her easy pressure against his leg. The occasional nudge when he stopped scratching behind her ears.

Kash looked at Nyx, then up to Chase. "We're worried about you, brother."

He took a few steps back. "And for the record. That forgiveness you're trying to find…" He motioned toward Greer, then back. "It's not at the bottom of a medic bag."

Chase stared at him, his tongue too thick to work, until Nyx finally trotted over to Kash, glancing back at Chase one more time before following Kash when he sighed and strode off, stopping next to Jordan. She smiled, nodding at something he said before they headed for the corner. What Chase assumed was further clearing of the facility. Maybe evacuating the residents if Faraday couldn't get the power back on.

Chase glanced at Greer. Head bent in conversation, she looked almost regal as she handled everyone. Allocating resources without losing her cool, all while constantly scouring the grounds. Guarding everyone's six.

She must have felt him staring, because she paused then focused on him, eyes narrowed, her head tilting to one side. The same expression she'd given him last night when she'd told him she'd hunt his ass down if he tried to ditch her.

He scrubbed a hand down his face, then grabbed his bag. Second night in a row he'd have to restock — not that having all his supplies had mattered.

Greer appeared at his side, palm resting on her weapon, gaze still searching the tree line. "I'm gonna be here a while. I'm sending Kash and Jordan home once they've cleared the building with Nyx. You should catch a lift."

He frowned. "And just leave you here? Alone?"

"Bodie and Eli will be here once they're back on shift. My apartment's not far. I'll be fine."

"Right up until someone targets you, next." He swung his bag over his back. "I'm staying. And you're not spending the night alone. You choose where, but… You're stuck with me."

He pushed past her. "I'll go toss my bag in your Bronco."

He struck off, the intensity of her gaze following him to the corner nearly crippling him. While he wasn't ready to act on what they'd been building for the past several months — allow himself to feel anything other than the fire raging beneath his skin — he wasn't about to compromise her safety.

Having her walk away was one thing. Allowing this bastard to hurt her…

He'd die before he let that happen because despite everything — his training, all his tough talk — he knew he'd never come back from that.

CHAPTER EIGHT

"Greer."

Greer jolted awake, nearly catching Chase in the jaw as he loomed over her, eyes narrowed, mouth pinched tight. She clutched her hand to her chest as she searched the room for some kind of threat before relaxing against the back of the couch, pain already creeping into her neck.

She scrubbed a hand down her face. "What time is it?"

"Early. Just shy of seven."

"Did Shirley call? Is there another body—"

"Nothing's wrong, it's just…" He sighed. "You were dreaming, and it didn't sound like a good one."

She let her head fall against the cushion as she blew out an exhausted breath, remnants of the nightmare still lingering in the shadows. Nothing concrete, just dead eyes staring at her from the darkness. A sense of familiarity that prickled the hairs on the back of her neck. "I don't really remember."

Chase nodded, staring down at her for a few moments before shifting back — reclaiming the chair on the other side of the coffee table. He didn't talk, merely eased onto the cushion, watching her as if he thought she'd vanish.

Several months' worth of wanting to be in this exact scenario — the two of them alone in her apartment — and he couldn't have been farther away if he'd tried. The distance between them larger than a fissure now. More like a chasm. The kind of expanse no bridge could span.

Irony at its best.

Greer rocked to her feet, stretching out her neck as Chase stood, still staring at her as if she were a ghost. "I can't believe I fell asleep out here."

Chase shrugged, shoving his hands into his pockets. "I tried to move you but…" He chuckled, though it sounded forced. "You get a bit *aggressive* in your sleep. Tried to deck me, twice."

She cracked a hint of a smile. "A girl can't be too careful." She pointed to the chair. "Did you seriously sleep in that?" She groaned when he simply stood there, shifting his weight. "You didn't sleep."

He glanced at the door, then back. "Your security system's not nearly as robust as mine. Zain would be disappointed."

"Then, it's a good thing Zain doesn't live here. And it's plenty secure. Haven't had to shoot an intruder, yet."

Chase scoffed. "With how easily someone could bypass that alarm, you wouldn't get the chance before you'd be dead."

His voice roughened on that last word, as if he'd caught himself a bit too late to stop it from clawing free. Hadn't wanted to jinx the future by putting the thought out into the universe.

She pursed her lips, wanting to walk the few feet over to him — sink into his arms. Instead, she rounded the couch to the hallway, stopped at the edge. "I'm going to grab a quick shower before another emergency springs up." She turned, pausing when the floor creaked behind her.

"Greer."

God, the way he said her name. It made her knees weak, her damn heart beat so fast she thought it would explode.

She took a fortifying breath, looking back at him over her shoulder. "Did you want to go first?"

Or join me...

She didn't say the words out loud, but damn, she wanted to. Wanted to wrap her arms around him, close her eyes and believe that everything would be okay, even if it was only for a moment.

Chase toed at the floor, looking like he had the other night when she'd thought he'd bolt. "I already had one."

"Then, feel free to make some coffee, unless you take after Zain and burn everything."

"I don't. And I would have already, but you've got less in your cupboards and fridge than we do, which I didn't think was possible."

Greer raked her hand through her hair. "It's been a long few days."

"Don't you mean months? Because you've been working insane hours since we met."

"My boss was a drug dealer. The sheriff's station has a lot to atone for, and I can't earn back everyone's trust by sitting on my ass."

"Pretty sure you're allowed to eat."

She sighed, barely pushing the breath out amidst the suffocating pressure all around them. As if he'd increased gravity in the center of her apartment. "I'll go shopping later."

"It's about more than just groceries. You need to take better care of yourself. Of your safety."

"Chase..." She paused, noting the tight press of his mouth. The hints of red on his cheeks. All that hypervigilance focused on her. Like the death vibe he'd given Faraday last night, and she knew this was about more than just coffee and milk. "I'll look into a better security system." She motioned toward her room. "After I shower."

He glanced down the hall, and she wondered if he'd insist on searching the shower before he deemed it safe enough for her to be alone. "I'll tell Zain he needs to fortify this place."

"Fine." She got another two steps in before he called her name, again. She turned, this time, repeating her mantra in her head. How she needed to give him time. Space. Anything to alter the cold reality staring back at her.

That somewhere between the kiss in the parking lot and Rhett's death, she'd already lost him.

Chase closed the distance by half. "I'm not trying to

be..." He huffed out a rough breath. "I've lost two people in twenty-four hours on my watch. I can't lose you to this asshole, too."

"Dismissing the fact we don't know for sure these two incidents are connected, yet, I'm not a regular civilian."

"They're connected. And there's nothing regular about this bastard, either."

"I'll be careful."

"I need you to be more than careful. I..." He fisted his hands, blew out another breath. "Go have your shower, just leave the door cracked open and lock the window. Just in case."

"We're on the fourth floor."

"I could still access that window if I wanted to, as could my team."

"Which suggests you're the ones I should be more concerned about." She turned and tossed, "I won't be long," over her shoulder.

She headed down the hall, opened her door and grabbed some clean clothes before heading for the bathroom. Water splashed in background as she readied the shower, then stepped inside, allowing the heat to ease the tension in her muscles. Calm the fluttering in her gut.

Talk about torture.

Looking back, she wasn't sure how she'd lasted all this time without acting on her feelings. How she'd managed to focus on work and not how his voice sent shivers along her skin. Or how just standing in the same room with him affected her way of thinking. Bent it until she'd subconsciously aligned it with his.

He was right about one thing. The killings were connected. She just wasn't sure whose attention the asshole wanted — hers or Chase's. Maybe his entire team's.

Answers she hoped to have today once she'd received more reports. Knew, for sure, what had killed Rhett.

Air ruffled the curtain, a cool swirl breezing over her skin. She frowned, inching toward the back when the curtain flung open partway, Chase's arm stabbing into the open space, her phone grasped in his hand.

She screamed. Nearly tumbled onto her ass before she clutched the curtain and held it against her as she whipped her head out. "Jesus, Chase, what the hell?"

He furrowed his brow, glancing at the phone, then back to her. "Shirley keeps calling. I figured it was important."

Greer allowed her head to tilt up. "Then, you could have just answered it and taken a message instead of scaring the crap out of me."

He shifted his weight on his feet. "If you'd brought your damn gun into the bathroom with you, I wouldn't have scared you."

"If I'd brought my Glock, you'd have a gunshot wound instead of the welt I'm going to give you on the backside of your head once I'm out of here."

"At least, you would've been able to defend yourself. What would you have done if I'd been our crazed killer?"

"I would have started with a kick to your nuts, followed by a few throat punches, which I'd be happy to demonstrate." She glared when he arched an eyebrow. "Just call the station and put it on speaker."

Shirley answered immediately. "Sheriff? Are you okay? I called three times."

Greer stayed behind the curtain. "I was in the shower. What's up, Shirley?"

The other woman sighed. "Sounds like you still are. And I'm sorry to call so early when I know you didn't even get home until after four, but Dr. Pike called. He wants to talk to you, in person, at his office."

Greer groaned. "By office I assume he means the autopsy room."

"Afraid so. He says it can't wait."

"Right. Please call his office back and tell him I'll be there as soon as possible."

"Will do. And Sheriff… try to remember to eat today."

"Says the woman who should have gone home an hour ago."

After she'd said goodbye, she nodded to Chase, and he ended the call, then crossed his arms. Looking at her as if he'd been vindicated.

Greer stared at him. "Are you going to stand there while I get dressed, too, or…"

He blinked, as if he hadn't even realized she was naked behind the thin fabric before carding his fingers through his hair. "I'll call Foster. He's already at the hangar since we're on call for the next few days. Get us a lift to Providence."

"I can drive."

"You heard Shirley. It can't wait."

His boots didn't even make a sound as he turned and walked out, vanishing through the door. Greer leaned against the shower wall. If this was an indication of how the day would progress, it was going to be another long one.

* * *

Chase stopped outside the autopsy room when Greer raised her hand before slipping inside. It had only been twenty minutes since they'd left her apartment, but it had felt like hours, each minute crawling past until he'd wanted to scream.

He glanced at the large silver doors. Rhett was back there. Spread out on one of the cold, stainless steel tables. Reduced to a number on a file. The sum of Chase's failures.

Foster moved in beside him before turning and leaning against the wall. He rolled his right shoulder a few times as he shook out that hand before shoving it in his pocket. He didn't talk, just stared at Chase until the man's unspoken questions grated on Chase's last nerve.

He grunted, shifting over to steal a peek through one of the windows, not that he could see anything important. "Whatever's burning a hole in your ass, buddy, just spit it out before you pop some of those screws in your shoulder lose from the strain."

Foster glanced at the closed door, then back to him. "Not sure you really want to hear what I have to say."

"Since when has that ever stopped you before?"

"Fine. What the hell's going on between you and Greer?"

Chase straightened. He'd expected Foster to talk about Rhett, about Chase's obvious fixation on everyone's safety. How he hadn't really slept, had barely eaten, since that night. Hell, his undeniable spiral into the abyss Greer had mentioned. Not this. "Nothing."

"Seriously? That's your answer?"

"Yes, seriously, because it's the truth. Nothing's happened."

"Which I suspect is the issue because if it had been any colder inside the chopper, my damn instruments would have frozen." Foster pushed off the wall. "You barely looked her in the eyes, and there's no missing the freaking walls between you, despite the fact you're dancing around her like a damn satellite, trying to protect every angle. I've never seen you this hyper-focused about someone's safety before. Not even after Sean died. So, I'll ask again. What the hell's going on?"

"Of course, I'm focused on her safety. Someone killed Rhett. Killed that nurse. For all we know, they're targeting Greer."

"Or this is all about Rhett, and they killed Stacey because she overheard something damning he muttered while coming out of that coma."

Chase clenched his jaw. "I can't afford to take that chance."

"Why? When you've made it clear she doesn't mean anything beyond a friend to you." Foster shook his head. "And honestly, that's up for debate, right now."

"What are you even talking about?"

"You. Sabotaging the best thing that's ever happened to you, because you haven't dealt with the past." Foster paced the width of the hallway before facing Chase, again. "We've all got demons, buddy. And we've all been fighting them since long before that damn flight. It took me and Zain nearly losing Mac and Saylor to finally pull our heads out of our asses. And Kash had to nearly drown before he grew a set. But you…"

Foster snorted. "You've been quietly treading water, pushing it all down while pretending you were healing. That you'd found some form of inner peace, all the while being secretly relieved Greer wasn't ready to commit. That you could stay in the friend zone while you waited for some kind of abiding forgiveness. Then, Rhett miraculously wakes up, and all the guilt you've been hiding finally starts to lift. And for the first time in your life, you took the kind of risk you can't train for. Until some bastard stole it."

Foster loomed closer. "I don't know what's going on inside your head, but if you don't shake it loose, she's gonna run. Not just from you, but from Raven's Cliff. From everything. Because if I've learned anything about Greer, it's that she's not the kind of person to come between others. And she knows, if she stayed, there'd always be a wedge between her and us, regardless of what we said."

He tilted his head when Chase went to break eye contact. "I know you don't think you're worthy, and I get you need time to work through this. Just don't take too long, brother, or the only woman you're ever going to love will be long gone. And you'll have to spend the rest of your life knowing you had your happy ending, and you threw it away because you were too fucking scared to believe you deserved anything other than endless suffering."

Foster straightened, clenching his hand as he rolled his shoulder, visibly pushing down some of his tension. He held firm, still standing too close, when the doors opened on a whoosh, cold air tinged with a slight chemical odor spilling out along with Greer.

She held one of the doors ajar, gazing between them as if she wasn't sure if she should interrupt or go back inside. "Everything okay out here?"

Foster stepped back and plastered on a fake smile. "Golden. You finished?"

Greer looked at Chase, lips pursed, some of the color draining from her face before she sighed. "Dr. Pike's willing to edge into one of those gray areas I mentioned last night, if you think you're okay to come in and hear what he has to say."

Chase moved forward, Foster's words still ringing in his head. Thoughts he'd unpack once he'd had some time to process them without the stain of Rhett and Stacey's deaths tainting them. "Totally focused."

She stopped him with her palm on his chest. "Before I do this, there're a few ground rules. One, nothing you hear goes beyond the team."

Chase arched a brow. "The entire team?"

"I'm not an idiot. I know how you guys operate, and I know you'll share the intel with Kash, Zain and the others. But if I hear any rumors, I'll arrest your asses for obstruction."

Foster nodded. "Understood."

"Second... I know you guys are tough sons of bitches, but..." She glanced over her shoulder for a moment. "It's different when it's someone you love on the table. And yeah, I know firsthand how that feels, so... Be very sure before you step inside because you can't uncross this line."

Chase looked over at Foster, his buddy's answer already evident in the way he narrowed his eyes as he drew himself up. "Not sure it can be any worse than finding him..."

Chase didn't finish, the truth already hanging between them like an omen. "Anything else?"

Greer opened the door wider, waving them in. "Yeah. Don't make me regret this."

Chase nodded, then followed Foster into the room. The bright lights glinted off the expanse of metal surfaces, that chemical scent saturating the air as they headed toward the tall man standing behind a silver slab. A white sheet glowed in the harsh light, the silhouette beneath more than a bit familiar.

Dr. Jonas Pike looked up, waving them over as he squared his shoulders, shoving the bridge of his glasses against his face. "Beckett. Remington."

Foster stopped a couple feet back. "Thanks for bending the rules for us."

Pike shrugged. "It's not something I do lightly, but considering the results, I felt you should be adequately prepared, just in case."

Chase swallowed, nearly choking on the lump in his throat. "So, these deaths are linked?"

Pike crossed his arms. "We'll get to that, but to start..." He waved at the sheet. "May I?"

Foster flashed Chase a quick side-eye, waiting until Chase nodded before answering. "We're ready."

Pike grabbed the edge of the sheet, then eased it down until he'd exposed Rhett's torso. That number glaring up at Chase like a hieroglyphic curse. Sharp. Unforgiving. He spared a quick glance at Rhett's face, swallowing against the crest of bile at the back of his throat.

Twenty years in the service. Rescues and missions that had scarred him in ways he couldn't put into words. Brothers he'd lost. Nightmares that haunted even his waking moments. And yet, seeing Rhett lying there, silent, almost vulnerable, eviscerated Chase to his core. Reminded him of all those reasons he'd stayed distant, just like Foster had claimed.

Without making eye contact, Greer shifted closer and squeezed his hand. Just her small palm brushing across his for a second before easing free. As if she knew even that light contact was too much.

That it threatened to take him to his knees.

Yet, her gentle touch anchored him. Calmed the panicky roil of his gut in a way no one else ever had.

Pike motioned toward Rhett. "You're already aware of Mr. Oliver's obvious injuries — the gunshot and knife wounds — but it's what I discovered during the autopsy that's relevant." He pointed to a small mark on Rhett's arm. "Do you know what this is?"

Chase leaned in closer, staring at the tiny hole for a few seconds. "Looks like a needle stick."

"Good eye. We're talking extremely small gauge."

"But the nurses always used the IV to give him any meds."

"Which I already confirmed with Dr. Tremblay, myself. So, how did he get it?"

"Wait." Chase inched forward. "Are you saying Rhett was injected with something that killed him?"

Pike blew out a long breath, glancing at Greer, and Chase knew everything was about to change. "Potassium chloride, actually, which is hard to determine as natural levels rise astronomically after death. But using liquid from the eye and some other techniques, I'm confident that whoever attacked him gave him a lethal injection likely five to ten minutes before you reached him. Just enough time to give the illusion of life before his body succumbed to the overdose."

Pike stood there, staring, before sighing. "What I'm saying is, there was no way your teammate could have been saved. No amount of intervention that would have brought him back. Diabolical, really."

Foster scrubbed a hand down his face. "Christ. What about Stacey?"

Pike shifted to the table behind him. "I haven't done the full autopsy, yet, but I did check her for puncture marks, and she's clean except for a suspicious one between her toes. Now, that's a popular injection site for anyone abusing a substance who hopes to keep it hidden. Nothing suggests that, but I won't know if it's the same MO or if this is something different until I get the results back. I can tell you that she recently got a tattoo on her hip of the number fifty-five."

"Damn." Foster glanced over at Greer. "Can we confirm with family or friends if she had the tattoo before last night?"

Greer nodded. "Faraday's sending over her file. He asked around for me and everyone's fairly certain she didn't have any tattoos."

Foster crossed his arms. "So, these are connected."

Pike shrugged. "I can't confirm that until after I have all the results, but I thought you should know, in case there're more victims. I'm not telling you not to provide advanced life-saving measures, but you should be aware that if this is the work of one man, it's possible none of his intended victims have a real chance at survival."

Greer stepped forward. "Thanks, doc. I'll look for a copy of your report once I'm back at the station. I'd appreciate an update on whatever you discover with Ms. Bradford as soon as you're able."

Greer motioned toward the door, ensuring it closed behind them before raking her hand through her hair.

Foster glanced back at the autopsy room. "That was... unexpected."

She looked them both in the eyes. "I'm really sorry about Rhett. I should have forensics back this morning, and I've asked for a rush on Stacey's. I also got a message from the DoD. They'll be sending me a heavily redacted file today." Greer toed the floor. "I know you guys are on call, but I could use some insight later, if you're around. I won't ask you to break any confidences involving national security, but I might have questions only you four can answer."

"We'll be as open as we can."

"That's all I can ask. Whoever's doing this is sending us a message. And it'd be nice to know who he's talking to before another body drops." She gazed fleetingly at Chase. "Now, I just need a lift back."

Foster waved toward the door, pinning Chase with a hard stare before following her. Chase looked at the autopsy room doors, chest tight, cold sweat beading his brow.

Potassium chloride.

He hadn't seen that coming. Hadn't considered all his efforts had been pointless. That he'd never had a chance to save his buddy. Knowing…

He wasn't sure if it stung more or eased some of the guilt. Either way, he needed to get a grip. Get his head out of his ass and into the game — figure out who this asshole wanted to impress. Not just to salvage his relationship with Greer, if he hadn't already destroyed it beyond saving, but because she was right.

This wasn't just a random killing. It was personal. And he had a bad feeling it was only the beginning.

CHAPTER NINE

"You need to go home."

Greer looked to her left, arching her brow at Bodie as he stood there, arms crossed, the Army Ranger in him surrounding him like a tangible shield. Similar to what Chase and his buddies projected, and what she assumed intimidated most people.

She took a swig of overly strong coffee. "You do realize I spend most of my free time around Chase and his teammates, right? They've got that death vibe down to a fine art."

Bodie shook his head, then walked over to the desk she'd braced her ass against. "You're a real buzzkill, you know that?"

"It's come up." She nodded at her whiteboard. "And I'll go home once I've stared at this board long enough that it starts to make sense."

"Right. Because sleep deprivation always helps with clarity."

"You know that old saying. You're either part of the solution…"

Bodie chuckled. "Maybe you just need someone with fresh eyes. Looks like you got forensics back while I was out dealing with frat pledges, so lay it out for me."

Greer sighed, then stood, walking over to the board. "Okay, we know…"

She trailed off as the door opened, Chase and the others walking through, a hint of wood smoke drifting along the breeze. They stopped just inside the threshold, scanning the room as if they'd thought they'd have to throw down. Maybe fight off a rogue band of tangos.

Greer arched a brow. "I didn't wire the place if that's what you're worried about."

Foster motioned to the room. "Actually, we're looking for the S.W.A.T. team you had waiting to arrest us because the way Atticus phrased it, you were on the warpath, and we're your targets."

"Seriously?"

"You know how he gets."

"First of all, you all have alibis. Chase was with me, and I know the rest of you were scarfing down pie at that new all-night café. Which is the real problem, because I doubt you'd planned on bringing us any. And second, I don't need S.W.A.T. I just need Jordan."

Bodie coughed. "Way to boost my ego there, Greer."

Greer smiled. "Please, the woman could take us all down without breaking a sweat. Which reminds me, before you lose your shit, Kash, she's out with Eli on patrol. Should be back shortly."

Kash chuckled. "How angry was she when you insisted Eli babysit her?"

Greer scoffed. "She's babysitting him. Eli doesn't know this county well enough to go traipsing off on his own, yet, and I'd rather not lose anyone else. Which reminds me, I heard your last rescue had a better result."

Foster headed for the coffee machine, pouring a cup before leaning against the wall. "We managed not to add to your caseload, so that's a positive."

"I appreciate that, and we can all use a win right now."

Zain ambled over to the whiteboard. "Can't help but notice there's not as much empty space."

Greer pinched the bridge of her nose. "It'd be more impressive if any of it gave me the answers. As it is, I've gone through financial and medical records, cell logs — had Portland PD track down a couple possible leads — but there's nothing in either of their backgrounds that points to a connection outside of Raven's Lodge, and nothing in either of their files worth killing over."

Foster nodded. "What about Rhett's military record?"

Greer snorted. "The three words per page that weren't blacked out have been extremely insightful."

"You did mention it was going to be redacted."

"There's redacted, and then there's the DoD laughing in my face."

Chase inched forward, meeting her gaze when she expected he'd skip over it — focus on the patch of air off her shoulder like he'd been doing the past couple days.

"Was Pike able to confirm if Stacey had been dosed, too?"

She pursed her lips. She could lie. Hide behind her badge in order to save his sanity a bit, but it wouldn't do either of them any good. Especially if there were more victims. "He just called."

"Potassium chloride?"

She glanced at Foster, then back to Chase. "Not this time. Apparently, it was a massive insulin overdose."

Chase's expression fell, his shoulders rounding slightly as if she'd punched him in the stomach. "She was diabetic? She didn't have a medical alert bracelet."

"That's because she wasn't. Which suggests our perp injected her for the same purpose as he did Rhett. To make you think you had a chance at saving her."

"Except where if I'd known, I could have countered it with glucose—"

"But that's the point. You couldn't have known, which also explains why he strangled her. It masked any symptoms you might have picked up on as part of the trauma. And Pike estimates she was too far gone by the time we arrived."

She took a step forward — nearly reached for his hand — before catching herself. Drawing back when he looked as if he wanted to crawl out of his own skin. She took a breath, then stared each of the men in the eyes. "We need to have a candid talk."

She stood her ground when the men all gave each other a look. One of those internal conversations she swore they all had with nothing more than an arched brow or a frown. "I'm concerned about the possible implications of some of the forensics."

She grabbed a couple photos off the board and held them up. "I assume you knew Rhett still wore his dog tags."

Chase nodded. "No way we were removing them until…" He swallowed, clenching his jaw before pushing out a rough breath. "Why?"

She handed him the first photo. "Someone inscribed a word on the back."

Chase stared at the photo, sharing it with his buddies. "*Abandoned*. What the hell does that mean?"

"I was hoping you might know."

Kash shook his head. "That word wasn't on there the last time we saw him."

"You're sure?"

"We checked them every time…" Kash clenched his fists before Nyx nudged him, then sat on his feet. "It was our way of showing him we were still there. Still waiting." He gave the dog a scratch. "I know that sounds crazy but—"

"It doesn't." She handed them the next image. "Then, I'll assume you don't know what *mercy* means, either? It was scratched on a similar dog tag found with Stacey."

Zain leaned in close, brow furrowed, red creeping along his cheeks. "No idea. Strange she doesn't have it around her neck in any of the other photos."

"That's because she wasn't wearing it. Pike discovered it lodged inside her esophagus. She'd likely tried to swallow it just prior to being killed."

Foster rolled his right shoulder. "As in, this asshole shoved it down her throat?"

Greer pursed her lips. "Considering she didn't have any military ties, I doubt it was hers. While it looks authentic, it's blank on the other side. And seeing as she was probably choking on it when he strangled her…" She locked her gaze on Chase. "Pike said it was impressive you were able to establish an airway."

Chase mumbled something under his breath, then focused on her. "Not that it did her any good."

"She was dead the moment this guy took her. Nothing either of us did was going to change that."

Chase looked away as he scrubbed a hand across his face before drawing himself up. Reinforcing all those walls he'd created over the past two days. "Have you ever seen anything like this before?"

She froze for a moment, the words sparking a wave of unwanted memories. How she'd stood in the war room, night vision cameras streaming on the monitors. The shouts. The explosions. The blood. All playing out in real time.

Zain sighed. "That's a yes."

Chase inched forward, squeezed her hand. One of the only times he'd initiated contact in the last thirty-six-hours — other than guarding her ass. "You mentioned you profiled extremist groups for the bureau. Were part of a number of JSOC units."

Greer toed the floor. "Sadly, I've profiled groups who participate in these kinds of rituals. Often as a way of weeding out anyone they deem impure or unworthy. Modern versions of old witch trials, I suppose. The fact our perp switched his MO — a different drug. Strangulation instead of shooting." She leaned against one of the desks. "It's more than a bit concerning."

Foster moved over to the whiteboard. "What about the numbers?"

The subject change eased some of her lingering memories. Allowed her to shove down the rest. "Obviously, they could be almost anything. Part of an address, a phone number, old mission log or an ID. Bodie's running algorithms to compile the most likely options. One possibility does come to mind, though."

Zain looked at Foster, then Kash and Chase before crossing his arms. "Geographical coordinates."

Greer hitched out her hip. "Did you just check with your buddies before offering that up?"

"Of course not."

"That muscle in your left temple tenses when you lie. And yeah, that's at the top of my list. No one goes to these extremes unless he wants us to figure it out. And with him using flash bangs, assault rifles and flares… This feels more field related."

Foster tapped his chin. "You think this guy's getting revenge for something that happened at this mystery location."

"If we're right about the numbers? It makes sense. His way of giving us his origin story."

Zain walked over to the board and grabbed the marker. "Forty-two and fifty-five. If we assume those are degrees, and you're looking for an area where something covert could have happened that wouldn't have made the evening news, there're only a couple options that aren't in the middle of an ocean. One being Russia, though I'd assume further south, where the steppe meets the mountain fringes. We're talking sparse settlements, and jurisdictional complexity. Easy to be off-grid yet reachable by small convoys. Prime landscape for extremists groups or abduction scenarios."

Foster nodded. "Could be the Russia–Caucasus corridor — thin on population, thick on deniability. Though, the other option is what... Kazakhstan?"

Zain nodded. "Sounds about right. It's all wide-open grasslands and semi-deserts with few settlements, long distances between towns, and minimal policing — good for a remote a training camp or bunker. And the border regions allow smuggling routes."

Greer stared at them. "You know all that? Off the top of your heads?"

Foster merely shrugged.

"Which means you've done multiple missions in both areas." She kept talking when they looked as if they might interrupt. "I'm not asking for details, though, since the intel the DoD sent me is useless, I'd appreciate it if you four could go through your old mission logs. Let me know if there were any ops that went sideways enough someone might come gunning for you."

"We'll have a look." Foster glanced at his buddies, again. "Are there any scenarios that don't involve us?"

"Sure." Greer grinned wryly. "Someone could be seriously pissed at me. I've green lit high asset retrieval missions to more places than I'd like to admit via those JSOC units, and not all of them were without casualties.

Or we're simply dealing with an opportunistic psychopath, and it's just a coincidence he started with Rhett."

"But you don't think so."

"Besides the fact I don't believe in them, between the dog tags, the military-style attacks and the way the vics were posed, I—"

"Posed?" Foster stepped closer. "What do you mean, posed?"

Greer glanced at Chase, arching a brow.

Chase blew out a harsh breath. "Rhett had IV tubing wrapped around him reminiscent of a rescue harness. And Stacey had the same kind of tubing wrapped around her neck, just like the mannequin in the utility room."

Foster's eyes widened. "There was a mannequin?"

Chase crossed his arms. "I wasn't sure how much Greer wanted me to say."

"Or maybe you didn't want us to conclude that you were this asshole's ultimate target?"

Greer stepped between them. "Easy. All we know for sure is that these two crimes are likely linked, and I've got a ton of work to do if I'm going to catch whoever's behind this. You four focus on those missions. I've already got a call into my friend Nick Colter. He's agreed to dig through the old JSOC files — see if anything pops up that gives him serious pause. But I think it's safe to say, none of your crew goes anywhere alone. And that's no longer a request."

Foster turned to face her. "Which means you, too."

"I'll do my best."

She twisted to tape the photos back on the board when the room swam for a moment, tilting beneath her feet. Chase grabbed her before she tripped into the wall, tugging her against his chest. Holding her tight as one hand slipped around her back, the other cupping her head.

Citrus and evergreen.

Just like in her Bronco that first night. The unmistakable aroma soothed her nerves. Quieted the voices she hadn't been able to muzzle since they'd found Rhett.

Since everything had gone sideways.

He tsked, pulling her tighter when she thought about easing back. "When's the last time you ate?"

She melted into his embrace, granting herself one moment before she finally pushed away, tucking some hair behind her ear. "This morning."

Chase scoffed. "You mean that half-eaten bagel on your desk?"

"I ate…" She let the words fade when he motioned to the stale bagel peeking out from a piece of twisted brown paper.

"That's what I thought." He stared down at her, a hint of a genuine smile lifting his lips. "C'mon. We'll head over to the café. Grab some soup or something before they close."

She looked at him. "You're not going to insist I go home? Sleep?"

"I know better. Though, we'll have that discussion later. Food, first."

A creak, followed by traffic noises in the distance. "Typical. Looks like we missed the good stuff."

Greer chuckled as Jordan's voice carried from the doorway, her amused tone impossible to miss. Greer glanced over her shoulder, putting a bit of space between her and Chase before shaking her head. "You're late. I expected you both back ten minutes ago."

Jordan shrugged. "Eli drives like an old man."

Eli rolled his eyes. "Just because I didn't tip the cruiser onto two wheels and manhandle it across some rickety old bridge doesn't mean I drive slow." Eli moved over to Bodie. "She's nuts."

"It wasn't that old." Jordan glanced at Kash, then back to her, and Greer knew there was more to the story.

Greer crossed her arms. "That's not really why you were late, was it."

Jordan shook her head. "We might have a problem. We stopped at the Lighthouse Café to get some coffee, and the owner, Josh Walton, came out and said that Anna Delgado didn't show up for work today, and he's concerned."

Greer frowned. "Anna. She's been working there about a year. Left an abusive relationship. Started fresh. Her ex is doing a dime in the state pen. Does she often blow off work?"

"Josh said she hasn't missed a shift since she started."

"When's the last time anyone saw her?"

Jordan glanced at Eli, then back. "Not since she went off shift two days ago. We did a welfare check. No one home. No signs of a struggle, but there were a couple sets of footprints in the mud along the property line by some trees."

"What kind of footprints?"

"Based on the tread, I'd say combat boot, size eleven. Had to be sometime after the rain ended early this morning."

Eli stepped forward. "But that area is on the boundaries of a state park with lots of trails. It could have been a hiker or dog walker."

Greer nodded. "Still, the timing's questionable. Let's—"

"Sheriff?" Shirley stuck her head around the corner. "Hate to interrupt, but I just got a call about a woman trapped on a cliff on the edge of Oswald Park. Description matches Anna Delgado. Normally, I'd just call Atticus, but in light of everything…"

"This caller leave a name?"

"Nothing. Said he was flying over in an ultralight. Couldn't help, then the line went dead."

"Damn." She looked at Foster and the others. "What's your take?"

Foster walked over to the map Greer had covering a large portion of one wall. "Landscape's a bit of a nightmare. Heavily forested with tons of blow down. Chase and Kash can rappel, but trying to get a litter back up without it getting caught up on deadfall and branches would be nearly impossible. Especially with the way the cliffs curl in on themselves. Creates this giant funnel. Best bet would be to anchor everything from the top and pull her up. Once she's on solid ground, we can probably airlift her — transport her to Providence."

Chase nudged her. "You know we have to respond."

"Of course, just… If you're using Saylor as backup, send someone with her. And I'll drive out — meet you along that fire road. If this is Anna, I'll need a statement if she's able. Some photos, just in case."

"Not alone."

"Chase…"

"Either you pick someone, or I'll ride with you." He stared her down. "With the way you drive, we'd probably get there around the same time anyway."

"Fine." Greer pointed at Eli. "Eli, you're with me. Bodie. Jordan. Hold down the fort, and unless there's a mass casualty event, you stick together on any incoming calls."

Greer shoved Chase when he hovered too close. "All right. I'll meet you guys there. Just be careful."

Chase stared at Eli until the guy inhaled, then nodded. Greer looked between them, but Chase simply turned and walked out, Foster's truck pulling out of the station lot a moment later.

She motioned to Eli. "What was that?"

Eli drew himself up. "Nothing."

"I was in the bureau for twelve years. I can handle myself."

"Of course. I'm just backup. Getting a lay of the land."

She glared at him, then headed for the door, stopping when Shirley stepped in front of her — held out a protein bar. The woman tapped her foot, waiting until Greer peeled back a corner — took a bite — before Shirley moved aside. Looked at Eli as if she planned on quizzing him once they got back as to whether Greer had eaten all of it.

Greer chewed on the bar as she ran to her Bronco. She needed to get ahead of this asshole before he left another clue. Or worse, he decided it wasn't worth drawing out and tried to take Chase's entire team down in one epic event.

CHAPTER TEN

"Chase. Brother, you need to breathe."

Chase clenched his jaw before eyeing Kash across the cabin. Nyx sat at his feet, harnessed and ready to deploy. Just like they'd done all those years in the service.

Except it wasn't just Chase and his buddies' lives on the line.

He looked out the window, watching the coastline rush past. Waves crashed against the unforgiving cliffs, long stretches of rugged forest terrain stretching toward the horizon. "I am breathing, jackass."

Kash leaned back in the seat, crossing his feet at the ankles. Looking way too relaxed. "Is that what you call this? Because you're practically frothing at the mouth."

Kash sighed when Chase flipped him off. "She'll be okay. She has Eli with her. Guy's hardcore. He'll have her back."

"He'd better because I'll hand him his ass if she gets hurt on his watch."

"Annnnnd he's back."

"Shut up." He fiddled with the edge of his harness. "I know Greer can handle herself, but this guy…"

Kash shifted until he had his elbows braced on his knees. "It's all pretty dark. And we'd understand if you need to focus on watching her six for a while. We can always get Seth or Randy to sub-in if trying to divide your attention gives you a freaking aneurism."

"Greer's going to give me the aneurism. And I'm not tapping out. I just need her to consider her own damn safety for once. She seems to think she's bulletproof."

"Then, it's a good thing she's got the hots for a medic."

"The hots? Seriously, Kash?"

"Don't hate the messenger." His expression sobered. "She's crazy about you. You know that, right?"

Chase snorted, nodding when Foster glanced over his shoulder and gave him the one-minute sign. "She was. Not sure she's looking for anything other than my ass in a sling right now."

"Maybe if you keep your head out of it like when you held her back at the station, she'll pivot again. Though, I agree she needs to take better care of herself. I swore she was going to tank before you caught her."

"And yet, I bet she still hasn't eaten anything." He stood when Foster started bleeding off some speed, heaving his medic bag onto his back before reaching for the flexible litter, only to have Kash grab it first.

Kash tsked. "You can get the doors."

Chase huffed, then opened the doors. Deep shadows engulfed the coastline, the last vestiges of light quickly fading along the horizon. He switched on his headlamp, scouring the cliffside — searching for a trace of their victim.

His comm unit crackled, then Foster's voice. "Got her. About fifty feet down at your ten o'clock."

Chase nodded as her limp form materialized in the strong beam. "Copy. Looks like her jacket snagged on a branch. Kept her from falling all the way down. Not sure how long she has before that wood snaps."

Kash clicked his mic. "I can rappel to that small opening just north of her. Limit the downwash. I'll set up anchors and send down a line. Have Nyx patrol the immediate area just in case we're not alone. Once the rope's ready, Chase can lower directly to her location then clip in. Assess the situation. Either way, it's not going to be pretty."

Foster gave them a thumb's up. "Saylor and Zain are coming in fast. She said this area's full of shoals and rocks, but she'll get in close in case things go sideways. Her usual insane tactics. Just be careful and take appropriate firepower with you."

Kash scrunched up his face as he tapped his weapon. "When don't we."

The rotor wash buffeted the cliff, thundering against the stone face as Foster brought the bird into a hover. Nose angled into the wind, Kash's rope snapping in the swirling drafts as it fell out the open doors, hitting the small patch of dirt below them. His buddy gave a mock salute, then launched forward, sailing down the line, one hand working the rope, the other holding his rifle.

He landed a few seconds later, cleared the area, then unclipped Nyx.

A few quick movements, and the rope slipped free, curling in the spiraling vortex before Chase reeled it in. Foster held his position until Kash had three anchor points set, the litter roped and ready with another line already tossed over the edge, fluttering in the wind a few feet from their patient.

Chase clicked his mic as Foster repositioned the chopper. "Heading down. I'll transfer as quickly as possible, so we don't risk blowing her off the cliff."

"Roger, and buddy…" Foster looked back across his shoulder, not budging an inch as he held everything steady. "Watch your damn six."

"Here's hoping Zain's got his game on, just in case."

Chase took a breath, then stepped off the skid, the rope humming through his hand, his boots skimming the air. Seagulls called nearby, his headlamp cutting a circle through the encroaching darkness as he approached the narrow ledge, the beam illuminating the pale rock.

The woman slumped against a pile of branches, her bleach blonde hair glowing in the harsh light. Chase slowed his approach, timing his landing with the gusting wind. He hit the stone boots first, scrambling for a hold before the downwash compromised her safety.

It took a couple tries to reach the other rope before he had it clipped through his carabiner, releasing his tether to the chopper.

Chase clicked his mic. "I'm clear."

Foster didn't waste a second, banking left, hugging the rock wall before heading off — circling nearby until they needed a pickup.

Chase grabbed some gear and readied a couple anchor points, securing the woman before the damn branch cracked and she tumbled the fifty-foot drop into the ocean. Once secure, he crouched beside her, removing enough supplies to run through her vitals — determine what level of screwed she was — before brushing back a tangle of hair from her face. "Kash? It's Anna."

Kash breathed into the mic. "Break it down for me, buddy."

"Airway's clear, but I've got reduced breath sounds on her right side. Pulse is weak with bouts of tachycardia. Skin's pale, lips bluish." He moved down her body. "Visible leg deformity suggests a fractured right femur. Femoral pulse present but thready. Minimal external blood loss, but I suspect massive internal trauma."

He secured a neck brace, then rubbed his knuckles along her sternum. "Anna? Can you hear me?"

She groaned, eyelids fluttering a few times before she managed to keep them open — look up at him.

He smiled, readying more supplies. "Welcome back. Do you remember me? Chase Remington. I'm with Raven's Watch."

She blinked, blacked out for a moment, then resurfaced, nodding ever so slightly. "I…"

"Don't move your head or try to talk too much. Just stay with me, okay? I've got you."

She gasped, then fisted his shirt. "Help…"

Chase snapped his gaze to hers for a moment before slipping a needle in her arm — setting up an IV. "Everything's going to be okay. Did you fall? Or did someone do this to you?"

Her chin quivered. "A man…"

"Got it. Just stay calm. I'll have us out of here in few minutes." He tapped his comm unit. "Everyone have their head on a damn swivel. Anna said someone left her like this."

Chase removed his vacuum splint and secured it around her thigh, lining up the straps. "It looks like you've broken your leg. I need to immobilize it before we can pull you up. It's gonna hurt, but I need you to stay still so we don't Peter Pan off this cliff, all right?"

She cried out as he removed the air, increasing the pressure as the splint molded to her leg — gave him the stability he needed in order to get her up the cliff.

Her grip eased for a while, before she pulled herself back. "Monster…"

Chase made eye contact. "It's okay. I won't let anyone hurt you. Just keep looking at me." He adjusted the IV flow rate. "Anna? Did he give you anything? Inject anything into your arms or legs?"

Tears welled in her eyes, a few slipping down her cheeks. "No… he…"

"It's going to okay. We just need to get you out of here." Chase tapped his mic. "Kash, send down the SKED."

Rocks and dirt rained down beside them, the rolled strip of orange plastic quickly slipping along the cliff face. Chase grabbed it as it settled beside him, bouncing in the gusting wind.

The anchors groaned, the rope creaking against the strain as he eased her against his chest long enough to wrap the sheet around her — snug the straps until the unit created a protective cocoon. She mumbled something under her breath, fading in and out of consciousness as he readied everything for the main haul.

He pushed a few meds, placed some warm compresses on the outside of her clothes, then radioed in. "She's stable. Double checking knots."

Anna reached for him, but he tucked her hand back inside.

"I know it's scary, but all you have to do is relax. Let us do the lifting. I'll be right beside you."

She blinked twice.

He clicked his mic. "Package ready. Start ascent."

The SKED shimmied, shaking as Kash started hauling from above, the outer layer screeching over the jagged rocks. They got her a few feet up before her eyes flashed as her breath hitched, a thin, whistling sound tightening into nothing. She arched, clawing at the webbing, a few tears leaking down her cheeks.

"Damn it, hold the main. She's got a tension pneumo."

Chase ripped open the kit, bracing her with his knees as he grabbed the needle — slipped it between her ribs. Air hissed through the open tube, some of the color returning to her cheeks as she sucked in a large breath, finally easing back in the litter.

Chase checked her breathing, relaxed a bit as it slowly equalized, before taping the tube in place. "Okay, we're good. Resume ascent. On her left."

The litter rattled, then inched up the cliff, rocks and dirt sloughing off as Chase pushed from beneath, keeping the edges clear from the stabbing branches and bramble. The gusting winds roared past as they neared the edge, the strong currents catching the SKED — almost knocking him off as the litter floated above the rock, swinging like a pendulum. He tugged his line taut, wrestling with the SKED until he locked it down — got everything stabilized. Dirt and leaves swirled around them in small eddies as he reached for the lip — held the litter secure as Kash wrapped his hands around the top.

A crack.

Clean. Sharp.

Echoing off the rocks as birds scattered from the trees.

The sound barely registered before Chase launched to his right, kicking off the rocks. He swung in front, determined to block any other shots, but she was already slouched against the webbing. Eyes open. Blood eating up her jacket.

Kash shouted something in the background, hauling the litter up and behind him onto flat ground a second later, rifle shouldered, return fire cutting up the tree line off in the distance where the cliff curled back toward them. What had to be several hundred meters off. More shots boomed from beneath, Zain adding to the mix as

Chase scrambled up the last few feet before moving over to Anna.

No pulse.

Just a steady flow of blood oozing from the massive chest wound.

He put pressure on it, relying on Kash and Zain to have his six when Eli popped up off the ground, rifle at the ready. Greer all but shoved him over, muttering to herself as she crouched low, looking as if she wanted to throttle Eli before darting over to the SKED.

Chase started compressions, cursing when every push only pumped Anna's blood out faster, an increasing pool puddling beneath her, staining the dirt an eerie black.

Greer pressed down on the wound, constantly scanning the grounds as Chase kept working, counting off the seconds in his head. Aware he didn't have the equipment to bring her back but unwilling to just quit.

She'd been down a few minutes when Greer grabbed his arm, waiting until he met her gaze before shaking her head.

He checked Anna's vitals.

No pulse. No hope.

Just the weight of his broken promise hanging in the air. The lingering echo of the shot still ringing across the cliff.

Greer pushed to her feet, nodded at the body as she tossed Eli her keys. "Grab a plastic bag from my trunk and lay it over our vic, then keep your ass glued to the stretcher. Get Foster on the radio. See if he can swing over and pick both of you up, then hightail it back to base. I'm going after the shooter. Kash. Chase."

She took off, hoofing it across the small clearing and into the forest. Chase and Kash caught up to her just as she started weaving through the underbrush, jumping over logs and darting around bushes. She didn't slow, despite the bramble clawing at her clothes. Likely scratching lines across her skin.

They hit a trail and really picked up speed. She waved Kash and Nyx ahead, Nyx barely held back by her leash. Her nose twitched as she slowed at a junction before turning left and taking them deeper into the park.

Chase stayed on their six, constantly checking behind them. Deep shadows covered the path, the thick canopy stealing any hints of light. He dimmed his headlamp when they came to another branching path, Kash slowing to a halt.

His buddy moved in beside him, keeping Greer positioned in the middle. Protecting her from any viable hit. "Guy's probably long gone, but based on where he'd likely been nesting, he's heading for the northeast fire road."

Greer nodded. "There's an obscure path up on the right. Cuts the distance in half. Won't be pretty, though."

Kash shrugged. "Rarely is. We'll take point. Let Nyx warn us if there's any hint of trouble. Just don't get shot."

Kash took off, boots kicking up dirt and gravel as he sprinted along the trail, angling right toward what looked like an old deer path. Nyx took the lead, keeping them on track, despite the overgrown ferns and roots covering the narrow path. Branches snapped across Chase's chest, thorns catching his clothes as darkness settled around them, just their narrow beams keeping them from tripping over logs or impaling themselves on broken stumps.

Nyx trotted to a halt, fur raised, a low, menacing growl just reaching him. Kash ducked down, signaling to the main trailhead opening up ahead of them. They switched off their lights, ducking behind a couple large boulders as they scanned the path. Chase kept Greer close, ready to cover her if he got even an inkling of an attack, when a shadow moved amidst the trees, a ghost of a glow shining from some kind of light at the perp's waist, his rifle just visible in his silhouette.

The bastard froze behind a massive pine, body hidden, head exposed just enough that when he tilted it slightly toward them, Chase knew he was looking back. As if he'd wanted them to see.

A laugh.

Deep. Maniacal.

Echoing through the trees. Mixing with the hints of fog just starting to weave through the canopy before he clicked off his light and took off, vanishing into the night.

Kash whistled to Nyx as he sprang forward, hauling ass down the last of the deer path then onto the trail, sprinting up it before heading back into the underbrush. A few twigs snapped somewhere up ahead, the odd bird cawing before taking flight.

Greer kept up, leaping over blowdown and barreling through bushes, Chase's dim light illuminating the path. Not much, but either she'd done maneuvers at night, or she had the instincts of a damn cat because she didn't miss a step. Didn't seem at all concerned she'd trip or fall down a hole.

An engine revved in the distance followed by gravel crunching beneath tires. Red taillights lit up the forest, skidding around a corner as they burst out of the woods and onto the old fire road.

Kash slowed to a halt, chest heaving, Nyx still tugging at her lead. "I'd let her go, but…"

Greer waved it off, bracing her hands on her knees as she sucked in air. "It's not worth the risk. He didn't even turn on his headlights."

Chase kept his gun at the ready, scanning the forest as he took a moment to breathe. "He wanted us to see him."

Kash nodded. "Bastard probably waited until he caught a glimpse of our lights. Not sure what that means considering he didn't attempt another shot."

Greer stared down the road, mouth pinched tight. "It means, this just got a whole lot worse." She drew herself up, cheeks red, every exhale creating a fine mist around her face. "We should head back. You guys can come out with Jordan and Nyx tomorrow if you're not on a call. See if you can find his nest. Until then, we regroup."

She turned — looked Chase in the eyes. "It's time to circle the wagons."

CHAPTER ELEVEN

Three dead.

All on her watch.

And she wasn't any closer to a viable suspect.

Greer closed her eyes as she leaned against her desk, images from the board following her into the darkness. Pike had prioritized the autopsy, and the crime lab had fast-tracked the forensics. Not that either had given much insight. She still had more questions than answers, and no way to guess who might be targeted next.

Other than Chase and his teammates.

The fact they'd gone twenty-four hours without another body only added to the tension because she knew the bastard wasn't done. Hadn't finished whatever mission he was on.

Hadn't exacted enough vengeance based on the cruel nature of his kills.

Salvation.

His last message. Burned onto another blank dog

tag, this time wrapped around Anna's ankle. What Greer assumed was the pair to the one the bastard had left with Stacey. The single word pooling dread deep in her gut because she'd seen various interpretations of salvation while working the joint-task-force missions, and they'd all carried a heavy toll.

She pinched the bridge of her nose. She'd barely slept in the past four days, and tonight wasn't looking any better.

The door creaked, a horn blaring in the distance before it cut off. A voice tsked, the familiar tone curling around her heart — squeezing it until it barely moved. Took all her strength just to keep it beating. She'd thought the time and emotional distance would lessen her feelings.

She'd been wrong.

If anything, she'd fallen harder. Chase's obvious pain tugging at the soul she'd left bleeding on her sleeve.

She scrubbed her hand across her face, putting her ever-present coffee mug down on her desk before glancing over at Chase and his buddies as they filed in. "Well?"

Foster stopped, looking over at Bodie as if the man held the answers before arching a brow. "Well, what?"

Greer resisted rolling her eyes. "Is everyone okay?"

He eased. "Fine."

"No one got shot? Or poisoned? Maybe infected with some kind of deadly pathogen that's about to wipe out my entire town?"

Zain coughed. "Is that even a thing?"

She stood, turned to face them. "Sadly, I've already lived that."

He shook his head. "No wonder you have trust issues."

"Just look me in the eyes and swear you didn't just get back from dropping another body off at the morgue."

Foster sighed. "If we'd had another body, we would've called you."

"No, you would've called Jordan or Bodie. Maybe Eli after he tackled me as soon as he heard that sniper shot the other day — as if I hadn't been a federal agent for twelve years. And you would've had one of them meet you at the hospital because you know, if one more person dies on my watch, I'm going to lose my shit."

Chase shook his head as he closed the distance and picked up her mug. "First, we need to switch you to decaf. Second, it was just a few routine calls. Nothing suspicious or deadly. And third, Eli's a former Ranger. It's in his blood."

"Please, I saw the look you gave him. And the only thing keeping me awake is the endless supply of caffeine."

"The only look was the one I give all my brothers if they're backing you up, and for the record, I'd expect Eli to tackle *my* ass if the situation warranted it. But consuming nothing but coffee is the real problem." He crossed his arms. "Have you eaten anything today?"

Greer pursed her lips, the half-eaten sandwich she'd gotten for breakfast lying accusingly off to her right. "I can eat when I stop this bastard. Sleep, then, too."

"Or, you can pass out from hypoglycemia."

"Are you always this dramatic?"

Chase leaned in close, sending a shiver down her spine. "Only when you're being incredibly stubborn."

"Says the man who hasn't slept, either. In fact, no one here has."

Bodie tsked. "You've been sending the rest of us home for regular breaks while you only catch a couple hours on your damn couch. And yeah, Chase ratted you out."

Greer gave Chase her best stink eye. "And that's the real reason I have trust issues."

Chase smiled. Not much, but more than he'd shown since Rhett's death. She gave him a quick once-over. He seemed... better. Not like before, but that death vibe had eased slightly, and he didn't look as if he wanted to crawl out of his own skin.

Bodie joined them, leaning against the wall beside the whiteboard. "None of this is your fault."

"My town, Bodie." She tapped her chest. "Which means it's my responsibility."

"I realize we're a relatively small county, but it's still too large for us to adequately cover twenty-four, seven." Bodie blew out a rough breath. "You're doing the best you can."

"And yet, I have the mayor questioning my competency on an hourly basis. And don't even start in on me with the town council."

"They're scared."

"They're not the only ones." She sighed, bracing herself against the edge of her desk. "I don't suppose forensics called back with some damning piece of evidence they missed?"

Bodie shook his head. "Nothing. No fingerprints. No DNA. Not so much as a fiber. Just the dog tag with *salvation* burned onto the back, and the bullet with twenty-four carved into it."

Zain walked over to the board. "You still think the numbers are coordinates?"

Bodie raked his hand through his hair. "I've run algorithms against other possibilities, but there're either too many numbers, too few or the option involves letters. Though, if it's some kind of file ID for a joint task, we'll need some serious hacking power in order to match it."

Greer tapped her desk. "I really doubt it's anything that encoded. This bastard's going to some extreme measures to get our attention — ensure his victims are found before they die. That takes timing. Preparation. Not to mention some brass balls. He wants us to figure it out. He's not going to make it some obscure reference we'd need to hack the freaking Pentagon in order to solve. Though, it does bring up a disturbing fact."

Foster groaned. "He's not done."

"At the least, we need another number." Greer let her head tilt back a bit. "At worst…"

Another three.

She didn't say it out loud. Didn't chance putting it out into the universe, but they all knew.

Foster glanced at his buddies, having another one of those creepy internal conversations before meeting her gaze. "I don't mean this the way it might sound. You're already spread thin, and if you keep up these insane hours, you're gonna do this asshole's job for him." He took a step closer. "You can't keep running on empty. You need more manpower."

She snorted. "If you've got a solution, I'm listening because I already have state running extra patrols along the main roads. Not that our guy is gonna out himself that way, but at least the rest of the town is a bit safer. And I've approved overtime and extra crews to process and gather evidence."

Foster inhaled, held it for a moment before sighing. "What about the bureau?"

"Wow." She placed her hand on her chest. "Now, you're just being mean."

"Greer, I—"

"I already called." She closed her eyes for a moment, reliving the roil of her stomach she'd experienced when she'd had to contact her old office. "Laid it all out. Requested assistance."

"And?"

"Apparently, there're another couple dozen sheriffs, police chiefs and joint task forces who all want help. The BAU is swamped. Their local office is understaffed and overtaxed. They did say I could use their lab if I needed it. Run any possible suspects through their more advanced databases." She snorted, bouncing her fist on her thigh. "Like that's what's holding me back from solving this thing."

She stood and paced across the room, resisting the urge to toss something at the wall. Expend a bit of her restless energy. "What I'm trying to say is, they turned me down."

Bodie coughed. "That's not what they said."

"It resulted in the same outcome."

"Except where they told you that you were already one of their best profilers, and if you couldn't figure it out, none of their people could, either, and that other departments don't have that advantage."

"Not exactly earning that praise, am I?" She startled when her cell rang before glancing at the screen. Nick Colter — CIA operative and one of the few people outside this room who she truly trusted. "Finally."

She put the call on speaker. "Nick. I hope this means you've got some good news for me."

A laugh floated over the line. "You know, Greer, if you keep asking me for these kinds of favors, you're gonna have to fly down to Langley and take me to dinner."

She glanced at Chase, noting the hint of red on his cheeks. "You're on speaker, jackass."

"What's wrong? Is there someone there you don't want to get caught flirting in front of? Like that guy you've mentioned? The medic?"

"Glad you're not making this awkward."

"Don't shoot the messenger, honey." He sighed, the heavy sound crushing any lightness from the room. "I went over your notes and all the evidence you sent, then scoured our joint operations. Based on those parameters, I narrowed the possible target groups down to two. You should have a file popping up on your encrypted server any second now."

"Can you give me the Cliff Notes version?"

Another sigh. Deeper. Rawer. And she knew he'd come to the same conclusion she had. "While I agree there're some disturbing similarities between the techniques and keywords your perp's utilizing, we both know the sheer skill of that last hit rules out most of the sleeper agents they'd be able to send your way. These people are savage and relentless, but they aren't marksmen. Most of the cult leaders and followers are low-level militia-trained at best. They rely on using mass-effect weapons and subterfuge to get their point across. Cleanse the undeserving. Definitely not the kind who'd be able to scheme to this degree while hitting a target at over seven hundred meters with dynamic forces in play. That…"

She pushed out a rough breath. "It takes years of extreme training."

"Sorry, Greer, I know that's not what you wanted to hear." Nick paused for a few moments, the silence more than deafening. "Look, I'm in the middle of something, but I should be finished in the next few days. If I haven't heard back from you, I'll check-in. If you're still in the thick of this, I'll be there."

Greer shoved back the wisps of hair that had broken free from her ponytail. "You could get into some serious trouble for that."

"Screw trouble. You've always had my back. And I swore I'd always have yours. Nothing's changed."

"You're just itching to play the hero, again."

"Again?" He chuckled. "I never stopped."

She smiled. "I'll go through the file, and I'll call if I need more help."

"You watch your six. And to everyone else who's listening, don't play around with this asshole. If he's this far gone, there's no way back."

He ended the call, the silence resonating through the room. Greer stared at her cell for a moment, the truth of Nick's comment hitting hard.

Foster cleared his throat, gaining her attention. "Seems like you've come to a conclusion."

She shrugged. "Nothing you boys haven't already considered. We all know that sniper shot was too difficult for the average person to make."

"You're thinking our guy's ex-military."

"Let's see what Nick sent before we make that final leap. Bodie?"

Bodie stopped typing on his keyboard. "Just decrypting it, now." He hit a few more keys. "Seems the last hurdle is a retinal scan. I've sent the files to your phone."

"Trust Nick to lean into his paranoia." Greer clicked on the file, waiting for the data to appear. "Okay, he narrowed these kinds of torture techniques down to a group out of Iran and one near the Carpathians. The first are more religious zealots. Extremely violent. Mostly go for those mass causality scenarios Nick hinted at. They've definitely got the know-how and the backbone to pull this off, but a single person hunting people one at a time... That's personal, and I'm not sure how they'd know about my involvement. Unless you guys also have a connection I'm unaware of?"

Foster shook his head. "Our top contenders are based in southern Russia and Eastern Europe. Missions that went seriously sideways. Multiple casualties. Though, if we think this is a former military man gone rogue, I'm not sure any of them fit. All military causalities were fatal."

She perked up a bit, staring at Nick's notes regarding his second option before meeting Foster's gaze. "Those Eastern Europe missions. I don't suppose any involved a group called the Legion?"

Foster froze. Looking her dead in the eyes for several moments before scratching the back of his neck. Glancing at his buddies as if he'd seen a ghost.

She stood. "Shit, that was your SAR team that went in with Dalton's crew."

Chase closed the distance. "You were involved in that?"

"I profiled the colony. Was able to predict a convoy. Got one of their own to turn, then green lit the entire mission." She closed her eyes, images from the drone's IR footage playing in the darkness. The ones that still haunted her. "Of course, he didn't know about the reinforcements their leader had called in until the bastards interrupted your extraction."

She swallowed, nearly puked. "I swear we didn't call for that missile strike. If it was the CIA or DoJ, it wasn't anyone in that room."

"Hey…" Chase reached out, took her hand. "That wasn't your fault. And we rescued all the hostages. Sometimes ops go sideways. Every soldier knows that going in, and we accept the risk."

"Just more blood on my hands that never quite washes off." She squeezed his fingers. "I don't suppose any of those extremists were highly trained?"

Chase snorted. "They were decent, but I didn't see anything to suggest they were our perp's level of good."

"And the men who didn't make it back?"

Zain stepped forward. "Dalton? He and his crew were hardcore. Had been Green Berets for over a decade. A medevac team went in shortly after the strike. They found dog tags, blood and bone fragments. They were all presumed KIA."

Greer nodded. "Agreed. But as I recall, they never recovered the bodies."

"From what we were told, there wouldn't have been much to recover."

Greer bit back the bile burning the back of her throat. She'd been watching that mission stream from a drone in the war room — had lived every second of it. While it had been only figures moving in that eerie green wash of night vision, she'd witnessed the missile strikes. Had felt the loss when the smoke had cleared and the entire area had been leveled.

Chase inched closer. "Hypothetically, if they had survived, do you think someone like Dalton could have been converted?"

She glanced at his buddies, then Bodie. "Despite their training, their strength, people can only hold out for so long. Some prisoners avoid the inevitable break by getting themselves killed, either by trying to escape or provoking their captors. Or they learn how to fake it enough, they integrate while biding their time. The ones who eventually crack..." She sighed. "They're taken apart down to their primordial ooze, then put back together with half the pieces missing."

"And you think that could have happened to those men?"

"Honestly? If it were all of you, I'd say no. You're definitely the kind who'd die trying to escape. As for Dalton... I don't know. But we've got military weapons, strategies and skill partnered with cult-level torture tactics. With words they've used in their manifestos inscribed on dog tags. It's worth considering."

Bodie stood. "If you give me their names, I'll see what I can find."

Greer moved over to her whiteboard and grabbed the marker. "There were four. Marcus Hodges, Carlos Rios, Royce Carver and Eric Dalton. If I remember correctly, Hodges was their comms tech, Rios their weapons' specialist, Carver was the team medic and Dalton was team leader."

Chase stayed close, as if he knew she was teetering on the edge. "Rios was in rough shape before that strike, as was Dalton and Carver. Only Hodges would have been able to run, but he didn't strike me as the type."

"Carver would be a logical choice with his medical background, but those kinds of torture techniques could have been ingrained during captivity. Who was their best sniper?"

Chase tapped his chin. "Any one of them could have made that shot, but Dalton and Rios had both trained as snipers."

Foster carded a hand through his long hair. "As much as I hate this idea is even on the table, it definitely warrants investigation. If nothing else to put their sacrifice to rest. What about that guy you turned?"

Greer stopped writing for a moment. "He died in the second assault."

"You're sure?"

She glanced back at Foster over her shoulder. "I saw it all play out in real time. So, yeah. I'm sure."

Foster grimaced. "I didn't mean…"

"It's okay. I know you've all experienced worse."

Chase reached over and eased the marker out of her hand, then placed his palm on the small of her back. "All right. Enough theorizing for a while. I'm taking you to the café to eat, then you're getting some sleep. And that's not up for debate."

Bodie crossed his arms. "Chase's right. You're working twice as much as everyone else. Time to shut it down for a few hours. Zain's gonna keep me company, and Jordan's going to hang with Kash once they're back from dealing with more frat antics. I believe it involved streaking, this time."

Greer laughed. "Those poor fools. Wait. Where's Eli?"

"He stopped to help state patrol with a tractor incident up Foster's way. I'm having him check-in every fifteen, and he knows to go directly back to my place and get some sleep once they're done. No detours. No stopping for anything without backup."

"It's almost as if you're trying to show me I'm not needed?"

"Not for the next several hours."

"Five, and I'll bring coffee." She looked at Chase. "Extra caffeine."

Chase shook his head, then motioned to the door. "Food. Then, sleep."

Greer scowled but grabbed her jacket and headed for the door. She'd take the break — give Bodie time to gather some intel. All she needed was a single lead.

CHAPTER TWELVE

It was official.

Chase needed to pull himself together — shove the guilt and uncertainty down until he needed a roadmap to find it — or he'd lose Greer.

She hadn't said that. Had sat quietly in her Bronco as he'd driven to the café, her hands clasped in her lap. Her gaze focused on the passing scenery. She'd been there, but distant.

Just like he'd been for the past few days. So focused on her safety, he'd been unable to see the toll the events had taken on her. Sure, he'd known she was exhausted. Pressured. That she harbored guilt. But hearing the tremor in her voice when she'd talked about the same mission he'd nearly died on — all the red in his ledger he still owed Rhett — it had all become painfully clear.

She was drowning, too.

It had changed him. Or maybe just lifted some of the shadows. And he'd finally understood what Foster and Kash had been trying to say.

That she was his redemption. His second chance.

He sighed as she sat across from him, chewing on her cheeseburger. Looking as if she wanted to be anywhere but there.

He reached out, gave into the urge to tuck some hair behind her ear. She startled at the light touch, pushing out a few frantic breaths before relaxing.

He'd done that to her. Left her questioning his intentions. If he'd thrown away several months' worth of friendship. Decided she wasn't worth fighting for.

He could fix it.

At least, he hoped he could. That their relationship hadn't cracked beyond healing. That there was still enough of them worth saving.

Greer chuckled. "Have I got something stuck in my teeth?"

He grinned. "No."

"Then, why the look?"

"I'm just trying to gauge how much I've screwed things up."

Those full, pink lips pursed into a slight frown. "Screwed what up?"

"Us." He waved between them. "This. I know I haven't really been there for you since…" He swallowed. "Rhett."

Greer leaned back in her chair. "I've nearly tripped over you a dozen times."

"I don't mean physically. But even then, it's been in an annoyingly overprotective way. I just…" Christ, how did he say he couldn't think about losing her without hyperventilating. "I'm not sure…"

She forced a weak smile, studying him for a few seconds before bracing her elbows on the table. "It's okay if you think we missed the moment."

That voice inside his head started poking at him as dread settled low in his gut. "What moment?"

"Ours." Her chin quivered. It wasn't something others would notice, but he did. Like an earthquake-level event that rocked him to his core. "I know I was the one who wasn't ready. Who kept pushing things off. And I suppose, I'll have to live with that if what's happened has changed things."

"What? No. I mean…" He pushed down the rush of fear. "Why do I get the feeling we aren't having the same conversation?"

Another quiver, then she stood, popped the last bite of her burger into her mouth before she tossed some cash on the table. "You're right. I'm tired. Can we talk about this later?"

She pushed past the table, walking quickly to the door. The hinges creaked, the cool night air rushing in as she stepped outside, her silhouette blending in with the shadows and fog just starting to creep through town.

Chase jogged to catch up, reaching her as she opened the driver's door before cursing and spinning. She stopped cold, trapped between him and her SUV. Just like that first night before everything had gone off the rails.

Before he'd gotten lost in the abyss.

He held firm, hating the way her eyes teared over. "Greer…"

She held up her hand. "You don't owe me an explanation. I get it."

He stopped her from shoving him out of the way. "Get what? Because if you'd let me stumble my way through the conversation, I was trying to apologize."

"For what?"

"Not being there for you the way I should have been. Getting lost in all that darkness. Having my head stuck up my ass. You pick." He sighed. "I'm not on the other side of this, yet. Losing Rhett…"

He pressed his hand against the vehicle. "Even knowing I couldn't have saved him, I still feel responsible. Still question if I deserve," he gestured between them, "all this. But I'm still crazy about you. A fact I'm scared nothing will ever change."

Greer stared up at him, eyes wide, mouth slightly open. As if she wanted to speak but couldn't find the words.

He smiled. "I don't expect the road back to be easy. I'm just hoping there's still one open for me."

Greer bit at her bottom lip, a couple tears breaking free before she fisted his shirt — stepped into him. Head pressed against his shoulder, her heart thrashing against his chest.

Definitely all the redemption he needed.

He gathered her close, holding her tight as the world faded for a moment, all the chaos and pain easing. He didn't take it further, content to simply stand there, entwined.

A throat cleared behind them. "I'm thinking you two

should spend more time in this parking lot. Good things happen."

Chase groaned as Kash's voice cut through the tender atmosphere, snapping him back. He hugged Greer tighter for a moment before easing away — looking over his shoulder. "Are you stalking us?"

Kash shrugged, one arm wrapped around Jordan, Nyx hugging his other leg. "Just stopped for some coffee before heading back to the station."

Greer sighed. "You already worked a full shift at Raven's Watch."

"And you already worked more than that." Kash tsked. "There'll be plenty of time for all of us to catch up on sleep once this asshole's behind bars. Until then, we need to spell each other off. That includes you."

"Men." Greer focused on Jordan. "You sure you're okay?"

Jordan tilted her head. "After twenty years running missions for Rook, pulling a few extra hours is nothing. I'm fine. The baby's fine." She waved at the Bronco. "Get some sleep."

Kash winked at Chase, the ass, before they headed for the café, looking way too relaxed. Or maybe Chase had simply forgotten how to play it cool. Box away any unwanted feelings. It had been second nature in the service. Since he'd met Greer...

He'd been floundering.

Barely stumbling through while holding it all inside. Having the medic part of him unravel this week...

That had been the beginning of his descent into oblivion.

Greer wrapped her arms around herself, looking more than a bit lost, as she shifted her weight from foot to foot. He grabbed her hand, led her around to the passenger side before opening the door.

He crowded her, holding her attention before she climbed inside. "Kash is an ass."

She gave him a small, genuine smile. "He's not wrong, though."

"I'll make you a deal. Come back to my place, where I know we'll be safe, and we can sleep on the couch, again. Or in the bed. But, we'll just sleep."

She arched a brow. "You promise not to get up in an hour and sit in a chair and stand guard? Because that's creepy."

He held up three fingers. "Scout's honor."

"Fine. But you're not earning a badge for this."

He closed the door once she'd buckled up, then rounded the grill and slipped behind the steering wheel. The engine growled as he pulled out of the parking lot and joined the late-night traffic. Fog rolled in off the ocean, threading through the trees and across the street as he headed for the property.

He waited until they'd turned onto the long winding road up the cliffside before giving her a nudge. "So, Nick Colter. Did you meet him when you shifted over to counterterrorism?"

Greer eyed him, obviously aware he was digging for intel. "He was still with the NCS. Had infiltrated a terrorist cell and needed a working profile for one of the newcomers. He was worried he'd been burned."

Chase nodded, constantly checking his mirrors. "How long did you two date?"

She twisted to face him, studying his profile for a while before shrugging. "We were on and off for about a year. Nothing serious. I was still dealing with Troy's death. Was well on my way to drowning myself in tequila."

"And he offered you a lifeline."

"More like a hint of light at the end of a tunnel. I still had to drag myself out, but..."

"Can I ask what happened?"

She shifted in her seat. "He got outed. Nearly died, then went dark. I tried to help, dragged his ass back from a few nasty places, but he wasn't ready to be saved. He resurfaced two years later. Sober. Focused. But by then, whatever we'd had was long gone."

She reached out and drew her finger along his arm. "He was joking about the dinner thing. The guy's in a serious relationship with some badass operative."

Chase glanced at her. "You're badass."

"I used to think so. But every time I do something remotely death defying, Jordan walks over and says, 'Hold my beer'."

He laughed. "Trust me, she puts us all to shame. And thanks." He winked. "For not calling me out on the obvious fishing expedition."

"We both have a past. But if it eases those voices in your head any, there's one thing Nick could never be."

He arched a brow in question.

She looked him dead in the eyes. "You."

He shook his head. "And just like that, you turn the tables on me, again. Looks like you're ahead by two."

"Only if we're keeping score."

"You're always keeping score, sweetheart."

She smiled at the endearment, looking as if she wanted to launch across the console — kiss him — when her eyes widened. She tapped his shoulder, pointing out the left side of the vehicle. "Chase. Pull over."

He frowned, swerving onto an old access road, his headlights mapping out the scene. Blue strobes throbbed in the distance, the mist pulsing like a heartbeat. Twin beams lit up the forest beyond, tunneling through the fog until the light bled into darkness.

Chase stilled, a volley of scenarios racing through his head before he pushed them all down. Breathed. "Looks like a cruiser."

"On a decommissioned forest road?"

"Bodie said Eli and one of the state cops were out here dealing with a tractor incident. Makes sense it might be off the main thoroughfare. But, we should take a look so you can tear Eli a new one for scaring you."

She drew herself up. "I'm not scared."

"That makes one of us."

Chase eased the SUV forward, bumping along the rutted track. Gravel kicked against the undercarriage before they slowed to a halt twenty feet back. The lone sedan sat off to the right, driver's door yawned open. Interior light gleaming yellow against the mist.

Greer scoured the area before slowly stepping out, weapon drawn. Chase followed suit, the Bronco lighting up the fog just like it had that night at the psychiatric hospital. Bringing all those memories flooding back.

How eerily familiar this felt.

Chase joined her at the front of her vehicle, scanning the area again as the cruiser's engine ticked in the background, the cooling fan whining from the strain before abruptly shutting off.

He nodded at the rear end. "Trunk's cracked open."

Greer wet her lips, a brief frown curving her mouth before she inhaled — removed any trace of emotion from her face. She pointed at the wedge of space. "Guess we check there, first."

They walked over, guns at the ready, turning a full three-sixty, before Chase grabbed the edge — mouthed a countdown. Greer backed up a bit, muzzle aimed at the trunk as he tossed it open, the large metal hatch blocking out the flashing blues.

The Bronco's headlights cast deep shadows in the large space, a hint of the jack peeking out from beneath a first aid kit. The flare box laid open, a handful scattered around the trunk.

Chase made a few hand signals, staying left as she veered around to the passenger side. They closed the distance in sync, peering into the back — bouncing the circular beams around the interior before continuing to the front. Greer opened the opposite door, sending a swirl of air through the cab.

The radio mic dangled from the rearview, the frayed cord sliced halfway down its length. The radiator hissed out front, steam slowly rising from the hood as the car's spotlight illuminated a circle of trees off in the distance, dust motes flickering in the bright light.

Chase nodded at the camera mounted on the dash. "Dashcam's set to record. Interior's warm. We must have just missed him."

Greer pulled back. "Missed him going where?"

"No idea." He paused as his beam caught something dark smeared across the outer pillar. "Shit. I've got a bloody handprint."

She darted around to his side, stared at the mark before bouncing her light across the gravel. "There's a drop beside the tire. Three more heading toward that patch of woods lit up by his spotlight."

"Maybe he hit an animal, but it took off, so he followed after it."

"God, I hope so." She grabbed her radio off her belt. "Bodie, Jordan. Anyone copy?"

A burst of static crackled over the airwaves, a muffled voice starting and stopping in the background.

She tried again — got the same unsettling response.

Chase palmed his cell. "No bars."

"He wouldn't go far. He doesn't even know his way around up here."

"We'll look for tracks. Follow if we can. Or we can backtrack until we get a signal, though, cell coverage is spotty up here, at best."

"He might not have time for us to backtrack." She motioned toward her Bronco. "You might want to grab your kit. And the shotgun in the rack. Code's your birthday — month, then day."

"I'd consider that romantic if the circumstances were different."

Chase raced back to the vehicle, slipped on his vest, then grabbed a bunch of gear and met her in front of the cruiser. He handed her a vest and the shotgun, tossing his medic bag across his back. "Point or sweep, sweetheart?"

She eyed him. "Are you going to stroke out if I take point? Because I'd feel infinitely safer knowing you have my six."

"I'll always have your six, but I'll be fine, just… watch your step. No telling what this might be. For all we know, it's a setup, and Eli's not even involved."

"Something tells me we won't be that lucky. Not that an ambush's lucky, but…"

He understood what she'd meant. Having their lives on the line was one thing. Involving others…

Chase fell in behind her as they picked their way across the grassy field, listening for any suggestion of trouble. Coyotes kicked up a chorus somewhere uphill as an owl dropped silently across their path, snatching something off the ground before vanishing into the night.

Greer stopped halfway through the field, pointing to a patch of ground. "That's his badge."

Chase closed in behind her, staring at the shield glinting in the yellow beam. "We'll leave it for now."

In case it's evidence…

He didn't voice his concerns out loud, but based on the slight slump of her shoulders, the rough exhale of breath, she already knew.

She glanced back at him. "Should we try calling his name?"

"It'll out us but... It's worth a shot."

"Elijah!" Her voice carried across the field, the massive trees throwing it back at her.

Chase scanned the tree line, but the beam only caught the mist — bleaching everything into a nauseating white.

They waited, breath held, the oppressive darkness crushing in around them.

A faint chirp.

Definitely mechanical. Like a beacon from a radio. They veered right, stopping at the edge of the field.

Chase went to one knee, tracing a faint boot print in the dirt. "I've got a partial print. Pine needles are kicked up all around. And there's a crushed fern. Someone definitely walked this way recently."

She nodded. "Fog's getting thicker. We'll have to dial back the wattage, or we'll end up blinding ourselves."

He toned down the flashlight, following her along a patchy trail until they reached an obvious fork. One curved down toward what he thought was a creek. The other continued upward, winding along a short embankment.

He tapped her on the shoulder. "Wait here for a second."

Chase darted up the embankment, searching for more prints before doubling back — heading toward the creek. A deeper imprint compressed the dirt several feet in, what looked like someone tripping their way along the trail. "This way."

Greer took point, again, shotgun at her shoulder as she followed the path toward the river, the distinctive rush of water drawing them down. Something crashed off to their left, twigs snapping as bushes rustled from the force. They turned, weapons raised, muzzles sweeping the darkness. Waiting until the noise had faded into the distance before continuing.

Another chirp.

Louder. Closer.

Greer picked up a bit of speed, waving at the mist when something clattered up ahead. Metal on rock, followed by a low thud. "Elijah."

Any peripheral noise cut off, the trees bending closer from the light breeze, as if straining to hear a reply.

They moved on, stopping when the creek ate up the trail. Cold vapor lifted off the pooling black water, and for a second, everything smelled like copper and decaying moss.

She bounced the tiny beam around the bank, inhaling at a dark object snagged on a bush.

Chase climbed over some deadfall, shining his light on the item. "It's his radio."

Greer inched closer. "Eli. If you can hear me, tap twice."

They waited, even the woods holding its breath as the cruiser's blue lights strobed in the distance. Nothing more than the occasional hint of color reflected in the fog.

Greer called a second time, staring into the darkness as if she could will Eli to appear. Make him materialize out of the foggy depths. Chase retraced his steps, still listening for a response when something thumped downstream. He paused, gaze searching the shadows, every sense on high alert, when the hollow sound echoed through the forest, again, followed by two light taps.

CHAPTER THIRTEEN

Greer inhaled, glancing over at Chase. Wondering if she'd simply willed the sound into existence. Chase snapped his gaze to the bank, shining his light along the mud until he zeroed in on a spot several feet downstream.

He lunged forward, crouching low. "I've got a knee impression and more blood."

She followed, breath held, her flashlight covering as much area as possible.

A gurgling rasp.

Low. Weak. Like someone breathing through a straw and failing.

They inched along, caught a hint of movement off the side of the bank.

Chase removed his medic bag, propped it on the bank, then jumped in. The surging current tumbled him forward a few steps until he leaned back — braced himself. He moved along the edge, stopping at a tangle of roots, clumps of moss and old leaves collecting along one side. Churning in the current as it eddied around the wood. He leaned down, highlighting a large hollow cave stretching beneath a massive spruce, one black boot poking through the weblike structure. "Eli."

Greer scrambled to the edge, slipping into the dark water. Branches clawed at her legs as she moved in beside Chase, spying Eli's face barely cresting the surface.

Chase held her back. "Stay here. Keep as much light on him as possible. I'll check for wires, then get him free."

She nodded, teeth already chattering, the beam shaking as she shivered from the cold. Chase drew in a deep breath, then dipped beneath the surface, the water quickly closing overtop his head.

Time ticked away, every second dragging on until she started searching the surface.

He should be up by now. Grabbing another breath. Telling her it's clear, unless…

A surge of panic before she shoved it down. Focused on keeping Eli pinned in the center of the beam. Trusting Chase was simply stronger than her. Better prepared.

Eli whimpered, mouthing what looked like her name before he bobbed beneath the surface, reappearing a moment later in front of the roots, Chase cresting the water beside him.

Chase dragged him clear, his head balanced on Chase's shoulder until they reached her. "Can you guide his head until we're back to where I left my bag?"

"Sure."

She swung the shotgun across her back, then cupped one hand beneath Eli's hair, keeping his face above water as they fought against the current, finally backtracking to the opening on the bank. Chase motioned for her to jump out, somehow maneuvering both him and Eli out of the water without having to hike the other man over his shoulder.

He carried Eli back to the main trail, then eased him down, shoving his wet jacket under Eli's head. "Easy, brother. I've got you."

Greer hovered nearby, shotgun sweeping the landscape, her stomach tied in knots. Images of Troy played in her head, that same helpless feeling flooding her system.

Chase did a quick body sweep, then rolled Eli onto his side, wincing when the man cried out. "I know, just bear with me. I need to see what I'm dealing with."

Pink bubbles frothed from Eli's shoulder blade, the odd fleck of blood splattering across his uniform.

Chase eased him back, then went to work, slapping on sponges and setting up an IV. He waved her over, pointing to the massive wound on his lower abdomen. "I need pressure. A lot, so use your knee."

She hesitated, her gaze flying to Eli before she shifted — pressed her knee into his stomach. He jerked, clawing at her for a few moments before his hands fell limp at his side, his eyes rolling back.

Bile crested her throat, but she willed it away, holding one of his hands in hers. Something to anchor him. Keep him this side of the light.

Chase checked his cell and cursed. "Still nothing.

We've got to go. Get him back to the Bronco. We'll call once we've got a signal. See if someone can meet us along the way."

She nodded, moving when Chase did his best to pack the wound. Thick dark blood stained the ground as Chase heaved the man onto his shoulder, shifting Eli's position until most of his weight centered over that wound — kept it from bleeding out.

Chase waved, and Greer took off, lighting up the path while checking for danger. Another sniper shot or a trip wire they hadn't noticed. Or one their perp had added after they'd passed by. A twig snapped beneath her boot, everything inside her jumping before she pushed it all down. Picked up the pace.

Chase followed behind, moving so fast, she wondered how his legs didn't buckle beneath the strain. His breathing measured. Strong.

This was the real Chase Remington.

The man beneath the easy banter and stunning smile. The medic who'd brought his brothers back from behind enemy lines. Who'd given everything, even when he'd suspected it was a losing battle.

The guy who never quit.

They reached the edge of the tree line as sirens sounded in the distance, more blue lights flickering in the fog. They charged across the field, Greer checking for more wires until they reached the cruiser, then over to her SUV. She flung open the back, just like with Rhett, helping Chase ease Eli onto the surface. Blood soaked his clothes, his skin an eerie gray.

Eli reached for her, his lips moving. What looked like, "You."

She shushed him and squeezed his hand. "Save your strength. Cavalry's nearly here."

Chase pushed more meds, looking back when Kash and Jordan rolled up in Kash's truck. They jumped out, Kash yelling something across a radio before taking point, Nyx vibrating at his side.

Jordan moved in close, mouth pinched tight. "Bodie called when Eli missed his check-in. Foster and Mac are already on their way. Luckily, they'd joined us for dinner. Were only five minutes from the hangar."

Chase gestured toward the street. "Let's get to the main road. Save whatever time we can."

That's all Greer needed. Two seconds and she had the door open, keys sliding into the ignition. Another couple and the engine revved, gravel spraying out from beneath the tires as she swung the Bronco around and took off. Keeping it as smooth as possible.

Chase muttered in the background, either to himself or Eli. The low sound sending shivers down her spine. She'd heard that same tone with Rhett, then the others. Chase's way of trying to bend fate — align it to his will.

She hit the pavement just as a chopper soared overhead, thrashing trees and branches as Foster banked hard to the right, somehow landing a heartbeat later. Greer swerved onto the shoulder, jumping out while the chassis still rocked beneath her, the engine humming in the background. Chase barely waited for the hatch to open before he had Eli in his arms as he raced toward the helicopter.

Greer beat him by a step, opened the doors wide, then gave him a boost. She hopped in, leaving her Bronco idling on the side of the road, closing the doors and strapping in before Foster lifted the machine and tipped it forward. The chopper shook, dipped a bit, then picked up speed, soaring over the towering pines as Foster angled it northward.

Chase hooked up more tubes, had the defibrillator on standby. That inevitable crash she knew lurked in the shadows, waiting to strike.

He glanced over at her, frowned, then checked Eli's vitals. "Greer. Sweetheart you look like you're going to tank."

She swallowed, nearly puked, but waved him off. How he had time to worry about her, too, mystified her. "I'm fine."

His frown deepened, but he didn't call her bluff, cursing as he pressed against Eli's neck. "No pulse." He leaned over Eli — started compressions. "Foster. Brother any more speed you can get out of this baby would be appreciated."

Another round of shaking as Foster urged the aircraft faster, the interior vibrating from the strain. An alarm sounded from the cockpit, crushed a moment later as Foster pressed in some buttons. Greer shifted closer, manning the bag as Chase counted it down, nodding whenever he reached zero, pausing only when he shocked Eli's heart. Eli lurched with each hit, that unforgiving tone sounding in the background.

Chase shook his head. "Come on, Eli. Hang in there."

Time blurred, freezing then rushing ahead. The chopper ride fading into a dash through the hospital. The frantic race filled with white coats and bright lights.

She stopped outside the trauma room, blood sticky against her skin, every muscle twitching. She shivered, too tired to worry about the bone-deep chill seeping through her veins. Her clothes reeked of death and old leaves, most of her equipment beyond saving.

A hand landed on her shoulder, the heavy weight nearly taking her to her knees. She glanced up, the undeniable truth written across Chase's face.

He curled his fingers around her arm. "You need to get into some dry clothes before you're their next patient."

She shook her head, focusing on the room. On the flurry of motion, everyone darting around in some form of controlled chaos. "I can't leave him."

"Greer. There's nothing more you can do but wait. You're not helping anyone by worsening your hypothermia."

She huffed but followed him to a locker room, grabbing a quick shower before pulling on scrubs and an oversized hoodie. Chase's or maybe Foster's. Either way, it took away a bit of the chill. Gave her back a modicum of humanity.

The hard vinyl chair creaked as she collapsed into it, elbows braced on her knees, hands laced together as she stared at the floor. Snippets of the night played in her mind. The ghostly cruiser, its blue strobes glowing in the fog. The mechanical chirp breaking the silence. Eli's eyes as he'd fisted her shirt — searched her gaze for something she wasn't sure he'd found.

People rushed past, wheeling patients along the hallway. Nurses called out vitals, the glass doors opened and closed as a clock marked out time, each tick stealing more of her sanity.

She'd failed.

Again.

Only this time, she wasn't sure she'd find her way back.

Footsteps.

Closing in on her. Dragging her from that edge as they stopped in front of her. Taking a breath, she looked up.

Chase stared at her for a moment, head tilting off to one side. "You're still shivering."

She shrugged. "I'm fine."

"No, you're not." He drew in a deep breath, then offered her his hand. "C'mon. Bodie's here. He'll take over."

Greer stumbled to her feet, tripping against Chase before drawing herself up. "I already told you. I can't leave until I know…"

Eli wasn't going to make it.

She knew it. That, despite all Chase had done, it wouldn't be enough. That Eli's fate had been sealed before they'd spotted his cruiser.

That in the end, it was all her fault.

Chase slipped his hand over hers. "You already know. He'd lost too much blood. Suffered horrific internal injuries. The only reason he even made it into the chopper alive was because the cold water slowed everything down. Bought him some time. Once I pulled him out…"

Greer looked at the room, noting the lack of movement. The unnatural silence suffocating the space. She scrubbed her hand down her face. "I can't…"

"I know."

She closed her eyes, tried to quiet her mind, only to have the images bounce back. Threaten to drag her under. "I need his clothes. We need a CSI team out to the site. I—"

"Bodie's on top of it." Chase shook his head when she opened her mouth to interrupt him. "Everyone's got backup and state's on scene. The best way to help is to give yourself some time to process everything. Grieve. You were barely holding on before, now…"

"I can fall apart once I end this bastard."

"You can't bring him down if you're so messed up, you can't think straight. I'm not telling you to throw in the towel. You just need a break."

"And if he strikes again?"

Chase clenched his jaw. "I think he's made his point clear tonight. To everyone."

Her chin quivered, all the pain and guilt burning her eyes. She turned away, swallowed the hurt, then nodded, heading for the exit without looking back. She stumbled her way to the helicopter, slipping inside the cabin without even looking at Mac or Foster.

Chase settled in beside her, close but not touching.

Just a warm presence if she wanted the contact. The helicopter rocked, the rotors picking up speed before they lifted off, the return ride noticeably calmer than the last.

A mix of bleach and lemon infused in the air, all traces of their race against time washed away. She glanced out the window, watching the fog creep below them, reflecting the glimmer of moonlight low on the horizon. Trees stood black against the indigo sky, a few stars punching through the darkness.

The rest of the trip passed in a hazy blur — landing at the hangar, then riding with Foster and Mac back to that pullout in the road. Chase jumped out, talked to one of the state cops, then slipped behind the wheel of her Bronco. She hadn't even realized he'd been following them until he pulled in behind Foster's truck, parked her SUV off to the right.

Mac moved in to give Greer a hug, stopping short when Greer wrapped her arms around her chest. Instead, her friend simply nodded, then followed Foster up to the main house before disappearing inside.

Chase shouldered up beside her, gently guiding her down the path to his door. The alarm chirped, a light burning down the hallway as she stepped inside, wincing at the firm thud of the door.

Every noise was too loud, every light too bright. Chase must have read her mind because he dimmed everything until only a soft glow remained. She wiped her palms along her pants, wishing she could just disappear when he moved in behind her — pressed his chest to her back.

She tensed, all the anger and guilt burning along her

skin. Threatening to self-combust from the simple pressure. She turned, fisting his shirt in an effort to shove him away, when he placed his hands over hers. Held her captive with nothing but the press of his palms — the comfort of his skin over hers.

The first sob caught her off-guard. Ripped a hole in her soul as it clawed free. She pounded her fists against his chest, still clenching the fabric as the next guttural gasp escaped. Punched right through those walls she'd spent a lifetime reinforcing, pulverizing them into bits of sand.

Chase held firm through three more rounds before wrapping his arms around her — holding her tight.

She sank into him. Any defense still standing crumbled within his embrace. And she would have fallen to her knees if he hadn't been bracing all her weight. Tears burned her eyes, each shuddering breath stealing more of her strength.

She wasn't sure how long they'd been standing there before she finally eased back, every nerve stretched tight, her heart thundering against the rush of emotions.

Chase didn't speak, just dropped a kiss on her head as he palmed her cheek, softly brushing away some of her tears. He tilted his head, looking at her as if seeing her for the first time before giving her a hint of a smile. "Greer…"

The way he said her name undid her. Pulled her in. She yanked him closer, brushing her lips across his, needing something to anchor her — stop her from falling into that abyss. Losing herself like she'd done with Troy. He tensed for one agonizing moment, their mouths touching as everything froze, waiting for some kind of sign.

She tightened her hold, closed her eyes, and leaned in.

CHAPTER FOURTEEN

Lethal.

That was the only way to describe Greer's current state. A mixture of gut-wrenching pain and unbridled anger. The kind that either ended in an all-out brawl or a tumble between the sheets. Opposite sides of the same coin.

Not that Chase had been unaffected. But for the first time since finding Rhett, he'd been able to see the situation through Greer's eyes. How each new victim stole a bit more of her soul. Sucked more light from her eyes.

Her fists tightened around his shirt, tugging him that last quarter inch until his mouth crushed down over hers, his fingers slipping into her hair. She moaned, stepping into him as she slid her hands up and over his shoulders, locking them behind his head.

Chase held her close, backing them up until they hit a wall. He pressed her against it, used the position to ravage her mouth before kissing his way down her neck

— nipping at her pulse point. Her breath hitched, her head tilting to one side before she grabbed his hoodie, yanked it over his head.

A flash of blue, then the hoodie hit the floor, puddling at his feet as he returned the favor — tossed hers somewhere off to their left. She paused for a moment, bottom lip snagged between her teeth, chest heaving before she launched into his arms — claimed his mouth.

He gathered her in his arms, then started moving, bouncing his way down the hallway, leaving a trail of scrubs. He kicked open his bedroom door, stepped inside, then turned and pinned her to the wall.

Greer didn't give him a chance to breathe before she had his pants down around his ankles, his boxers hugging his knees. She palmed his chest, skimming her hands along his ribs, then over his shoulders. Looking as if she wanted to climb her way up his torso.

A tug of the drawstring at her waist and her pants dropped to the floor. A heap of blue against the brown hardwood. She'd forgone any underwear, nothing but soft, pale skin gleaming in the hint of moonlight spilling through the windows.

Her muscles jumped as he smoothed his hand over her hip and across her ribs, brushing the side of her breast then back along her jaw, burying his fingers in her mass of auburn hair. The silky strands tickled his palm, and he knew he could spend a lifetime staring down at her like this.

Eyes heavy lidded.

Skin flushed a light pink.

She shivered, though he wasn't sure if it was from the river or his touch. If she was half as wrecked as he was.

A smile, then she wrapped one leg around his back, used his shoulders to lever up — rest her elbows next to his head. Just a rim of green visible, those gorgeous eyes searching his.

He scooped her up, hands positioned under her ass, his sheer size pinning her to the wall. She held his gaze, nostrils flaring, breath panting past his cheek before he settled between her thighs — slowly eased inside.

She inhaled as her head fell back, exposing the long, sleek line of her neck. He mouthed her skin, licking and tasting, pressing forward until he bottomed out. Her breath left her on a moan, his name whispering in the space between them.

Chase fisted her hair, kept her face level with his as he inched back, stopped just shy of slipping free. That razor's edge between not enough and all-in. Greer tugged him closer, resting her forehead on his as he reclaimed every inch, the force jostling her against the wall.

"God, Chase."

That set him off.

Had him starting up a punishing rhythm. In. Out. Faster. Deeper. Angling her hips until she started chanting his name. Scratching at his scalp as she anchored her fingers in his hair.

Her breathing kicked up, her heart pounding in sync with his as he hit that sweet spot — damn near finished on the spot.

She tensed, nails digging into his muscles, body shaking before her eyes rolled back, her mouth opening in a soundless scream. He kept moving, fighting the fire burning beneath his flesh. All the heat they'd been building over the past several months sparking to life. Dragging him under.

He lasted maybe three more minutes before the coil snapped, and everything went supernova. A blinding white light that left him gasping for air. His forehead resting against the wall, every ragged breath drawing in more of her.

Greer clung to him, her face buried in his shoulder, her arms locked around his neck. A few tremors shivered through her — he just wasn't sure if it was from the hypothermia or the sex.

The thought lifted some of the euphoric haze — allowed him to take stock. How he hadn't even fully stripped, his boxers still hanging at his knees, one leg of the scrubs wrapped around his ankle. He hadn't even thought about protection, though, that didn't worry him nearly as much as he would have imagined.

Greer sighed, the soft sound jacking up his protective instincts. He eased back, her legs still snugged around his hips, her fingers anchored in his hair. She blew out a shaky breath, finally pulling away enough to look him in the eyes.

He smiled, dropped a soft kiss on her lips. "God, you're beautiful."

That earned him a small tilt of her mouth. Not quite a smile, but he'd take whatever he could get considering the circumstances.

He brushed back a few errant strands. "You, okay?"

Her chin quivered, like in the restaurant. "Jury's still out."

The next round of shivers got him moving. He managed to kick out of his clothes, then carried her into the bathroom. He twisted on the taps, grabbed some towels, then ushered her under the warm spray. He didn't talk, just stepped inside, took her in his arms.

Greer melted against him, seemingly content to simply stand there, water cascading over them, the weight of their combined guilt adding to the steamy air. He pulled her close, his chin resting on her head as he drew lazy patterns across her back. Time stopped, nothing registering beyond the patter of the shower, how her heartbeat matched his.

He managed to give them both a quick wash before stepping out — wrapping her in one of the thick towels, then heading back to the bedroom. He placed her on the edge of his bed, going to his knees in front. Tucking her wet locks behind her ear. "I swear your lips are still blue."

She shrugged, looking as if she wanted to say something before closing her eyes — pushing out a shaky breath.

He cupped her jaw, waiting until she finally met his gaze. "Whatever you need, if I can swing it…"

She smiled, traced her thumb along his jaw. "I…" She swallowed, coughed, then leaned in. "I just need you."

He kissed her palm. "I can manage that. You want the left or the right side?"

She snagged her lip, inhaling before getting lover-close. "I don't want to sleep. Not yet."

He nodded, dropped a kiss on her mouth. "Then, let's get you comfortable. This could take a while."

* * *

Greer stared up at Chase, her heart thundering against her ribs, her pulse somewhere in the triple digits. The man was breathtaking. From his Hollywood good looks to his boyish charm, he'd stolen her heart from the moment they'd met, and she doubted she'd ever get it back.

Chase tilted his head, grinning as if he knew she was hopelessly in love with him. That if he hadn't stepped up tonight, she would have spiraled. Lost herself in that darkness.

Images played in her head. White mist rising off black water. Blue lights strobing against the fog. Eli's bloody hand gripping her shirt. His blood sinking into the dirt.

A tsk, then Chase had her in his arms, looming over her as he took her back on the mattress. "I'm not going to let him hurt you."

She palmed his cheeks, staring into his hazel eyes, wondering if she'd ever loved anyone this much. Trusted someone with more than her life. "Love me."

He smiled, the simple tilt of his lips kicking up her pulse, until it thundered inside her head as he tugged the towel free. "That's a given. But I'm not above showing you, again."

He moved slowly, helping her scoot to the middle of the bed, fanning her hair out around her. His skin gleamed in the muted moonlight, his muscles flexing as he went to his elbows, looking at her as if she held the answers. Or maybe just his heart.

She smoothed her hands along his chest, frowning at the purple patch smeared across his ribs. "Is this from that round you took protecting me from the flash bang?"

He sighed. "It's nothing."

"It looks like a slash of death. God, Chase…"

He lowered until his chest compressed hers, his mouth no more than a breath away. "There's no limit to what I'd do to protect you. You know that, right? No risk too great, no sacrifice too big."

"I don't want you to sacrifice yourself for me."

A shrug. "I know."

"How about we both just focus on living?"

"Amen to that. I just needed you to know…" He dipped down, nuzzled her nose. "There's no future without you in it."

She inhaled, his words slowly sinking in. Easing the emptiness that had taken root after Troy's death. Filling the spaces she hadn't realized were there.

He kissed her.

Soft.

Coaxing.

The exact opposite to their no-holds-barred sex against the wall. When she'd needed something raw. Primal. An escape from the pain and guilt. Unlike now, where every brush of his hand, every press of his lips, acted as an anchor. A tangible link that grounded her to this moment.

To him.

Chase shifted to her neck, arching her against him as he moved down to her shoulder, sucking at her pulse point until she thought she'd scream — every inch of her hyperaware. Like having her senses dialed up to eleven.

He smiled against her skin, teasing her with barely-there caresses before wrapping her legs around his hips — slowly sinking inside.

Forever.

That's what this felt like.

Lying there, completely entwined, his breath feathering across her neck, his skin heating hers, she couldn't imagine going back to longing glances over dinner. Nights alone in her bed, dreaming of this moment.

She wanted more.

Wanted to taste every inch of his skin. Trace every muscled band. Watch him as he gave himself over to her. But more than anything, she wanted to feel safe. Unburdened.

She wanted him, with her, for the rest of her life.

Chase slipped his arms under hers, closing his fingers around her shoulders. Holding her tight as he devoured her mouth, tangling their tongues before finally easing back. He winked, then dipped to the left, effectively changing their places.

He helped her straddle her legs around his, every inch still deep inside. She rocked her hips, grinning at the way his jaw clenched as he closed his eyes — grunted out a harsh breath.

Greer went to her elbows, her hair falling in a curtain around them. Chase reached up — speared his fingers through the right side as he dragged her mouth to his. She gave herself over to the kiss, moaning when he started moving. Long, measured stokes designed to take her to the edge but not over. She met each thrust, angling her hips, hitting that sweet spot as fire laced through her veins, her breath kicking up.

Shadows moved across the room, the soft moonlight painting his skin, highlighting how his muscles flexed as he levered up — trapped her between his chest and thighs. She pulled him closer, needing every inch touching as she let her head fall back, still rising and falling with every thrust.

Chase threaded his fingers through her hair, tugging her in until her gaze locked on his. "No closing your eyes or looking away. I need to know you're here. With me."

She palmed his face. "There's no one else I'd trust like this."

He smiled, kissed her, increasing his pace until her ragged breath sounded around them, every thrust threatening to send her over. Heat coiled low in her belly, a haze blurring her vision as she teetered on the edge, that fire burning white hot inside her.

Chase stopped, rolled, again, starting back up the moment her back hit the mattress. Hard and fast, staring down at her as if he needed to memorize every moment. She tried to hold his gaze, failing when the next stroke hit home, tipped her over.

She gasped, spots flashing across her vision, the heat burning up her skin as everything exploded. Chase kept moving, coaxing a few more spasms out of her before he stiffened, emptying inside her in a series of jabbing strokes.

His breath panted across her shoulder, his weight crushing her into the bed, but for the first time in forever, all she felt was safe.

Time ticked in the background, everything fading until Chase sighed — pushed onto his elbows. He took a few more deep breaths, his massive chest brushing against hers before he nuzzled her nose — dropped a soft kiss on her lips.

Love.

No other explanation for way her stomach clenched, or how a simple smile made her heart flutter. Had her wishing they could spend the foreseeable future wrapped up in each other's arms.

He shook his head, brushing his thumb along her cheek. "Not sure I want to know what you're thinking because the way you're looking at me…" He whistled. "It's even more intense than that night in your Bronco. Before I screwed everything up."

Greer teased her fingers through his hair, loving how the soft strands slid across her skin. "Doesn't look screwed up to me."

"Only because you're incredibly forgiving."

"Grieving isn't a crime. You needed time. Space. I don't want you to change. To push it all down. We both know how that ends. If you hadn't been there for me tonight..." She would have spiraled. Gotten lost in the pain and the guilt. And she wouldn't have made it back, this time. "I needed more than just a hint of a light. I needed a safe place to fall."

She palmed his cheek. "I needed a lifeline."

Chase pressed into her touch. "Seems only fair, seeing as you saved me, first."

She closed her eyes, a few tears slipping free. She wasn't sure if they were from his words or maybe leftover from earlier. A mix of love and guilt. But she didn't care as long as he held her — kept her grounded.

A kiss.

Soft.

Loving.

Then, he eased free and rolled to the edge of the bed, hanging his head as his shoulders drooped a bit. "So, not that I'm worried, but we didn't use..."

She sighed. "I have an implant. Not that I've ever fully trusted it before, but..." She pushed up and wrapped her arms around him from behind. "I'd be lying if I said I'm having a hard time caring if it works or not."

He glanced back at her over his shoulder. "Does that mean you're not going to shoot me in the ass if we somehow got pregnant?"

"Pretty sure I'm the one who'd be puking and craving ice cream, but no. We're good."

God, his smile. As if she'd just told him he'd won the lottery. It eased any inklings of doubt.

"You're way past good, sweetheart." He rose, turned,

then gathered her into his arms. "Another quick shower because your damn lips are still blue, then sleep. The real world can intrude later. First, we get to live in our bubble a bit longer."

"You still promise to hold me all night? No creepy watching in the chair?"

"All night."

"Chase." She held his gaze as he placed her on her feet in front of the counter. "I really don't know what I would've done if you hadn't…"

"You would have pulled through. Found a way to keep going. Not because anyone asked you to. But because they didn't. Because you're hands down the strongest person I know. It took me nearly a week to crawl back to the light." He leaned in closer. "To realize *you're* my light. That you brought me back, so… It's okay if you need to break. I won't lose any pieces."

Tears pooled in her eyes — slipped free while he readied the shower. She took his hand when he offered it, holding still for a moment. "What if I can't rebuild them?" She swallowed. "The walls."

He eased her in close, kissing her softly. "Then, you can come inside mine. I'll keep you safe. Who knows, maybe we'll learn that we don't really need them."

"We'll share your walls?"

"Why not? You've already got my heart."

His words stole her breath. Not that he hadn't hinted at it. What being crazy about her meant. But hearing him say it…

She squeezed his hand. "I guess it depends on if you snore or not."

CHAPTER FIFTEEN

Love.

It all seemed so simple now. How he'd been fighting it all these months. Shoving it down because he'd been scared. How he'd gotten buried beneath the guilt. The pain. But now that he'd given in…

He couldn't go back. Couldn't lock it away. Not after she'd trusted him to bring her back from the edge. To be her lifeline. He hadn't been lying. She'd saved him, first. Given him a reason to regroup — step up. He wouldn't fail her.

Chase pulled Greer a bit closer, breathing her in as he stared into the darkness. Rain pattered against the roof, the faintest suggestion of gray light brightening the room. She'd fallen asleep a heartbeat after curling into him, the easy weight of her head on his chest, her arm looped over his waist, settling something deep inside. And he knew this was what forever felt like.

She whimpered, twitching against him until he

rubbed her arm — eased the furrow on her brow — then drifted off. She'd been dreaming most of the night, none of them seemingly good. Likely reliving the past week. All the pain, the loss.

Finding Eli like that...

Chase would be lying if he'd said he hadn't been worried she'd spiral. And not just a little. The kind of backward slide that fed on darkness — preyed on guilt — until only a shell remained.

That would have been him if she hadn't stuck by him. Refused to let him drown. And that simple truth had changed everything. Brought it all into sharp focus. He'd meant what he'd said. He couldn't see a future without her in it. He'd already wasted months treading water — looking for forgiveness only he could give. Now that he'd stopped sabotaging their relationship, he knew exactly how he wanted it to play out.

And failure wasn't an option.

He closed his eyes, content to lie there, holding her, watching the shadows dance across the room when his cell buzzed, the vibration shaking the nightstand. Greer startled, jumping awake before groaning — snuggling back against his chest.

He chuckled. "Easy, sweetheart. It's probably just Foster."

She sighed, drawing her thumb across his chest. "What time is it?"

"Not quite seven."

Another groan. "You should've woken me hours ago."

"Why? So you could fall on your face from sheer exhaustion? It's only been five hours. Barely enough to qualify as rest."

"Everyone's tired."

"But not everyone's had to face what you have."

Greer pushed onto her elbow. "Other than you."

Chase reached up — brushed back some of her wild hair. "And you made sure I didn't fall through the cracks. I'm simply trying to return the favor."

Greer smiled down at him, and his damn heart stopped. Just froze in his chest for a moment before kicking back up. Leaving him breathless as he tugged her close — slanted his mouth over hers.

Definitely forever.

Greer smoothed her hand across his chest, tracing each band, looking as if she had something wicked in mind, when his damn phone buzzed, again. She laughed, snagged it off the nightstand, then handed it to him. "Looks like Foster's pissed you didn't answer his first one."

"Foster's gonna get my boot up his ass." Chase read the texts, all that heat cooling.

"Judging by the slight frown, I'd say it's not just a proof of life request."

"Bodie needs to talk to us. He's up at the main house."

Her smiled dropped, all the light in her eyes dimming. As if hinting at last night's events had flipped a switch. Taken her to the edge of the abyss, again.

Chase typed a quick reply, stopping her from rolling off the bed with an arm around her waist. He pushed up, holding her captive as he leaned in. "We'll figure this out."

"Before or after I have more blood on my hands?"

"Greer..."

He let the rest of the words fade. She didn't need a pep talk. Or reassurances. She needed action. Results. Something tangible to put her faith in, and token promises weren't going to cut it.

Instead, he drew her in, dropped a soft kiss on her lips. "No more playing by the rules. We've got more... questionable contacts. It's time we went off-script."

"Whoa, easy there, slugger. Before you go all *John Wick*, maybe we should hear what Bodie has to say."

"Fine. But I mean it. I'm not letting this fucker hurt you."

That earned him a small smile. "I know." Another kiss, then she scooted off the side. "I don't suppose you've got some sweats I can borrow? I really don't want to put those scrubs back on."

"They'll be big, but..." He rummaged through his closet and tossed her some clothes, pausing to watch her slip into them. "You really are stunning."

She glanced over her shoulder at him, giving him a long slow sweep. "Says the man who looks like he just walked off a movie set. Not that I'm complaining."

Chase tugged on some clothes, met her at the door. "You sure you're okay?"

"Not even close." She tiptoed up. "But I've got you, so I will be."

"Hell, yeah, because I'll be watching. No more

skating by on half a bagel and a gallon of shitty coffee." He pulled her close. "I've got your back."

He ushered her out, darting up the path to Foster's place — avoiding the worst of the puddles lining the trail. Fog wove through the trees, the warm lighting from the main house casting long shadows across the ground. Greer stopped beneath the overhang outside the kitchen door, biting at her bottom lip, looking more than a bit apprehensive.

Chase turned to face her, shaking off some of the rain. "If you're not ready…"

She shook her head. A bit too fast to be convincing, but he got the message. "I just need a minute."

"Whatever it takes, sweetheart."

Her mouth quirked as she drew in a few deep breaths, rubbing her free hand on her thigh before nodding — following him into the house.

Foster looked up from his coffee. "Sorry to get you both up so early."

Chase waved it off. "We were already awake."

Kash met them at the counter, handing them both a cup. "Figured you could use the hit."

Greer clasped the mug in her hands. "I always need the hit."

Chase thanked Kash and took a sip, damn near groaned. "Any issues?"

"Nothing since…" Kash trailed off, coughing as if something was stuck in his throat. "State's securing the scene until it's been cleared. They're fast-tracking forensics, but they already sent Bodie copies of their photos. He's just in the other room. He'll be in shortly."

Greer nodded, leaning against Chase when he shouldered up beside her — pressed his chest into her back. He dropped one hand to her hip. A small show of support. She wasn't alone.

Kash grinned, the bastard, turning when Bodie strode into the kitchen, hair slightly messy. Mud and grass staining his uniform. Fatigue lining his brow.

Bodie spotted Greer and slowed, looking as if he wanted to drag out whatever he had to say. "You look like shit."

Greer snorted. "You look worse. What couldn't wait?"

Bodie sighed, glancing at Chase, and Chase knew the situation had only gotten worse. "I've got preliminary forensics from the cruiser. Our perp's not leaving much up to deliberation, anymore. But first…"

Bodie glanced at Zain as the man walked in, tablet in hand. "Someone's been a royal pain in my ass since he heard about the incident. Said you weren't answering your cell."

Greer frowned. "Everything got soaked in the river. I was letting it all dry out before charging it. And honestly, I wasn't in the headspace last night to really care."

"Which is why he's been ringing me since four."

Zain stopped at the counter, leaning the tablet against a couple mugs before turning it.

Greer groaned, looking at Chase before shaking her head at the man glaring at them from the screen, arms crossed, a scowl curving his mouth. "Nick? What the hell?"

Nick Colter merely stared at her, eyes darting to the side when someone yelled in the background. "Why the fuck didn't you call me last night?"

Greer braced more of her weight against Chase, as if needing the strength. "You know why."

"I thought it was you." Nick scrubbed a hand down his face. "I got a call from a buddy in Portland PD saying there'd been a fatality in the Raven's Cliff sheriff's department. That local SAR had rushed the officer to Providence, then you don't pick up my calls!" He swallowed, looked as if he wanted to punch his fist through the screen. "I thought you were dead. That I'd missed something or just all 'round screwed up and you'd…"

Greer bowed her head. "I'm sorry. You're right. I'd be livid if you'd done the same. I just… I couldn't…"

Nick grunted, shifting his gaze to Chase. "I assume you're Remington."

Chase squared his shoulders. "It's Chase."

"I know. How is she? Really?"

Greer coughed. "I'm standing right here, jackass."

Nick barely spared her a quick side-eye. "I know. I can see you, but we both know you'll give me some bullshit answer about soldiering on. Pulling yourself up by your damn bootstraps. Everything but how you're really doing, so I'm asking the damn medic because he knows that after spending seven years with Delta Force and another ten with the NCS, I'll know if he's lying."

Chase held her close. "She's riding that razor's edge between wanting justice and going full-metal jacket. But she's functioning, which honestly, is about all anyone can ask after everything that's gone down."

"And you've got her back?"

"The only way this asshole's getting to her is if I'm dead. My team, too."

Nick narrowed his eyes, staring at Chase for a good thirty seconds before nodding. "I'm holding you to that, PJ. At least until I can get there."

Greer inhaled. "You finished your op?"

"No, I'm going rogue."

"You can't go rogue." She cocked her head to the side when he simply stared at her. "Nick. I've already got enough ex-military testosterone suffocating me. The last thing I need is the freaking CIA sending a squad here to bring you back. Besides, we need your help, and you can't break a bunch of security protocols for me from here."

"It's about to get incredibly messy here. If I don't break ranks, now, I won't get another chance for maybe a week."

Greer sighed. "You know I love the sentiment, but I've already got one hell of a team. So, don't get arrested."

Nick glanced at Chase, again, as if measuring how accurate Greer's claim had been before pushing out a rough breath. "Fine. But if you get yourself killed, we're gonna have one hell of a conversation." He rolled his shoulders, visibly pushing down his unrest like Chase had done a thousand times. "Now, about this bastard who's decided you're all his personal vengeance puppets... Bodie filled me in on your theory about

Dalton's crew. That maybe they're not as dead as everyone thought."

Bodie stepped up. "Nick and the others have already seen this, but it's definitely looking like that mission is at the heart of this case."

Bodie spread out a bunch of photos, the images making Chase's heart skip a few beats. "These are from Eli's cruiser."

Words and numbers scratched across the inside of the trunk, along with what looked like a note.

Greer shook her head. "No. We checked the trunk before venturing into the woods. None of this was there."

"We figured as much. The creep gave us all the numbers, this time, in degrees and minutes. Nick confirmed the coordinates match that compound from the mission you were talking about — involving the Legion. And he said the word *sacrifice* that the creep scratched across Eli's dog tags is another word from their motto — *Salvation from sacrifice*."

Chase flipped through the various images. "What about his dashcam? It was set to record when we arrived."

"All it picked up was the two of you heading for the tree line, then you racing back after."

"So, our guy turned it on, not Eli." Chase held up one image. "Leaving a note's new, but it's hard to read it in the photo. What does it say?"

Bodie glanced at Nick on the tablet, then sighed. "We're not exactly sure how it applies, but it says *I'll double back*."

The words hit Chase like a hammer, dropping his stomach to his knees before it reared up — nearly clawed free. How many times had he heard those three words reverberate in his head? Woken in a cold sweat, his own voice echoing in dark? And all because of that one night.

That one mission.

Greer grabbed his hand, snapped him out of his thoughts. "Chase?"

He hung his head for a moment, explosions echoing in the background. That wet rattling sound as Dalton tried to breathe. How the men had looked at him, as if they knew Chase had been lying.

He glanced over at his buddies. They knew, even if they hadn't discussed every detail. — repeated every word. They'd all shared in the trauma. Just like with Sean and Rhett. The dark side of their brotherhood.

Chase raked his fingers through his hair. "That's for me. It's all been for me. The IV tubing, the staging. Killing Anna when he could have easily killed me, instead. He wants me to know that I can't save everyone — hell, anyone — because I didn't save him. Save them."

Greer reached for his hand, not giving him the choice to pull away. "You can't possibly save everyone."

"No, but I made a choice. I picked those two hostages over my four brothers. I promised them I'd double back — help them get to the medevac chopper. But then I took a couple hits to my vest, those missiles turned everything into white light, and Rhett pulled me out. One of the few times he ever left the damn helicopter."

Zain shook his head. "You're neglecting to mention the part where you'd already saved them. Carried Rios out from inside that building. That you pulled Dalton and Carver behind cover after they'd been hit." He leaned in. "You didn't abandon them. You did your job. Civilians, first. They knew that."

"Apparently, at least one of them disagrees." Chase eased back. "Caleb Rios likely died before the missiles hit. Eric Dalton had a GSW to his upper shoulder — sounded as if it might have ricocheted into his lung. Royce Carver had multiple shrapnel wounds — was bleeding pretty heavily. I tried to stop it but... Only Marcus Hodges was a hundred percent before that attack."

Greer inched closer. "I green lit the mission. If I'd done my job properly, I would have anticipated the added resistance. Had a contingency for it, and you wouldn't have had to choose."

"You can't plan for everything. That's just the reality of rescue missions. They're dynamic. Regardless, how would Dalton's team even know you were part of the op when you were a few thousand miles away in Langley?" Chase tapped his chest. "We didn't."

Greer glanced at Nick.

Chase frowned. "What's with the look?"

Nick sighed. "You didn't tell them."

Greer toed at the floor. "My location didn't seem important, especially when we're all dancing around national security."

Chase glanced at his buddies, again. "You were there?"

"I was at our command post about a hundred miles east." She hitched out a hip. "Did you really think I was able to profile a foreign group, anticipate their movements *and* turn one of their own from some boardroom in Virginia?"

"Did Dalton's crew know that?"

"They were the ones who intercepted the convoy, extracted my asset, then put him back in. I met with all of them on multiple occasions before that initial mission, then a few times afterward to coordinate the hostage retrieval."

"Greer." Nick's voice boomed through the room. "You're not the only one responsible. I was the one who uncovered their group, who brought you onboard. If we're handing out blame, then there's enough for all of us. None of which matters. Our only focus is stopping whoever survived before they up their game because based on what Bodie told me, Eli was different. No fake call to ensure you made it to the scene before he died. No second measure. And our guy doubled back while you were in the thick of it to leave clues."

Nick leaned back in his chair. "I'm not a profiler, but that seems like an escalation to me."

Greer inhaled. "Shit. Bodie, take Zain and get over to the café. I want all their video feed. And get every ATM and traffic cam surrounding the place. Nick's right. Chase had been coming back to my apartment for the last few days, so how the hell did the bastard know we were heading this way unless he overheard us talking?

Knew he didn't need to make a fake call because we'd drive right past Eli's cruiser — see the lights?" She tapped the counter. "He must have left just before us, then watched it all play out."

Bodie nodded. "On it." He paused for a moment. "I left you a set of new radios at the door."

He took off with Zain, the door slamming shut in the distance.

Nick cleared his throat. "Before I realized it wasn't you... I had our satellite sweep the area. I'm sending you a photo. I'm not sure what's off to the left, but it was in the vicinity."

Chase minimized the video and opened the image, staring at the white spot poking out from a small clearing in the trees. Definitely not part of the landscape. "Is there a tower out that way?"

"You've got to be kidding me." Greer expanded the image. "It's like he's a magnet for trouble."

"Who?" Chase stared at the image again. "You know what that is?"

"It's a telecommunications array. On top of an RV." She scoffed. "As in our neighborhood conspiracy theorist Buck Landry."

Chase looked again. He didn't quite see it, but he wasn't going to question her. "Think he's still there?"

"He's not." Another ping as Nick obviously sent a second image. "I've had my guy following it, just in case I needed to fly out and exact some revenge. I've just sent you where it was as of five this morning. Hasn't moved since. Your guy probably thinks he's safe. Not sure if he'll have anything useful, despite being right on top of it, but it's worth a shot. Coordinates are with the image. I'll get my people scouring everything they can get their hands on for evidence that Dalton or one of his guys ventured back into the country. It's a long shot and will likely come back way too late, but…"

"Thanks, Nick. I owe you." Greer closed off the connection, glancing up at Chase, her green eyes flashing in the light. Looking darker than usual. "You up for a ride? It's time I had a chat with Bucky."

CHAPTER SIXTEEN

Greer bumped her Bronco along the old, rutted forest road, closing in on the dot pulsing on her GPS. Thick, dark clouds filled the horizon, blocking out any hint of sunrise. The rain had picked up, falling in steady sheets as the wind pushed the trees in a violent dance, branches thrashing against each other in the early morning gloom.

Chase stared out the passenger window, constantly scouring the landscape, then rotating through the mirrors — rearview, side, repeat. Occasionally checking over his shoulder. That situational awareness she'd often admired in full swing.

He shook his head. "Does this guy always park in the middle of nowhere?"

She shrugged. "He thinks everyone's spying on him. After our last encounter, he's taken his defensive tactics up a notch. Damn hard to find him if he doesn't call in and want a visit."

Chase nodded as he patted down his vest. "And you're sure he's not a threat?"

"He might toss some tin foil your way, but otherwise, he's pretty benign. Overlooking that whole grenade fiasco."

"Grenade?"

"The one that got stuck under Saylor's seat. Nearly took her and Zain out because Buck forgot he had some live ones in his little treasure box. Didn't Zain tell you?"

"Remind me to kick Zain's ass later." Chase arched a brow. "And that seems to be going around."

Greer sighed. "I didn't think my location was relevant. Up until last night, we didn't even have the area narrowed down. And who would have thought any of the men could have survived. That they'd hunt us down. It's crazy. Besides, I'm sure there're a hundred missions you can't talk to me about."

"You're right." He pursed his lips, leaned closer. "How about I make you a deal? The next time some psychotic ex-teammate comes gunning for either of us, we'll tell each other everything, security be damned."

She smiled. "Deal."

She slowed as she entered a small clearing, Buck's motorhome parked off to one side. Green camouflage netting covered everything, the tiny squares fluttering in the gusting breeze, only the tall array poking out the top.

She parked to the right, jumping out as soon as she'd turned off the engine. It ticked, the fan humming in the background for a while before everything cut off.

Leaving an eerie silence in its wake. Just like Eli's cruiser last night.

Chase looked at her across the hood, tilting his head as if reading her mind. "There's nothing we could have done. No way we could have saved him. He'd lost too much blood before our perp put him in the river."

"Why doesn't that make me feel any better?"

"Because the truth won't bring him back."

The thought hit her hard, and she turned, headed for Buck's door. A generator hummed somewhere behind the vehicle, a few strings of lights connected to the nearest tree. The stairs creaked, rocking the RV a bit as she rapped on the door. "Buck. It's Sheriff Hudson. We need to talk."

The chassis squeaked as footsteps sounded behind the door before it cracked open.

Buck peered out through the sliver of space, gaze darting to Chase before focusing back on her. "How did you find me?"

She grinned. "I'm an expert tracker."

He glared at Chase before directing it back at her. "You're supposed to come alone."

"And you're supposed to call me if you witness any criminal activity."

His gaze darted to Chase, again. "I can't help you."

"Buck—"

"The last time I helped out, those bastards shot me."

"You made a deal with mercenaries to spy on Saylor. You're lucky they didn't kill you, which they would have if Zain hadn't saved our asses." Greer hitched out a hip.

"Four people are dead, Buck, including one of Chase's teammates and one of my dep…"

She swallowed. She couldn't say it. Couldn't get her tongue to work. "I know you were right next to where Eli was murdered, last night. And I know you never park this rig unless you're investigating a theory. So, show me."

He frowned, opening the door a bit wider. "Show you what?"

"All the photos you took. All the different walls you've got inside."

He stood a bit straighter. "I don't have any."

"The sheriff's department bought you this motorhome as a show of appreciation for your cooperation in our last endeavor. I can just as easily impound it. Now, are you inviting me in, or am I'm pushing past you?"

Buck paled, his hand holding the door trembling. "Fine, but… I didn't see anything. I swear. Not before…"

Greer backed up, swung open the door, then followed Buck inside. She got a whiff of stale coffee and vinegar, most of the light blocked by cardboard taped over the windows. Photos and trail-cam footage cluttered the walls, a number of old maps pinned off to one side. "You've set up your own dark room. That's new."

Buck shuffled on his feet as Chase closed in behind her, tall, unmoving. That death vibe rolling off him in waves. He scanned the walls, frowned.

Buck chewed on his thumbnail, eyes darting back

and forth. "I decided to switch to a digital camera after you took all my stuff. Now, I just print out the important ones, but I still have my backup."

"I didn't take your stuff. It got destroyed along with your RV."

"Same difference." He shifted restlessly, hands fisting and releasing at his side. "See? I don't have anything."

"Don't have anything?" Greer walked over to one of his boards. Blue strobes colored the fog, the driver's door hinged open. Clear enough she knew if she looked closely, she'd see the bloody handprint. "Jesus, Bucky, this is Eli's cruiser. Exactly how we found it."

"I..." Buck cringed when Chase took a calculated step closer. "I... I didn't do anything wrong."

"I know you didn't hurt Eli, but did you see who did?"

"No, I..." He banged his head with his right hand. "I've been following the lights. That's all."

"What lights?"

"The ones that have been popping up all over town and in the woods. First, at that old crazy hospital. Then, out by the park. I've seen them from my boat, too, along the coastline. Up in the forest." He leaned closer. "They're back."

"Who's back?"

Buck looked around, then pointed to the sky. "Aliens."

Greer yanked off a bunch of the photos, sorted through them before stopping on one shot. The trunk, wide open. The Bronco's headlights catching a silhouette in sharp relief. Tall. Muscular, a rifle slung across his back. She didn't recognize him, but something about the image felt familiar. Either the shape of his body, or the stance.

Chase moved in beside her, took the photo gently from her hands. The muscle in his temple jumped as he clenched his jaw, muttering a bit under his breath. He held the image out to Buck. "Do you know who this is?"

Buck snagged his bottom lip. "He's part of the lights."

"Did you see him at the other places you saw the lights?"

"Yes, but..." Buck checked his six, again. "He disappears."

"Where were the lights last night?"

Buck frowned, then pointed to one of the other images. "The old prospector cabin. That's why I parked close by. I wanted to get proof he's preparing for an invasion."

Chase nodded. "And is he?"

"Why else would he take Eli?"

Greer edged in next to him. "So, you did see the guy take Eli."

"No, I..." Buck banged his hand against his head, again. Harder. "I heard Eli shouting, and I was going to go after him, but then you two showed up, so I stayed hidden. I'm supposed to track. Take notes. Look for hidden threats. But I don't engage unless..." His voice trailed off, eyes slightly unfocused.

Chase tapped the photo. "When did this guy come back?"

Buck blinked a few times. "After you followed Eli. He only stayed for a few minutes, then left."

"Which way did he go?"

Buck shrugged. "He just... vanished."

Chase groaned, shaking his head.

Greer changed places. "Let's focus on the lights. How long have you been seeing them?"

Buck toed at the floor for a few moments. "Since I started photographing Saylor."

"That was nearly a year ago. Why didn't you tell me all this last month?"

"Because it wasn't part of Saylor's board."

Greer bit back any harsh response, reminded herself she wouldn't get any information out of Bucky if she lost her cool. "Okay, let's all take a breath. Why..."

A blast of static drowned her out, followed by intermittent chatter, too broken to distinguish any words.

Greer grabbed her radio. "This is Hudson. I missed that. Say, again."

More crackling, more broken words until Bodie's voice cleared for a second. "Atticus... attacked... missing."

She stilled, heart lodged in her throat, a cold sweat breaking out across her skin. She glanced at Chase, then tried the radio. "Bodie? You're still broken. Did you say Atticus was attacked? That he's missing?"

Nothing, then a few choppy words. "Ambushed..."

"Shit." She tamped down the rush of fear. The cold reality that if they lost one more... "Chase. Can you try the radio in the Bronco?"

Chase rushed out, boots hitting the metal stairs, then gravel crunching in the background. A distant chime followed by low murmurs.

Greer hooked Buck's arm. "I need you to show me every photo of where you've seen the lights."

Buck chewed at his bottom lip, then darted around the RV, tearing off pictures from various stashes before spreading them out on the table. "That's all of them."

"Any on your camera you haven't developed yet?"

Buck frowned. "Maybe."

Greer resisted the scream trying to claw free. "Can you check? It's important."

He muttered something under his breath, then grabbed his camera — started hitting one of the buttons. Chase reappeared at the door, brow furrowed, mouth pinched tight.

Greer took a step toward him. "Well?"

Chase visibly pushed down his shoulders, exhaled. "Transmission was still garbled, but it sounds like Atticus and one of the other pilots were ambushed while fueling the choppers. That there were flash bangs and tear gas. Travers, the other pilot, was taken to Providence, but there's no sign of Atticus."

"Damn it." Greer turned back to the table. "These are all the places Buck's seen the lights. Assuming this is our guy, maybe he's taken Atticus back to one of these locations. An area the bastard hasn't targeted yet."

Chase nodded. "Which means we rule out the psychiatric building, the park next to the Lodge and anything close to the other two sites."

He shuffled the images, pushing some to the side

until only a couple of locations remained. He tapped the table. "This looks like a fire lookout tower or maybe a ranger cabin. The other... Is that some kind of facility?"

Greer turned to Buck. "Where did you take this?"

Buck leaned over. "From my boat. It's down the coast a bit. By that cove Saylor and Zain were interested in."

Greer slapped her thigh. "It's that decommissioned water treatment plant. The county switched to lines from the north a good twenty years ago. As far as I know, it's been vacant ever since."

Chase groaned. "In other words, the perfect spot for a hideout."

"He's not there."

Greer froze as Buck's voice filled the room. She turned. "Say that again?"

Buck shrugged. "He's not there."

"How do you know?"

"Because I saw the lights at the old fire watchtower. That's why I parked here. I thought he might come back."

Chase crowded the man. "You saw the lights this morning?"

Buck puffed out his chest a bit, looking oddly confident. A glimpse of who Greer suspect the man had been before he'd fallen apart. "Are you deaf? I just said that."

Chase glanced at her, eyes narrowed. Slashes of red across his cheeks. "How far is the tower from here?"

"Not far if you drive." He laughed. "Too bad you can't drive."

Greer stepped between Chase and Buck, shuffling Buck back against the wall. "Enough. I need you to focus. Atticus' life is on the line. We can't afford to be wrong. Why can't we drive?"

"Because the road's got laser eyes!"

"Laser eyes?" She inhaled. "You mean he's wired it. Has laser trip beams."

Buck rolled his eyes. "That's what I said. And they're good. It'd take a while to disarm them. I could but…"

Buck could disarm trip wires?

Greer made a mental note to ask the man about that, later as she pointed to the photo. "Is there another way up?"

"There's an old mule track that weaves through the woods. Overgrown. Hard to follow. I've gone up it a few times, but it's really muddy and slippery from the rain. I tried this morning, but…"

"Well, you're not alone, now." She motioned to the door. "Let's go."

Buck shook his head, grabbing ahold of the driver's seat. "I'm not going anywhere."

Greer loomed in close. "I know this isn't easy for you, but we'll never find the path in time. I need you to be our guide. Chase and I'll handle whatever's there. I just need you to get us to that tower."

Buck glanced at Chase, then back to her. "I need a new telephoto lens."

"Deal. Now, move." She snagged his elbow. "And Buck, don't try to run off. This guy — the one with the lights — he's really dangerous."

Buck nodded, then pushed to the back of his RV. He grabbed a backpack, started chucking in supplies.

Chase brushed past her. "I'll grab my medic bag and some gear. We can radio Bodie and Raven's Watch, in case they can hear us. Just… remember that saving Atticus is more important than catching this guy. That he's not worth dying over."

"Understood. It'd be nice to do both, though."

Chase nodded, then ran off, clearing the steps before disappearing beyond the door.

Greer collected the photos, staring at the silhouette of the tower rising above the pines, like a sentry keeping watch. This was it. Their one chance at stopping whoever had survived that mission. Finally ending the rampage. She just hoped they'd be enough.

CHAPTER SEVENTEEN

Chase grabbed some survival gear and shoved it in a spare backpack. Not that he thought they'd need any, but he prided himself in being prepared — a feat this perp had pushed to the limits — and he didn't want to risk Atticus or Greer's life because he'd cut corners. Left a vital piece of equipment behind. He'd spent a lifetime carrying rucksacks and men across enemy lines. He'd put his trust in all that training, now.

Greer met him at the Bronco. "I relayed our intentions on both channels. I realize our guy could pick up on the transmissions, but it's worth the risk." She handed him one of the radios. "You should carry one, too, in case…"

He clipped it on his belt, then handed her the pack. "It's not much. Some carabiners and webbing. A length of cord and a few medical supplies."

She didn't ask any questions, just slipped it over her shoulders. "Bet it's a quarter of the weight yours is."

He simply smiled. "What I wouldn't give to have

Nyx right about now. Bet she'd pick up on that asshole's scent — lead us right to him."

Instead, they had Buck Landry — conspiracy theorist, and the guy they were betting Atticus' life on.

Chase wasn't sure what had shocked him more. That Buck had recorded their guy's movements during an imagined alien invasion, or that their perp had been stalking Chase and his buddies for nearly a year. All without them realizing.

He sighed. He could question his competency later, after they'd rescued Atticus.

God, he hoped Buck was right. That their suspect had brought Atticus back to the watchtower. If he hadn't…

They wouldn't have enough time to reappropriate their resources, assuming their calls eventually got through. That his team would have his back like they always had.

He rolled his shoulders, looking Buck in the eyes. "Okay, Buck. You take point, just… be careful. And don't out us before we even have a chance to assess the situation."

Buck scoffed. "I told you. I know how to track. I just don't like…"

He trailed off, leaving the rest unsaid, then headed off, angling toward a narrow opening on the far side of the clearing, seemingly indifferent to the soaking rain. Chase waved Greer ahead, taking up the rear. Constantly checking their six as they crossed the gravel lot, then ventured into the trees.

Chase glanced up the path, though, path was

stretching it. More of a slight depression in the undergrowth. Fewer ferns and bramble. The odd bent branch. Nothing the average hiker would look twice at.

He saw the trail. How the needles and mud had been flattened ever so slightly. The hint of a boot tread on the fringes. Likely when Buck had tried to scale the hill this morning. But any variances could be easily missed, which made Buck's presence a key Chase wished they didn't have to rely on. Not when the man looked as if he'd spent too much time shouting at the wind. Seeing shadows even when there wasn't any light. Though, his remarks about tracking — disarming bombs — definitely sparked some questions.

Mist threaded low through the trees, veiling the distance, shifting shapes at the edges as they moved in a stacked line, weapons still holstered in case they slipped — needed both their hands to prevent a looming catastrophe. They angled right, one side of the trail sloughing off into a steep ravine, blowdown and dead wood crisscrossing the hillside.

Buck stopped, made a few hand signals, before taking another questionable track on their left. Even more remote than the last, only the occasional bent fern as any indication the line was passable. The guy continued up, pausing every so often to stare at the trees — sniff the air.

Chase studied him, trying to decide if Buck was crazy or gifted as Chase trailed after them, boots sinking into the mud, each step leaving a print behind. Chase avoided any twigs, every footstep measured. Controlled. Heel to toe. Maintaining his balance in case the whole damn side of the hill gave out. Greer followed suit, not an ounce of energy wasted as she surveyed the landscape, gaze searching the shadows, pausing at locations he'd questioned, too.

She had great instincts, moving like a wraith through the fog. Keeping Buck from slipping whenever his shoes lost traction — sent him sliding off toward the ravine. They traveled in silence, any noise muffled amidst the patter of rain — the constant dripping that sounded in the background.

They crested a small, rocky ledge and pivoted onto a larger track. Not quite a main trail, but it opened up a bit. Stopped the endless ferns from soaking through their pants.

Greer slipped on a root, stumbled back until Chase caught her arm — steadied her. She reached for his hand, used it to regain her balance before she smiled her thanks, the brush of her skin over his — a flash of warmth in the cold rain.

He lingered, her breath ghosting next to his shoulder until she'd synced her breathing to his. Calmed the flutter of her pulse at the base of her neck. A small nod, and she struck off, head on a swivel, muscles tensed and ready to react to a dynamic situation.

Buck led them through a long, narrow clearing, the air heavy with freshly cut cedar. Patches of sawdust dotted the scrubby ground, a discarded jerrycan resting against a stump. They hit the next thicket, sticking to the non-existent trail as it wove higher, a hint of lighter sky showing through the canopy.

The underbrush thinned as they reached the top, the

lush ferns giving way to heaps of pine needles beneath thick trunks.

A snap.

Sharp.

Deliberate.

Somewhere off to their right. Too heavy for a deer. Bear, maybe, though Chase doubted it. They stopped, listened for movement, scanning the mist for a glimpse of a shadow, but the rain distorted the sound — made every drop a false echo.

A crow cawed overhead.

Sudden. Jarring. Then nothing.

Buck veered left, walked another hundred yards, then stopped. He crouched behind a fallen log dotted with moss, pointing two fingers at his eyes, then his hand toward the tree line.

A faint glow flickered between the tree trunks, the amber hue moving from right to left. Muffled grunts sounded above the rain, a low thud rumbling through the air. Chase took lead, picking his way through the deadfall to the edge of a clearing. The surf thundered faintly beyond the cliffside, another storm cell crawling across the horizon, rain hampering the visibility.

The abandoned lookout loomed high above a rocky knoll, separated from the access road by that narrow ravine. An old footbridge spanned the gaping chasm, the fast-moving water churning beneath heading toward the ocean.

Greer pointed to a lone truck parked across the crest of the gravel road, the gray sky spilling through the windows, showcasing the empty interior.

Chase panned left, searching for the source of that light, when a hint of movement caught his attention. He squinted, water trickling down his neck, the scent of dead leaves saturating the air, when a figure moved onto the bridge. Tall. Muscular.

The guy looked up when thunder echoed in the distance, his gaze searching the heavens before he picked up his pace — trotted off the other end. His right leg lagged a bit, a slight limp throwing off his gait as he headed along the gravel road, gaze searching the forest. A bolt of lightning forked across the sky several seconds later, the brief flash highlighting the guy's face.

Chase froze. Stomach knotted. Chest squeezed tight. He glanced at Greer, noted her wide eyes and ashen skin. She'd recognized the man, too.

Marcus Hodges.

Older. Wilder, with a darkness radiating off him that dimmed the growing dawn. Prickled the hairs on Chase's neck. He closed his eyes, tried to shove down the pain and guilt, but it was useless. Knowing he'd been the catalyst. That if he'd remained conscious long enough to drag his ass back, maybe he could have prevented this.

Saved them.

Greer grabbed his hand. Strong. Unyielding.

She'd help him move on. Find the kind of future Rhett had wanted Chase to have. They just needed to finish this.

Chase readied his weapon, took a breath, then moved out, Greer matching his stride. He leveled his Sig at the truck, zeroing in on Hodges as he stepped beyond the flatbed, box clasped in his hands. He looked haggard. Broken. As if he'd stared into the abyss too long — had let it stain his soul.

Chase clenched his jaw, forced the name past the lump in his throat. "Hodges."

Their gazes clashed. Held, Hodges' eyes widening a second before a cruel smile shaped his lips. He snickered, tossed the box, then took off, darting behind the truck as Chase's round hit the quarter panel an inch from his shoulder. Footsteps pounded the ground, quickly fading into the next roll of thunder as he moved out of range, his lithe form bobbing along a rough path.

Greer raced ahead, skidding to a halt once she was parallel with the end of the bridge. Atticus slumped against the bank on the far side, wrists zip-tied, ankle tethered to a post with a short leash. He roused, lifted his head enough to meet their gazes.

The older man coughed, shivered, then motioned toward the path snaking along the ridge. "Don't just stand there, Remington, run the bastard down."

Chase looked at the bridge, then back to the fleeing silhouette, history replaying in his head. How he'd been forced to choose that fucking night. All the dominoes that had fallen since.

Greer gave him a shove. "Go. I'll get Atticus." She rolled her eyes when he simply stood there, debating. "Chase. I can cross a damn bridge without you backing me up. I've got Buck. You're taking the real risk. But we both know you're faster and stronger, so, go. Just don't freaking die on me."

Chase grunted, then took off, tearing down the

access road, gravel popping, boots flying, as he veered onto the trail skirting the bluff. Salt hung heavy in the air, the wind sharper. Colder.

Hodges bobbed along the path, that limp more pronounced as he avoided boulders and logs, wasting some of his precious lead as Chase vaulted over the barriers, quickly eating up the space.

Lightning spread like a web across the sky, the white light framing the scene — Hodges looking back over his shoulder, mouth still curved into a smile. The man ducked under a low branch, disappeared for a moment until Chase popped out the other side — spotted him heading down a lower fork.

Chase followed, scrambling over brush and debris, closing the gap, again, when Hodges stopped — headed for a flat rock jutting off the edge. He reached the stone plateau, then turned, hands at his side, strong. Resolute.

Chase slowed, looking for an ambush as he jogged to a halt, weapon zeroed in, chest heaving. He held firm, that voice inside his head screaming. "End of the road, Hodges."

The name croaked out. Low. Raw. The word tripping across his tongue.

Hodges laughed. Deep. Loud. The haunting sound echoing along the cliffs. "What's the matter, Remington? Have you seen a ghost?"

Chase stared at him, taking it all in. The scars. The shadows. The vision of a man who'd faced his demons and lost. "I thought you were dead."

Another laugh. "I bet you did. Made it real easy to go

on with your life. Pretend you didn't leave us all there to die."

"I didn't…"

The words fell flat, the meaning lost to the roaring wind. The crash of the waves beneath them.

Chase took another step, mud splattering the bottom of his pants, rain soaking through his jacket. "I know nothing I say will change your mind, and you're right. Believing you were dead did make it easier. But if we'd known you'd survived, that there was a chance…" He shook his head. "We would have come back."

"You would have come back? That's what you want me to believe? Because you looked us all dead in the eyes and swore you'd do just that. Then, more men came, started beating on us before the world exploded and everything we ever knew ceased to exist."

Hodges glanced over the edge. "Do you know how many times I prayed to be in this exact position? In charge of my own destiny? To choose whether I lived or died? But that doesn't matter because *you* would have come for me."

"I can't change the past. But I'm here, now. Just… walk over here. Let me take you in. I'll get you the help you need."

Hodges chuckled, shaking his head as he balanced on the lip, swaying back and forth as if he didn't care which way he fell. "Poor Remington. He's afraid he'll lose another one. That I'll become one more stain on his prestigious record? Like Rhett? And Eli? Did you promise them you'd have their backs, too?"

"I failed them. I know that. Just like I failed you and

the others. But it doesn't have to go down like this. You've suffered enough. Aren't you tired of running?"

"Tired? I spent four years rebuilding myself. Picking up the pieces you broke apart. Finding a way to exist while trapped in the darkness. Losing everything. Everyone." He leered at Chase. "I'm not running. I've finally come home."

He stepped back, foot skimming nothing but air, his body hanging in that space between standing and falling before he crumpled. Chase dove at him, catching a fistful of jacket, Hodges' weight dragging them both down. Chase dropped his weapon, clawed at the rock, digging in the toes of his boots, as his chest crested the edge, a huge breaker kissing the shore — spraying up the side of the cliff below them.

One boot caught on a root, grinding them to a halt, his right arm stretched beneath him, the nylon slowly slipping between his fingers. Rain poured off his jacket, falling around Hodges like a waterfall as the mud shifted beneath Chase, slowly inching him closer.

He tightened his hold, hand cramping, his grip loosening from the rain. He tried curling Hodges toward the lip, the sheer weight countering his efforts. "Damn it, Hodges, help me. Use your other hand."

Hodges hung there, smiling, staring at the ocean as if it held some form of salvation. "Still trying to be the hero. Even after all I've done." He reached up — grabbed Chase's forearm. "Rhett called out for you. At the end. Your name was the last thing he said."

Bile crested Chase's throat, but he swallowed it. "I'm not letting go."

"Then, let's both go for a ride."

He twisted, his jacket slipping free from Chase's fist as he wrapped his fingers around Chase's hoodie — pulled. The momentum split the root holding their weight, the unforgiving force pulling him down.

He scrambled for a handhold, nails scratching against the stone, toes digging into the mud before the world shifted and everything rushed past.

CHAPTER EIGHTEEN

Greer watched Chase's silhouette fade into the rain and the fog, his footsteps crushed beneath the roar of the water as it rushed beneath the bridge, the dark mass churning with logs and brush.

Buck moved in beside her, shielding his face from the driving rain. "I'm not sure that bridge is sound."

She gave it a once-over. The old wood looked tired, beaten, as if waiting for the right stressor to pack it in. But the cable handrails were taut, the weathered planks cracked but firm. "Hodges walked over it. Dragged Atticus across it, too."

"I know but…" Buck tapped his temple. "He sees ghosts, too. Misses what's right in front of him."

Greer studied Buck, seeing him in a slightly different light. One she'd delve into once they'd gotten Atticus free and on this side of the bridge. "We can't leave Atticus over there. He's already shivering. Just… take this. Keep broadcasting our location and that we need backup. Pray they can hear us."

Buck palmed her radio, started talking, as Greer moved to the end of the bridge, testing out the first few planks. The wood creaked, the entire bridge swaying with the gusting winds, but the boards seemed solid. Trustworthy.

She ventured out, taking each step slowly. Methodically. Distributing her weight in case one of them gave way. Water spit at her from between the cracks, slicking the wood as she inched her way across, the metal cable sliding through her closed fist.

She crested the halfway point, started picking up speed, when lightning spread across the sky, everything around her standing on end. She froze, waiting for the moment to pass when another fork shot out of the clouds, flashing bright white as it struck a guy-wire, exploded in a ball of sparks.

A metallic crack lit the air as the bridge shook, the resulting vibration humming through to her bones. The nails on the planks hissed as electricity strummed through the wood, the high-pitched tone singing around her. The right handrail twanged, the anchor bolt on the far side shearing beneath the strain as mud and gravel sloughed into the ravine, tumbling into the raging river. The cable sagged, then dropped, hitting the wooden planks with a resounding snap. Splitting the one beneath her heel in half.

Greer scrambled for a secure hold, most of the planks behind her crumbling into the water, leaving only splinters of the wood still held beneath the nails. Buck waved her back, but she knew she'd never make it.

Instead, she continued forward. Slowly, planting

each step before taking another. Staying low. Alert. Ready to bolt to the other side at even an inkling of more trouble.

The rain kicked up, soaking through her clothes, running in rivulets down her neck. She neared the other side, still shuffling like a damn drunk, when a log rose out of the water, tumbling over itself as it rushed toward the bridge.

Greer dove for the edge, wedged her fingers through a crack — locked them around one of the last boards a moment before the massive stump crashed into the bridge, splintering the support beams before continuing on, taking half the structure with it.

The remaining section dropped, smacking the surface like a skipping stone before twisting with the current, more of the planks tearing free. She hit hard, mud spraying across her face, the lower half of her body quickly submerging. More debris clawed at her clothes, nearly pulled her off before she reached for the next board — dragged her ass out of the water.

Shivers raked her body as she collapsed on the far bank, chest heaving, every breath misting in the thick air. Atticus called her name, the desperate tone snapping her back. She pushed to her feet, stumbled over to him. Skin pale, lips a cool shade of blue, he looked more ghost than man. An obvious head wound glared up at her, his hair sticky and matted with blood.

She crouched beside him, checked his pulse. "Atticus? Can you hear me?"

He grunted, lifting his right ankle. "I'm not dead yet, Hudson. But that bastard, Hodges, tied me to the damn post. This entire section's undercut. Only a matter of time before it collapses."

She nodded as she removed a knife from her belt. "Let's get you free, then we'll assess."

"Assess what? The bridge is gone. No other recourse but to take shelter in the tower until Mac or Foster get their asses out this way."

Greer laughed. "I can always count on you for your positive outlook."

"I'm old. Still breathing is about as positive as I can get."

"You're not old, you're crotchety. Now, hold still."

It took a few passes to slice through the zip-ties, the blade slipping in her grip from the rain, the deep-seated cold seeping into her bones. Atticus shook out his wrists once she'd freed his hands, looking more than a bit relieved.

Greer moved to the tether, shaking her head as she started sawing through the line. "Rope's thick. This might take a few minutes."

Atticus grumbled something under his breath. "Not sure we have many of those left."

"Well, if you'd rather start gnawing at it, be my guest. Otherwise, I'll keep going with the knife."

"Glad you still have your sense of humor. We'll need it when everything goes to shit."

Greer laughed. "I honestly don't know how Mackenzie puts up with you."

Atticus relaxed against the ground. "She doesn't really have a choice."

Greer shook her head, still working the rope, when

another lightning pulse brightened the sky, the nearby thunderclap shaking the ground. The wind increased, bending trees along the perimeter, an ominous shift tightening the air.

She sawed harder, finally cutting through the last few fibers. The line to the post fell, a finger of white amidst the muddy brown. She turned back to Atticus, gave him a quick body sweep. He cursed when she pressed on his right side, his breathing labored with a distinctive wheeze rattling through his chest.

Atticus shoved her away. "I'm fine. Nothing a stiff drink won't cure."

"You've got a nasty head injury, and what I suspect are a couple cracked ribs. Nothing life threatening, yet, but based on how badly you're shivering — the blue cast to your lips — hypothermia's already kicking in."

"You worry too much, you know that Greer?" He motioned to the tower, every small movement drawing a resulting grunt. "We should take cover before it gets any worse."

She nodded, helping him up, when a crack split the air, another strike lighting up the sky. The bolt hit the tower, arcing down the side, splitting the wood with an ear-piercing hiss. Flames shot out from the base, licking at the raised platform as the ground shook, more cracks filling the air.

The tower swayed, then tilted, bending toward them at some ungodly angle. The support beams cracked, everything sliding forward as the tower pitched, hanging on a forty-five before finally giving way.

Greer grabbed Atticus by the arm, took him with her

as she jumped into the water, sinking beneath the dark surface just as the tower hit the bank, shattering into several pieces. Chunks hit the water, stabbing at them like spears before the current took over — dragged both of them downstream.

Silt and debris clouded the water, stinging her eyes when she opened them, trying to get her bearings. She hit a rock, nearly blacked out, before the current spit them out. Greer crested the surface, gasping in air, Atticus coughing and spitting in front of her. She held on, kept his head above the surface, the torrent bouncing them off the stones like a pinball. She reached out, snagged a root, then slammed them against a midstream boulder.

Atticus clawed at the wet surface, finally scrambling halfway up as Greer hauled them the rest of the way, collapsing beside him on the cold rock. Thunder rumbled overhead, more lightning sizzling around them.

She took a moment to breathe, chest tight, every inch bruised from the punishing rocks. But at least they weren't dead.

Yet.

Atticus groaned, and she pushed herself upright. Skin ashen, hands shaking, the man looked a breath away from death.

She leaned over, checked his pulse. "Shit."

He coughed, shoved her off. "Don't be so dramatic. I've been hurt worse and still dragged my ass from behind enemy lines."

"Maybe we'll get lucky, and some tangos will pop up. Motivate you."

He chuckled, cursing as he grabbed his ribs. "You did that on purpose."

"Maybe a little." She glanced at the shoreline, sighing at the dark edge undercut by thick mud. No way to scramble over it in these conditions. Not that the other side was any better, the bank a mass of fallen pine and bits of broken bridge. A patchwork of deadfall she'd be lucky to climb over without impaling herself.

Atticus tsked. "Don't even think it. Even if you scaled one of the sides, you'd be knocked unconscious before you ever reached the edge. The current's too strong, too choked with branches. We're lucky we landed here without major injuries."

Greer rubbed where she'd headbutted that boulder. "Speak for yourself."

He smiled, grunting when the rock shifted, a large log bobbing to the surface a moment later. "Though, staying might not be an option for much longer, either. River's rising, and it's only going to get more congested."

She motioned to her backpack. "Chase threw in some gear. I could probably tie us on, but…"

"Not a good option if we suddenly need to escape."

"Lightning can't strike three times, can it?"

He rolled his eyes. "And now, you've jinxed it."

She smiled. She had to hand it to him, the old coot was ice under pressure. Calm. Steady, despite his obvious injuries. The pink froth he tried to hide when he coughed, sputtered flecks of blood across his shirt. Or how his shivering had eased from violent to barely there. A sure sign that hypothermia scenario was already in full effect.

Atticus shifted his gaze toward her. "I'm fine. Worry about how we're getting off this rock."

"I'd try calling for backup, but I gave Buck my radio. And my cell's smashed."

"They'll be here."

"I'm not sure they even know where *here* is. We tried, but… Coverage sucks."

"Buck's a bag full of crazy, but he's a good man. Did you know he's ex-military?"

Greer coughed. "Buck Landry? The guy who thinks I'm secretly harboring aliens? And not the kind who simply need papers. That Buck?"

Atticus nodded, holding his side. "He wasn't always… He was a Marine, ordinance specialist by trade before he joined the Raiders, became part of MARSOC. He was deployed mostly in Special Reconnaissance missions — where he picked up all those uncanny tracking skills — until he got on the wrong side of car bomb. Damn thing rattled more than just his nerves. Wasn't the same after that. Sees danger everywhere but has trouble processing it. Realizing what's real and what's ghosts from the past. He doesn't like to talk about it, tends to set him off, so I've never mentioned it to anyone. But, he's still got those instincts, and I doubt he simply stood there, watching us get swept downstream."

"Let's hope I owe him an apology, then."

A crack.

Sharp. Deep.

Like the sniper shot that day on the cliff.

Greer turned. Stilled. Stared at the top half of the tower as it barreled down the river, punching through overhanging logs and decimating boulders. It surged up, looming black against the next flicker of light.

No time to think. She just grabbed Atticus and rolled them to the edge, hooked her arm around a stabbing branch wedged on the side. She curled over him, bracing for impact as the wreckage slammed the rear end, nearly knocking them loose. The boulder scraped across the bottom, tilting off to the left as it shifted with the force, plunging them waist-deep into the river.

The steep angle slipped them farther over, the rock jutting out at a forty-five, beams and wood still trying to shove it downstream. She held on, judging when she'd have to give up — let the current take them before the rock fully flipped and pinned them to the bottom — when a beam tunneled through the rain and the fog, catching them in a wide circle.

The helicopter appeared out of the mist, rotors bending the trees, kicking up white caps across the river. The machine steadied, then a blast of light as the doors opened, a lone figure descending out of the gray sky.

Greer closed her eyes, focused on not letting go, until Kash landed on the rock, a couple harnesses strapped to his vest.

He shook his head, pulled some slack, then went to work, securing the first harness around Atticus. Hands flying, everything calm. Steady. He checked the attachments, gave the other man a wink, then jumped into the water, bobbing in front of her as if it was nothing. She swallowed, slipping a bit when the branch cracked — dropped her another foot.

Kash inched closer, somehow countering the current as he grabbed her jacket — held firm. "I've got you."

She nodded. Way too fast, more like a bobblehead on a dirt road, but he played along. Kept working that harness until it circled her chest. She groaned at the increased pressure, all those bruises burning to life before he yelled into his mic.

A blast of downwash as the rotors took the load, then they popped free, rising above the water just as the rock gave way, tumbling down the river before slowly sinking beneath the surface, the raging torrent quickly closing over top.

They spun, every rotation threatening to hurl what little coffee she'd had that morning across Kash's chest before they cleared the skid — got yanked inside.

She hit the floor, a dull thud echoing through the cabin as Kash stepped inside, looking every inch the warrior he'd been.

Jordan loomed over her, offering a hand before pulling her to her feet. "I'm starting to think this is some kind of competition. See who can pull the most outrageous stunt because that…" She whistled. "That looked insane."

Greer collapsed on the seat, wrapping the blanket Jordan handed her around her shoulders. "All I did was jump in the water. Everything else was the river."

"Right. Nothing heroic at all."

Greer nodded at Atticus. "You okay? Hodges didn't give you anything, did he? Some kind of injection?"

Atticus batted Kash's hands away. "Hell, no. The bastard was too busy rambling on about Chase and his teammates. Not that he wasn't batshit crazy before, but whatever screws he still had busted lose during the drive to that tower."

Greer inhaled. "Chase. Wait. He went after Hodges. He—"

"Foster and Zain headed his way. They'll see his ass comes back in one piece. You just worry about staying awake. You're even bluer than last night, and I didn't think that was possible."

"I can't. What if Hodges hurt him? What if he's out there, waiting... I need—"

"To be safe." Kash inched closer. "Chase is the toughest son of a bitch I've ever met. But he'd break if anything happened to you, so... Rest. His brothers'll have his back. Now, let's go get Buck before I end up throttling him. The jerk won't stop broadcasting over the radio, despite us telling him we were already on it. Something about you giving him an order."

"Call me crazy, but I might have to give the guy a job."

Kash rolled his eyes as Greer relaxed against the seat, staring out the window, willing the clouds to lift enough she'd catch a glimpse of Chase — some form of proof she hadn't lost him. But the rain only kicked up harder, everything closing in around them.

Fate.

That's what it all came down to. She only hoped that this time, it'd end in her favor.

CHAPTER NINETEEN

Free fall.

His stomach up in his throat, breath held as he slipped over the edge — dropped.

Hit a ledge ten feet below them. A narrow rock formation that shook as they slammed onto the slick surface, the sudden stop stealing his breath.

Chase groaned, pain sparking through his chest, then into his skull, scattering his thoughts. He rolled, nearly puked, then pushed onto his hands and knees. Hodges twitched beside him, glancing at him across the wet stone before clambering to his feet — catching him with a knee to his ribs.

Chase tumbled onto his ass, avoiding the next attack by sliding right, hugging that sheer drop before rolling away, putting as much distance between them as the small ledge allowed.

Hodges snarled, teeth flashing white in the lightning. "You can't save them all, Remington."

Chase remained alert, ready to react as he mapped out the available space. Four steps. That's all they had. "It's over. The only way you're getting off this hunk of rock alive is with a chopper."

"Who said I wanted to live?"

"Hodges. Brother, this isn't you. I don't know what they did to you, but this isn't what you trained for. What you dedicated your life to. You're the hero. Please, let me help you."

"This is what happens when heroes fail."

He lunged, catching a piece of Chase's jacket as he pivoted. They tripped, fell back to the surface, sliding a few feet from the force. Hodges slipped off the other side, legs dangling mid-air, chest notched against the edge. Chase grabbed one arm, securing the other man as he hooked his elbow around a root — anchored them.

Sweat beaded his brow, the rain sloughing off mud and rocks, shimmying that ledge lower.

Hodges laughed, not even bothering to hold on. "You can't outlast this ledge, Chase. Sooner or later, you'll either have to let go — save yourself — or we're both falling."

He grunted, hands shaking, every muscle cramping. "Not... an... option."

"Dying's not so bad. It's coming back that sucks." Hodges reached up — clamped one hand around Chase's forearm, squeezing until Chase's fingers numbed. "You don't get to bring back all the pieces."

"Then, let's not die."

Thunder, only deeper. Bouncing off the cliff, shaking

the ledge a moment before a chopper roared overhead, banked left, then circled back. A spotlight ate up the rain, the beam settling on them as the helicopter hovered over top, the rotors kicking up the loose rock.

Salt spray misted up the cliff face, swirling with the eddying winds as the doors opened, a familiar silhouette stepping off the skid.

Chase held steady, staring at Hodges as Zain lowered next to them, the gusting winds swinging him across the cliffside. "It's now or never, brother. You need to show me your other hand, so I know it's safe for Zain to help you."

Hodges tilted his head. "Don't you trust me?"

"Hodges…"

Chase clenched his jaw, then nodded at Zain, twisting so his buddy could loop a harness around his chest — lock him in.

The rock groaned, an eerie screech echoing across the ridge as Chase braced his feet, released the root, then dragged Hodges onto the ledge. The other man collapsed on the surface, eyes unfocused, mouth open as if he'd lost his will to fight.

Chase motioned for Zain to stay back. "On your feet."

Hodges chuckled, stumbling to his feet, eyeing Zain. "So predictable. Ironic, you're so eager to save me, now. Five years too late."

"I…"

A low rumble shook through the stone, mud and gravel raining down from above, tilting the rock toward the ocean. Chase lunged at Hodges, snagged his arm before the ledge dropped out beneath them, the line catching their weight.

They snapped to a halt, Hodges dangling beneath them, the line spinning from the increased downwash as the chopper slowly rose. Chase locked his other hand around the man's arm, fighting to hold on when Hodges looked him in the eyes.

Hodges reached up — pulled himself a bit closer. "You'll never be free Remington, because in the end, you won't be able to save her."

A glint, then a flash of pain along Chase's side — hot and bright. Blood bloomed against his shirt, bleeding through the fabric, dripping onto the rocks below.

He kicked at the knife, dropping it into the next surging breaker before Hodges released his hold, nothing but Chase's flimsy grip keeping him steady.

Chase grunted. "Damn it, I can't…"

Another laugh, then he fell, body disappearing into the surf. Nothing surfacing as the waves crashed against the shore, his voice still ringing across the cliff.

Zain grabbed him, holding Chase steady as they crested the chopper, got dumped inside. Bodie snagged some bandages, pressing them against Chase's ribs as Chase stared out the open door, watching the ocean curl in on itself. A light bounced along the water, slowing as it reached the impact site.

Zain claimed the seat beside him. "Saylor's backing us up. Took one of Bodie's buddies with her. If there's anything to retrieve…"

Chase let his head fall back against the seat, cursing

the hot line against his ribs. "I can't imagine what it took to turn him into…"

Zain clapped him on the shoulder. "You gave him a chance. That's more than I might have done."

"Didn't change anything."

He'd failed. Again.

A habit he needed to break.

He took a breath, inhaled. "Shit, Greer. Atticus. They're with Buck at that old tower—"

"Mac and Kash already picked them up. They're halfway to Providence. Seems there was a lightning strike. A trip down that river…"

"Of course, there was. I swear, she invents trouble just to give me a damn heart attack."

"She's not the only one. Rest, Foster's itching to have a come-to-Jesus moment with you, so… You'll need your strength."

* * *

"I don't need any pain meds. Just give me some clothes and tell me where the hell Greer is."

Greer sighed as Chase's bellow reached her from outside the exam room, the weight of his words lingering in the air. She stopped at the doorway, peeked around the corner. Foster stood with his arms crossed, mouth pinched tight as he stared at the silhouette beyond the curtain.

He glanced over at her, waving her in as he shook his head. "You talk to him. He might listen to you."

She dodged around the curtain, smiling at Chase as

he sat on the gurney, boxers slung low over his hips, all that muscled flesh gleaming in the harsh fluorescent light. The man was stunning.

He caught her gaze, the furrow along his brow lifting. As if seeing her quieted the voices. Slotted everything into place. "God, I thought you were in the ICU or something. All they said was there'd been a concussion, broken ribs with some minor lacerations to a lung." He curled his fingers. "Are you okay? Should you be walking?"

She laughed, placed her hand over his as she stepped up to the bed. "You might want to let me answer one question before you ask five more. First, I'm fine."

"I can see the bruises peeking out from your scrubs."

"Turns out, rocks aren't that forgiving." She shushed him when he grunted. "I have a small bump on my head and some cuts and scrapes. Nothing life threatening. Unlike you… Knife wound? Really?"

His shoulders drooped, some of the light leaving his eyes. "I thought…"

She stepped in, wrapped her arms around him, avoiding the bandages covering his left side. "I know. And I'm sorry. I guess I never stopped to consider that he was a victim, too."

Chase pulled her close, his breath feathering across her shoulder, the warmth of his body finally chasing the chill from hers. "It doesn't change what he did, but…"

She eased back, brushing her thumb across his jaw. "So, what's this about not taking any meds?"

He stilled, the tension returning to his muscles. "It's not my thing."

"Not abusing drugs is a thing. Not taking appropriate measures to mitigate your pain is something else." She cocked her head to the side. "Obviously, there's a story here."

Chase looked over her shoulder at Foster.

Foster merely shrugged. "It's your secret to share, buddy. I haven't said a word."

She cupped his jaw. "If you'd rather not, it's okay."

Chase grunted as he shifted on the bed, holding his side with his other hand. "My dad was a great guy. Hard-working. Fun. A real family man. Then, one summer, he crashed his motorcycle. Had to have a bunch of surgeries. I guess the pain was pretty bad because the doctor kept prescribing him narcotics. Morphine, then other pills. He never talked about it, just always mumbled something about being cursed. That it wasn't his fault. But within six months, he became this angry, violent addict. I used to tell people that he only got mean when he was itching for a fix, but the truth is… He was always mean. High. Low. Sober. Drunk. It became his default personality."

She dropped her hand to his, squeezed it. "I'm sorry. No one should have to live under that kind of threat."

"My brothers and I got really good at reading him. Knew when to steer clear — stay over at a friend's. It worked for a while until this one night…" Chase closed his eyes, took a deep breath. "He was supposed to be working late, but he came home early, completely wasted. Swinging at anything that moved. My mom managed to calm things down — get him into bed. The house went quiet. The kind that felt heavy. Wrong. Then, the floor creaked, footsteps padding down the hall. I'm not sure why I jumped out of bed, climbed out the window, but…"

He swallowed, looked as if he might puke. "There was a pop. Like the night just split open. Loud. Clear. Then, another. And another. Dogs started barking, lights flew on, sirens wailed in the distance. It took the cops five minutes to get there, but it was too late."

He stared down at his hands. "They found him on the landing, self-inflicted wound. The gun still warm beside him. Blood everywhere. Nothing breathing but the walls. The memories bleeding out on the floor. Since then…"

She nodded, still holding his hand. "You're worried it's inside you, too."

"Can't really take the chance."

"I get it. Easier to err on the side of caution."

Chase glanced at Foster. "See?"

"Though, would a man with that kind of darkness in his soul try to save a killer? Simply because he'd once stood for honor? Been part of the brotherhood?" Greer inched closer. "Do I seem like the kind of girl who'd fall head over heels for a man I couldn't trust with my life, no matter what state he was in?"

Chase stared at her, eyes narrowed. "Did you seriously just play that card?"

"What card?"

"The love card?"

Her heart fluttered as the word slipped free, hanging between them like a promise. She smiled, dropped a gentle kiss on his mouth. "I believe I did."

The shadows eased, all that tension melting away. "Not fair."

"What's not fair is me telling you I love you, and you not saying it back."

He stilled, eyes wide, red creeping along his cheeks. He opened his mouth, closed it, then laughed. Low. Genuine. "Say it, again."

She brushed some hair back from his eyes, all the tension from earlier lifting. "Okay, but that means I'm ahead by two."

"Greer…"

"I love you, Chase."

"Damn straight." He tugged her close, planted a searing kiss on her lips. "And I love you more."

"Saying the word doesn't make it real. You're gonna have to prove it."

"Challenge accepted."

"Now, about the meds…" She tsked when he frowned. "I know you've taken them before. So, what's the catch?"

Foster cleared his throat. "Generally, one of us has to promise to tackle his ass to the floor if he so much as twitches while on them."

Greer smiled. "I like the sound of that." She trailed one finger along his shoulder and down his chest. "You. On the floor beneath me. Count me in."

Chase coughed, grimaced. "That's not exactly what he meant."

"My interpretation."

"Greer…"

She hitched out a hip. "Foster? How many times has one of you had to tackle his ass?"

Foster started counting on one hand before chuckling. "Not once."

"That's what I thought."

Chase shifted on the gurney, eyes a bit wild. "And if this is the first time?"

Greer laughed. Damn, she loved him. "I'm an ex-federal agent and the sheriff. I can handle myself." She shook her head when he simply stared at her. "Fine. I'll bring my taser to bed. Now, take the meds, and let's go. I might actually be able to sleep tonight."

He snagged her hand as Foster mumbled something about getting him some clothes. "You know I'd never forgive myself if I ever hurt you, right?"

She leaned into him, drinking in the subtle hint of pine. Either from their trek through the forest or just his natural scent. "I know, which is why it's my turn to hold you, tonight."

The nurse reappeared, handed Chase a pill, then stood there, watching.

Chase mumbled something under his breath, then downed the tablet, staring at her when she didn't move. "I'm not opening my mouth to prove I swallowed it."

The nurse shook her head. "Good luck, Sheriff. He's definitely the worst patient we've ever had."

Greer arched a brow. "I see you're making friends everywhere you go."

He looked up at her and frowned.

She sighed. "It'll be okay. Promise. Now, let's get out

of here before that kicks in, and Foster has to carry your ass."

He snagged her arm. "I meant what I said. I love you, Greer. More than you'll ever know."

Warmth, burning away the chill that had settled in her bones. And all from those three words.

She moved into his arms, claiming his mouth in a dangerous kiss. "I love you, too. And once those stitches start falling out, I'll show you exactly how much."

CHAPTER TWENTY

"Morning, beautiful."

Greer blinked awake, staring into the darkness until her eyes adjusted, Chase's handsome face slowly appearing out of the darkness. She glanced at the clock, groaning at the early number. "You realize we don't have to be at work until seven, right?"

"Not waking you up to go to work, sweetheart."

She tilted her head, arched a brow. "And your side?"

Chase grabbed her hand, ran her fingers across his ribs. "Stitches are already falling out."

"Are they? Or did you take some scissors to them before you woke me?"

He placed a hand over his heart. "Are you questioning my honor? That's cold, Greer."

"But true." She brushed her thumb across his brow. "The bridge of your nose wrinkles when you're busted."

He smiled, and her heart fluttered, either too fast or too slow, the shaky rhythm highlighting how far gone she was. How deeply she loved him.

He shook his head, toying with the ends of her hair. "Fine. I might have helped them along, but the wound's closed. And I'm already cleared for work—"

"Not sure it counts when you clear yourself, but…" She laughed when he rolled his eyes. "Sounds like you have something in mind."

He shifted over her, elbows braced on either side, his mouth a breath away from hers. "Do you know how hard it's been holding you every night, breathing you in, and *not* making love to you?"

She arched her hips, pressing into his groin. "I have an idea. Not that it's been any easier for me." She lifted her head and nipped at his lower lip before kissing her way to his ear. "I've been on edge all week."

The muscle in his temple jumped as he worked his jaw, sucking in air then pushing it out. "Looks like we're on the same page, so do me a favor." He threw back the covers, trailing his fingers down her side, over her hip to the top of her thigh. "Get comfortable. This might take a while."

She inhaled, snagged her bottom lip as he inched his way down, licking and sucking every inch until he settled between her legs. Her fingers landed in his hair as a warm breath feathered across her flesh. "I swear, Chase, you put your mouth on me, and it'll be over in less than a minute."

He dropped a kiss on her inner thigh, and her stomach clenched in anticipation. "That just means I get more time to enjoy you in other ways. Though, I bet I can drag it out a bit longer."

"I… God."

She pressed her head into the pillow, every nerve burning white hot as he mouthed her skin, teasing her with a long, slow lick. Taking her to the brink in a single heartbeat.

She fisted her hands, reminding herself not to tug on his hair too hard as he hummed against her groin, each tiny vibration sparking a reaction.

Heat coiled low in her belly, every swirl of his tongue arching her higher until he placed one muscled forearm across her hips — held her in place.

That unraveled her. The weight of his arm, the strength of his grip drawing a guttural moan from deep in her chest as he slipped a finger inside her — hit that spot.

She died.

Right there on the bed, hips pumping, his name ringing off the walls, every thought bursting into tiny specks of light. The room faded, that searing heat lulling her into a numbing haze until he pressed a kiss to her lips, smiled down at her.

Chase grinned, looking more than a bit victorious. "You weren't kidding. Talk about a hair trigger."

"That's all your fault. Looking the way you do, all that smooth skin and bulging muscles holding me all week. You're lucky I lasted beyond the first pass."

"Barely."

She laughed, swatting at him as he settled above her, holding her close as he inched inside, bringing all that heat scorching back. Greer wrapped her arms around his neck, needing more skin, more weight…

More him.

Chase paused, tilting his head as he stared down at her, his eyes edging toward green in the waning light. He smiled, and she was lost.

She threaded her fingers through his hair, dragged his mouth to hers with little more than a soft tug. He deepened the kiss, seemingly content to lie there, waiting.

Chase nuzzled her neck, sucking at her pulse point as he slowly inched out, then slid back in, stealing what little breath she'd gasped. Tears pooled, then fell, all those walls a distant memory.

He mouthed her shoulder, brushing his cheek across hers, gradually upping the pace until need took over, the cords in his neck straining before he let loose — pounded her into the bed.

Greer hung on, body strung tight, her release just out of reach before he shifted his hips — hit that spot again.

She shattered.

Splintered like the light streaming behind her closed eyes. Chase kept moving, riding that high before he stopped, grunting through his release.

Greer clung to him, chest heaving, as time faded in and out, the light beyond the window gradually brightening. Her alarm sounded on the nightstand, Chase's chiming in a second later before he reached out — silenced them.

A smug smile curved his lips when she finally found the strength to open her eyes, take stock. He didn't move, just rested on his elbows, looking at her as if she'd quiz him later. See if he'd memorized every line, every freckle.

A soft kiss, then he brushed back her wild hair. "Now, that's a good morning."

"Right up until you expect me to move because… damn…"

He nuzzled her nose. "I'll carry you to the shower."

"And aggravate your ribs more than that did?"

"What ribs?"

A sob caught in her throat, all that love pouring out. "God, I love you."

Chase stilled, shaking his head as he eased free. "You're going to make me earn that claim I made about loving you more, aren't you?"

She shrugged. "As I see it, I'm ahead by at least three."

"Not for long. But since we're talking about how much I love you… Move in with me."

Greer coughed, pushed onto her elbows as he rolled to the edge. "Move in?"

"It's not like you haven't been staying here full time since…" He let the words fade for a moment. "We both work insane hours. I just want to spend every free one with you. Which is difficult if we live in separate spaces."

"Is that your way of saying my apartment's too…"

"Far. It's way too far."

"It's fifteen minutes away."

Chase leaned over. "I think I just proved we can do a lot in that amount of time."

"It was over thirty, but you've got a point. It's not

like my place ever really felt like home, it's just…" She palmed his cheek. "Are you sure? It's not too fast?"

"Fast? Since when is nearly a year of pining fast? Maybe this part of our relationship's new, but I've been all-in since we met. And yeah, I'm sure. Nothing I want more than to hold you every night. Wake up with you every morning."

She traced his lip with her thumb. "And just like that, you're ahead."

"Hell, yeah." He scooped her into his arms. "We'll grab your stuff after work. And we can change whatever you don't like."

She held him close after he placed her on her feet. "Just promise me the guys aren't going to bust in every morning."

"Not every morning."

She shoved him toward the glass door, showering and dressing before heading into the main area. His phone buzzed, rattling across the counter before he snagged it.

Chase sighed. "Kash has coffee waiting at Foster's if you're interested."

"Now *that*, I can get used to."

Chase tugged her in for a soul-searing kiss, then ushered her out, holding the kitchen door at Foster's before motioning her in. His teammates turned as they walked in, a round of smiles tilting their lips.

Greer took the coffee, savoring the rich smell as she leaned against the counter. "This really should be illegal, Kash."

Kash shrugged. "Gotta give you both a reason to leave the house."

Greer chuckled. "Trust me, the townspeople give me more than enough."

Kash nodded, looking between them for a while. "So, when are you two gonna make this a permanent arrangement?" He coughed when Jordan swatted him.

She sighed. "Forgive him. He's a rescue."

Greer grinned. "Already have."

"No thanks to you, brother." Chase moved in beside her, looped one arm around her waist. "Which reminds me, we're moving shit tonight, so... trucks. Her place. No excuses."

Foster groaned. "Don't you live on like, the fourth floor?"

Zain swatted Foster in the chest. "What's wrong, tough guy, afraid of some stairs?"

"Hell, yeah. I've seen how you jackasses move couches, and we're guaranteed to get at least one piece of furniture stuck." He tapped his chin. "I don't suppose there's a way I can sling everything?"

Greer sighed. "Easy, boys. All I need are my clothes, a few photos and a trunk of my brother's old stuff."

Zain arched a brow, glanced at Chase, then nodded. "No problem."

"Great. I'll grab pizza and beer after. As a thanks."

Chase nudged her. "No dessert?"

She smiled. "Don't worry. There'll be plenty of dessert."

Zain groaned. "Annnnnd, they've moved into the PDA phase of their relationship."

Chase flipped off his buddy, joking with his teammates before heading out — riding with Greer to the station as Kash pulled in behind them. "Everyone on shift today?"

"Yes, but even if they weren't, I'll be fine." Greer tapped her service weapon. "Like you once told me, I'm familiar with both ends of a rifle."

"Just be careful."

"You're the one going back early."

She gave him a quick kiss, laughing when he pulled her in for a second. Longer. Deeper, waving at Kash when his buddy honked the horn. "I'll drop by later if it's quiet."

"Looking forward to it."

Greer watched them drive off, then spent the day running routine calls, constantly glancing over her shoulder. Scanning the shadows. While she couldn't quite place it, something felt off.

The feeling had just started to ease when she stopped by the hangar, smiling at Chase and his buddies as they walked in off the tarmac, dirt smudged across their faces.

Chase grinned, dropped a kiss on her mouth. "Slow day?"

Greer groaned and punched him lightly in the arm. "It was, but now you've jinxed it, and all hell's gonna break loose."

Chase laughed. "How didn't I know that you're superstitious?"

"Only when it's justified." She motioned toward the chopper. "Good call?"

"Just a couple hikers who thought climbing down those cliffs by Oswald would save them time. Nothing fancy." He tugged her in close. "Does this mean you're done ear—"

A sharp blast of static cut him off, Shirley's voice sounding over Greer's radio. "Sheriff? You there?"

Greer shook her head. "See? Jinxed it." She hit the button. "Go ahead, Shirley."

"Buck just called in. Said he's got something he wants you to take a look at. That it can't wait."

"Of course, he does. Tell him I'll be there in twenty." She punched Chase lightly in the arm. "If I'm late, you're buying the pizza."

"I thought I was responsible for dessert."

"You are dessert."

He coughed. "Pizza it is, then." He nudged her. "You still thinking about hiring Buck as an informant?"

"Crazy, I know, but… If it makes it okay to keep tabs on him, ensure he's got enough essentials, then, it's worth the charade. Besides, he's had two solid leads over the past few months. I'd say that's worth the effort."

"You going out there alone?"

"Bodie and Jordan are already on another call." She sighed when he simply stood there, staring. "Hodges is gone. Nick's crew did a thorough sweep of all available surveillance footage. He found where Hodges slipped into the country — captured images of him stalking us for the past several months. And in every shot, the guy was alone. Same with the CCTV footage Bodie uncovered near the café. Hodges was in that truck.

Watching all by himself, so... It's over. Besides, I'm going to see Buck. He's the epitome of paranoia. I'll be fine."

"Still..."

"Chase. I love that you're passionate about my safety. And as hard and painful as it's been, I'm already talking to new applicants. I plan on hiring more staff so the county's properly patrolled. I realize I can't do it all myself, and honestly, I'm highly motivated to have more time away from the station. But there're times I'll be alone. It's the nature of the job. I do, however, have you on speed dial in case things go sideways."

He nodded, allowed the subject to drop. Not that she blamed him for being apprehensive. Today wasn't the only day she'd obsessively checked over her shoulder. Watching for anything remotely out of place.

More of those black boots looming in the darkness.

But sooner or later, she had to shake it loose.

Find some normalcy — grant herself some measure of forgiveness.

Chase followed her out to her Bronco, standing beside the door as she buckled in, scanning the surroundings, then looked back to her. "You sure you've got everything?"

"If I break anymore gear, I'll have to reprimand myself." She reached out, held his hand. "I'm sure coverage will be crap, but I'll text you as soon as I'm back in range. Give you an ETA."

"I'll come looking if you're late."

"I'd be disappointed if you didn't." She shoved the stick in reverse. "And for the record, thanks."

He leaned in the open window. "For being overprotective?"

"For asking me to stay this morning. It means more than you know."

"Gotta keep proving that *more* claim when you continue to outshine me." He dropped a quick kiss on her nose. "Be safe."

"You're the reckless one who hangs from helicopters."

He shook his head as she backed up, spinning her SUV before jumping onto the main road. She checked her GPS, inputted Buck's latest location. He'd moved, again, not that she blamed him. Though, discovering he'd been ex-military had put a new spin on his actions. Explained why he was obsessed with reconnaissance. Photographed every detail.

Her vehicle bounced along the gravel road, splashing through puddles as she turned onto a long, winding spur. Clouds covered the sky, a few errant raindrops splattering against her windshield.

Buck's motorhome appeared at the end of the road, situated in a small clearing. No camouflage netting, this time, just a few pine boughs laid across the top, more resting against the side.

She parked off to one side, shoved her Bronco into first and stepped out. A hint of smoke wove through the air, Buck's campfire circle positioned to her right. A gust of cool air swirled around her, picking up a bunch of loose pine needles and tumbling them across the gravel. She left the keys in the ignition, just in case, then headed for Buck's door.

As she reached the steps, something about the air prickled the hairs on her neck. Too thick, or too quiet, not a hint of birdsong chattering in the trees. She knocked, took a step back, senses on high alert. "Buck. It's Greer."

Nothing.

Just that eerie silence stretching over the clearing.

She pounded, again. Harder. "C'mon, Buck. You called me."

Footsteps. Softer than usual, the RV barely moving. A creak, then the door slivered open, Buck's wild eyes peering out. He stared at her, then over to her Bronco. No words, just his intense stare followed by a quick shake of his head.

Greer moved — backed up and drew her weapon as the RV door burst open, Buck tumbling onto the ground, arms locked behind him, some asshole in fatigues looming in the doorway. She got off two shots — hit the guy square in the chest — before she caught one high in the shoulder. Reeled backward.

The guy jerked, dropped out of sight, his body armor taking the brunt of the hits as she slammed into the ground, the report echoing through the trees. She rolled with the force, staggered to her feet as Buck gained his, yelled at her to run.

She grabbed his arm, shoved him ahead as they tripped toward her Bronco, blood dotting the gravel. Ears ringing from the report. Her vehicle door yawned open, that chime sounding around them. Loud. Incessant.

It hit her then. That Eli hadn't been mouthing *you*.

He'd said *two*. Had tried to warn her with his dying breath. And she'd missed it.

Something jabbed her shoulder blade, sent an icy ribbon weaving through her muscles. She blinked, fell, everything blurring into gray.

Buck landed on the ground beside her, legs twitching, his low moan crushed beneath the sound of crunching gravel.

A figure appeared over her, head cocked off to one side before he smiled. Bent low. "Hello, Greer. It's been a while. I can't tell you how surprised I was to find you and Remington together. Talk about serendipity. Only Colter's missing, but I'll pay him a visit, next. Now, try to stay conscious because, it's time we got the band back together."

CHAPTER TWENTY-ONE

She was late.

Chase paced the length of the hangar, pausing each pass to stare at his phone. It had been nearly two hours since Greer had headed off to Buck's, and she still hadn't texted. Not that it necessarily meant anything. Cell coverage was spotty around the county, and she could have gotten tied up on another call. Was merely talking to a farmer out on one of the rural lanes like she'd done a thousand times before.

That fact didn't stop him from worrying. Obsessing, really. Like he'd been doing every day since they'd stopped Hodges. Some deep-seated fear that he'd missed something. That it wasn't quite over. That he could still lose her.

You won't be able to save her.

Those words sounded in Chase's head. They'd been looping through his mind all week, like some kind of prophesy.

Zain shuffled in beside him, clapping him on the

back. "She's probably helping some local find his missing cow."

Chase nodded, the voice in his head already screaming. "Not like her to forget to text, though."

Zain nodded, no witty comeback like Chase had expected. "Did you try the station?"

Chase snorted. "And be that guy? She's the freaking sheriff. I have to let her do her job without hyperventilating every time she's a bit late from a call."

"True." Zain looked him dead in the eyes. "Or, you call Shirley and find out where she is. Screw what anyone else thinks."

"You're supposed to be the voice of reason."

"Not storming over there *is* being reasonable."

"Does Saylor know about this side of you?"

"Hell yeah. Loves me anyway."

Chase palmed his cell when the damn thing rang. He juggled it a few times, nearly dropping it on the hangar floor before shaking his head. Tapping the screen. "Remington."

"Where the hell is Greer?"

Chase frowned. "Nick?"

Nick grunted. "Who else would it be? Is Greer with you?"

"She's out on a call. Should be back soon. Why?"

Silence, then Nick muttering to himself.

Chase put the guy on speaker as his buddies gathered around. "Nick. If Greer's in trouble, you'd better start talking."

"I'm sending you a photo. Open it."

Chase's phone pinged, the message popping up on

the screen. He tapped the icon, waited as the image loaded, then stared at the picture of a guy walking through an airport. Clothes mismatched as if he'd yanked them off a rack in a hurry.

Chase zoomed in on the man's face. Froze. Chest squeezed tight, heart vibrating uselessly against his ribs. "Is that Royce Carver?"

Nick huffed. "I wasn't sure with the obvious burn marks and scarring, but… He looks older. Frayed."

"Why the hell are we just seeing this now?"

"Because we'd focused on Hodges. On tracking his movements until one of my guys came across this." Nick blew out a rough breath. "It's from nearly a year ago."

Chase fisted his hand at his side, stilling the urge to punch a hole in the wall. "So, this means what? It's not over. Hodges wasn't acting alone?"

"It means we need to track down Greer and get her ass somewhere safe while I mobilize a team. This isn't just about you and your buddies anymore. After all that shit you told me Hodges ranted about, this is a threat to national security." He paused, something tapping in the background. "I'm on the next flight out. I'll be there in six hours."

"If she's not answering her phone, I doubt she has that long." He held the cell off to the side. "Foster, fire up the chopper. Zain, get Bodie to text us Buck's location. We'll check with Shirley but…"

Another ping, Greer's name showing at the top of his cell.

Chase inhaled. "Greer just texted."

He switched to her thread, opened the text.

Nick practically growled into the phone. "What the hell does it say?"

"Nothing, it's coordinates. Foster…"

Foster glanced at the numbers, then punched them into his phone. "It's thirty miles south of here. Near that decommissioned water treatment facility. The exact point's in a river just up from the coast. Some kind of old trestle bridge."

Kash frowned. "Why would she send us that?"

"She wouldn't." Chase swallowed the rush of panic, shoving it all down until nothing remained but cold determination. "It's Carver."

Zain covered his phone for a second. "Bodie says she hasn't checked-in since she headed off to Buck's. He's sent the location, but…"

"She's not there. *He* has her. Nick? I'm gonna have to call you back."

Chase ended the call, then hit Greer's number, heart in his throat, sweat slicking his palms. He clenched his jaw, counting the rings before the line picked up, nothing but heavy breathing on the other end. "What do you want?"

No response.

Chase grunted. "Damn it, Royce, I know it's you. So, stop fucking around and tell me what the hell you want, because this is obviously some kind of game to you, and I can't play along if I don't know the rules."

Silence, then a low, grating laugh. His phone rang, the incoming video call from Greer's cell.

Chase switched over, breath held, anger burning

beneath his skin as the screen flickered, Royce's face filling the frame.

The guy grinned. "I have to hand it to you, Remington. I thought you'd need a few more clues to figure it out."

"Where's Greer?"

"She's with me. She's fine…" He grimaced a bit. "Well, mostly fine. She's alive."

"Show me."

"You're getting ahead of the play."

"I don't care. Either show me she's still breathing, or this becomes a hunt."

"It always was, but…"

The screen flipped, the sight dropping his stomach. He'd tied her to a chair, head bowed forward, her auburn hair sticking up in every direction. Blood stained her right shoulder, more splattered across her shirt. Gunshot wound, though, he couldn't tell how bad. If it'd gone right through or ricocheted somewhere far more deadly.

Royce sighed. "It's been a while since I used my skills to save anyone, though, I didn't do half bad."

"I'm the one you want. Why didn't you just knock on my damn door?"

"Oh, I want you, Chase." The camera flipped back to Carver, the left side of his face marred with burns and scars, just like Chase had thought he'd spotted from Rhett's room that last night, when that figure had walked past. "I want you to suffer. To know how we felt, lying there, waiting for you to come back. Killing you would be too easy, but this..." He laughed. "This way you get to choose."

"Choose what?"

"Who you're going to save. You see, I brought along another friend..." Carver angled the phone until Buck appeared behind him. Similar position minus the blood. "It's just like old times."

"Just tell me when and where."

"I assume your teammates already plotted the coordinates. Be here. One hour. No helicopters. You can catch a lift from that boat captain your buddy Everett's in love with. Bring him and Sinclair, though, in the end, it'll come down to you." He pulled the phone away, then stepped back into the frame. "I mean it. If I hear one hum of a rotor, see Beckett's face anywhere close to me — I'll kill them both. See you soon, Remington."

The line cut off, eerie silence filling the room. Chase stared at the screen, Greer's image playing in his head. He never should have left her alone. Vulnerable. If she died...

He'd be lost, and nothing would bring him back.

Zain clapped him on the shoulder, snapping him out of his thoughts. "Saylor's readying her Zodiac. She'll have it running by the time we get there. I'll pack... everything, though, I'm sure he'll make us discard any weapons."

Foster had his chopper on the tow cart. "I know he said no helicopters, but I'll find a place to set it down before he knows I'm there. Mac, too. We'll get her back."

Chase looked his best friend in the eyes, his own

uncertainty mirrored in Foster's, then grabbed his medic bag. He tossed in extra supplies, strapped on his Sig, then made a beeline for his truck. Nick rang his cell, but he let it go, typing out a quick text as he slipped behind the wheel — got the engine purring.

Kash jumped in with Nyx, tossing more bags in the back. "Bodie's on his way. He'll head out with Foster, while Jordan flies with Mac. In case we need a double rescue because there's no way we're making Greer wait."

Chase merely nodded before he peeled out, Zain following behind. He took the road at an insane speed, his wipers tapping out a steady rhythm. He hit the turnoff a few minutes faster than usual, bumping his way down the winding lane before skidding to a halt in front of the pier.

Saylor looked over at them from behind the helm, the Zodiac's engine chugging in the background. She seemed oblivious to the wind and the rain, waving them over as the last of the light bled into black.

The boat dipped as they piled on, crowding under the canopy as Zain tossed in the lines, then jumped onboard. Saylor hit the throttle, guided them out, the surf pounding the shore, spraying across the bow and down the sides. The wind howled across the deck, dropping the temperature as she picked up speed — skipped the damn vessel across the water like a stone.

Chase stared into the darkness, heart hammering, his sanity a distant memory. He couldn't talk, could barely breathe, as they headed south, each minute another chance for him to lose Greer.

Kash bumped his shoulder. "Your head in the game?"

Chase glanced at him. "Completely focused."

"We'll get her back. Royce obviously has something grandiose planned. That'll be his undoing."

"Unless he's set it up so there's no way to win."

"We've beaten the odds before, brother. We'll do it, again. Ride or die."

Ride or die.

No hesitation. No doubts.

Just his team against Royce. And Chase wasn't about to lose.

Saylor wove across the water, her spotlight accentuating the height of the waves. She somehow timed each surge perfectly, shooting out of every trough before the crest curled over — capsized them. A mix of fog and rain rolled across the surface, bleaching everything into a dull white.

Lights flashed along the shoreline, homes and beaches slowly turning into rugged cliffs and oversized boulders. Saylor danced around a few rocky islands, then angled the boat toward the shore, easing off the throttle.

The mouth of a large river gaped black against the surrounding white caps, the start of the last portion of their trip. Saylor took the junction, continuing along, her nav screens glowing bright in the darkness. She rolled the throttle back as the bridge materialized out of the mist, the large structure looming in the distance.

The Zodiac swayed against the rolling waves before she slowed to a halt fifty feet back from a makeshift dock. She peered at the water, though, Chase had no idea what she saw other than dark, foreboding depths.

She checked a screen, then shook her head. "Sorry guys, this is as far as I can take you until I can deal with that line strung across the water."

Chase jumped up, headed to the side. "What line?"

Saylor pointed to the surface several feet in front of the bow. "See where the water's rippling all the way across? It's hard to see, but someone's strung a line or maybe a vertical net. I'm sure I can dispose of it, but it'll take me some time and you're almost out of yours."

Chase looked at Kash, then Zain, but they both shrugged. "Is your dad Poseidon or something because I can barely see the ripples, let alone the rest of it."

Saylor shrugged. "I can't intubate someone, so..." She eased the Zodiac through some bulrushes to the edge of the bank. "I'll take care of it, then circle under the bridge, in case..."

She didn't say it. Didn't need to. While Chase didn't know what Royce had planned, he suspected the bastard hadn't brought them to this location if he wasn't going to utilize the landscape. And after the lengths Royce had already gone to with his other victims, Chase imagined this scenario would put the others to shame.

Chase tugged her in for a quick hug. "Thank you. I owe you."

Saylor waved him off. "Bring Greer back in one piece, and we're even."

Chase flicked on his headlamp, grabbed his bag, then jumped out, slogging through the mud and the reeds until he reached a rough trail, the yellow beam accentuating the rain and the fog. Kash and Nyx took point, Zain bringing up the rear as they hiked along the path, then up the embankment to a grassy knoll. A light snapped on at the far end of the trestle, a long figure standing tall.

Carver walked forward, exposing his face to the harsh light. "You made it, and with a minute to spare. I'm impressed."

Chase took a calculated step. "You knew we would. Let Greer and Buck go, and the four of us can have a chat."

"That's not very sporting of you. I brought you here for a reason, Remington. A do-over. See if you can make a difference, this time."

Two more lights flashed to life, their yellow circles mapping out the eerie scene. Buck, trapped in a spillway, only his head and shoulders above the water, the inbound tide rising with every surge. And who Chase assumed was Greer, her dark silhouette visible through the window of a truck positioned on the trestle.

Chase looked at Kash and Zain, then back to Carver. "What the hell, Royce?"

"I told you. You have to choose." Royce pointed to a bag hooked around a post in front of them. "There're proximity collars in that bag. Exchange them for the weapons I know you're packing."

Zain collected their sidearms, walked over and grabbed the bag, tossing the weapons inside before retrieving three metal collars. He handed them out, then clipped one around his neck, Chase and Kash following suit.

Chase crossed his arms. "Now what?"

The collars clicked, then hummed, a green light illuminating the front.

Royce held up his hand. "They're live. Consider this my way of replicating that night. How we were all forced to stay together. I've got explosives wired to both Buck and Greer. If you three wander more than thirty feet apart before they're disarmed…" He chuckled. "Let's just say you won't have to worry about saving anyone."

"I thought this was about me having to choose?"

"I'm getting to that. As you can see, they're both in need of a rescue. Buck… He's only got about ten minutes before the water covers his head and that spillway becomes his coffin. And Greer…"

Royce waved his arms wide. "I really outdid myself. There's an old freight car positioned up that hill on the far side of the bridge." Royce held up a small unit. "Once I hit this button, the brakes blow, and the car slowly starts to descend. I don't even know how long it'll be before it hits the truck, but… I think you get the picture. Choose who you save first. Pray you have enough time to attempt the second. Or, abandon one of them altogether. Your choice, but the collars don't deactivate until you win the game. And that only happens if you either save them both, or they die."

"This is insane. Let them go, and I'll stay."

"Just like you stayed back in that compound?" He shook his head. "I've been waiting five years to show you what your decision cost me. Now, we'll see what it costs you. And in case you thought you'd just come after me, instead, I've got a deadman's switch in my hand. It went live with the collars. Same deal. It shuts off if you win the game. Let's see if honor's your prime motivator, or if you'll sell your soul for the woman you love."

Chase looked up at the freight car. Large. Unyielding. It loomed overtop like a scythe waiting to fall. An unknown, unlike Buck, the rising water brushing the tops of his shoulders now.

Kash shook his head. "No one would blame you if you wanted to focus on Greer."

"She would." Chase scanned the area for a trail down. "Buck's in the most immediate danger. We save him, first — go from there. I just hope…"

"We won't let you down, brother."

"You never have. And once we save Greer, it ends."

CHAPTER TWENTY-TWO

Chase sucked in a deep breath, tamped down the fear and the doubt, then took off. A loud boom echoed through the night, a low rumble slowly filling the air. Sparks flickered amidst the rain, that freight car jerking, then inching ahead.

Kash picked up the pace, edged ahead, Nyx leading the way as they bounded down the trail toward the spillway. They hit the staging area moving in perfect sync, boots pounding the muddy ground, drifting no more than ten feet apart. Chase left his medic bag on the bank as Kash motioned for Nyx to stay before they jumped over the barrier and onto the rocky shore.

A slimy layer of algae covered the stones, the rocks giving way to brackish water as they waded into the center. The ebb and flow worked against them as they swam to the grate baring off the culvert tunneling into the hillside. Buck coughed, spat out water, each roll hitting his chin. A blue tinge colored his lips, deep tremors racking his body.

Buck grunted as they neared, motioned toward the bridge. "No, no, no... This isn't right." He shook his head, looking like he wanted to bang it against the grate. "What are you doing? Save Greer."

Chase shoulder up beside him, cursing when a similar collar around Buck's neck blinked on. "She's got a bit of time. You don't."

He chewed on his bottom lip, closing his eyes for a moment before sucking in a breath — looking Chase dead in the eyes. "The bastard shot her. She needs you more than I do."

"Even if that's true, we just armed that collar around your neck. You heard Carver. No going back, now. Not that we would have left you here, regardless." Chase grunted. "He's got a flack jacket with C4, and chains with a lock around his wrists. I packed some cutters in my medic bag, but I can't tell if the jacket's wired to the restraints."

Buck's teeth chattered, but he shook his head, again. "It's not. That asshole doesn't how to wire bombs properly. I could disarm it if my hands weren't bound."

Zain huffed. "If you can disarm the bomb, how come you didn't know you had live grenades the last time we faced a threat together?"

Buck shrugged. "I forgot. Things get... mixed up inside my head. I see patterns and threats, and I get so focused, I can't always remember who I really am." He looked around as if checking if someone else was listening. "Atticus knows."

"Knows what?"

"It's what I used to do."

Zain grinned. "You were an ordinance man?"

"Once, before the Raiders, and I got blown up."

"A Marine? Looks like our luck just changed. Hang tight, we'll be back."

They headed toward the river, Zain and Kash stopping twenty feet back while Chase continued to the bank. He grabbed some supplies, then returned, handing Zain the cutters while Kash did his best to lift Buck a bit higher — give Zain more time as he plunged beneath the water.

Chase held up some tubing with a mouthpiece attached to one end. "If the water rises to your chin before we get you out of here, you can breathe through this."

Kash sighed. "Five minutes already."

Chase looked up at the rail line, judged how far the damn freight car had already traveled, the scant distance easing a bit of the tension. Though, once it hit the steeper incline, it would pick up speed. Cut their available time down exponentially.

Buck cursed when the next wave covered his head before retreating. "This is all wrong. You need to go."

Chase shook his head. "You know we can't do that, even if we weren't all linked together. Greer would never forgive herself. You know the code. No one left behind, brother."

Buck's jaw flexed as he narrowed his eyes, looking oddly calm. Nothing like the other encounters, where he'd cowered or tried to run off. This version seemed focused. Determined, as if the past few hours had given him a glimpse of his former self.

Buck nodded, breathing through that mouthpiece as Zain resurfaced for a moment, then went back down. Time ticked away, each second drawing them closer to failure until Zain crested the water, nodding at Buck.

Zain coughed a few times. "We're good. Just the jacket. Buck's right. It wasn't connected to the chains or the grate."

Buck freed his arms, then they started swimming, dragging their assess out of the spillway and onto the shore. The gusting wind sliced through their wet clothes, the rain now falling in sheets.

Buck waved them off when Zain tried to examine the jacket. "I told you... He didn't do it right. I'll fix it later. Greer, first."

Chase looked the man dead in the eyes. "You know you have to stay with us, right? Or..."

Buck shoved Chase toward the trail. "I know I'm not generally... together. That I don't always know what's real. And I know for a fact that asshole ain't human, but... I won't run. I swear."

Chase glanced at his buddies, then took off, hoofing it up the embankment. His legs burned as they climbed the steep slope, finally cresting the tracks at the top. A distant rumble shook through the wooden structure, the metal rails singing as the freight car inched along, slowly picking up speed.

The trestle snaked across the river, the narrow bridge standing tall against the sky. No railings, just a small signal platform halfway across — the only glimmer of refuge along the expanse.

They jumped onto the track, headlamps lighting up

the slick ties as they took off down the line. The wind howled across the open space, tunneling along the river and shoving them sideways every other step. The ground gave way to air, the rippling water staring up at them through the gaps. The creosote-soaked ties gleamed in the yellow light, the rain-drenched surface slick beneath their boots.

They hit a gap, jumped, caught their balance on the other side and kept going, that damn car picking up speed. Shaking the structure as it crested the top of the hill — slipped down toward them.

They reached the truck and fanned out, Zain and Kash on the driver's side, Chase heading for Greer's silhouette on the other. He stopped short of touching the vehicle, peering in through the window, instead. Head bowed, uniform dark with blood, she looked like Rhett had when Chase had found him. Alive, but barely.

A collar around her neck clicked on, the green light casting an ominous glow across her face.

"Don't touch anything."

Buck's voice rose above the wind and the rain, the whine of the metal wheels chugging along the tracks. He motioned to her vest. "There's something off with her vest — that wire snaking down her leg. Let me check the chassis, first."

Chase frowned. "You think Carver rigged it?"

Buck kneeled in front. "He's like the voices in my head, always nattering away. Doing two things when they only need one."

Buck ducked down, crawled under the front end.

That train car moved faster, looming closer as Buck

cursed underneath then popped back up. "That wire's being fed by a metal plate. We need to move the truck a foot, but only that or it hits another, and then..." He made a gesture with his hands. "Boom."

"You sure?"

Buck looked at Chase, then Zain and Kash, eyes wide. He started hitting his head with the heel of one hand, mumbling under his breath.

Chase grabbed his shoulders. "Buck. Greer's counting on you. We just need you to hold it together a bit longer. *Semper Fedelis*, brother."

Buck snapped his focus to Chase, glancing at the truck before visibly pushing it all down. "One foot."

He dove under the truck again, calling it out as Chase and his buddies manned the bumper — started pushing. The vehicle shook, barely inching back, extra resistance holding it in place.

Kash grunted. "Bastard probably engaged the parking brake. Wants us to use too much force — hit that next plate."

They dug in, giving an extra boost, when it gave — damn near rolled right past the mark. They switched their grip — stopped it just shy of going too far.

Buck accepted Chase's hand as he crawled out. "We're good."

Chase darted to the side, ignored the increased rumble as the freight car hit the bottom of the hill, started eating up the distance. He yanked on the handle, slammed his shoulder against the door when it wouldn't budge, then tried again.

The hinges creaked, the door finally wheezing open. He slipped in, checked her vitals. Pulse fast, thready. Skin so damn white he wasn't sure how she'd survived this long.

Their collars blinked, then shut off, the ends popping open. Chase glanced at hers, its green light openly mocking him. What Chase suspected was Royce's contingency plan. That he'd had no intention of letting the two of them walk away.

Chase ripped off his collar, then opened her jacket. That vest glared up at him, wires and putty in a patchwork across the fabric. A thick rope looped around her waist, disappearing beneath the seat. He rummaged through his bag — grabbed a scalpel.

Buck crowded in the other door, tracing the wires. "I need something to cut these."

Chase coughed. "Let's just get her out."

"I told you. He did it wrong. It won't shut off like the others. I can fix it."

Chase grunted, then handed him some surgical shears. "Don't blow us up."

Buck went to work, looking way too calm considering the circumstances, cutting three of the wires while Chase hacked at the rope. He shrugged. "Fixed."

Chase glanced up. "What about the collar."

"It can't do anything to her, now." As if to prove his point, Buck grabbed the ends and popped it open, dropping it on the floorboards with an audible clatter.

"Thanks, buddy. I owe you."

Buck turned to his own vest, fiddling with the lines

when Kash moved in behind Chase, that car howling along the tracks, rolling onto the bridge.

Kash pushed out a rough breath. "Chase. Brother we're out of time."

"I'm almost through. You three go."

"We're not leaving you."

"We'll never make it to the far side before that train hits the truck and the force blows the wreckage all the way down the track. Once she's free, I can head toward the train — beat it to that signal platform. Get in front of the explosion and ride it out."

Zain scoffed. "Are you insane? We'll jump together."

Chase kept cutting, looking over at Zain. "She won't survive the fall, even into water. Go. We'll be okay."

Kash grabbed another knife, started sawing. That train bearing down on them, everything shaking from the strain. The fibers frayed, bits falling off before the line gave, the ends landing on the seat.

Chase scooped Greer into his arms, dragged her across the seat. "Go."

Zain shook his head. "Royce won't let you walk away, and if we jump, you won't have backup."

"I can handle Carver. That platform's barely wide enough for me and Greer. We won't all fit. Go."

The train filled the horizon, the entire bridge rocking. Some of the ties cracked, the weight shaking a few of the support beams free.

Kash hooked Buck's arm, took him over the edge before the man could argue. Zain gave Chase a hard stare, then jumped, the impact sounding a few seconds later.

Chase got Greer clear, juggled her against his shoulder, then hauled ass, taking the ties two at a time as he headed for the small platform twenty meters away.

The freight car loomed closer, sparks shooting out from the wheels, that high-pitched whine like a siren's scream. He slipped on one of the slats, nearly fell before palming the next tie — shoving off.

He hit the last few meters running full out, that train only seconds away from sweeping past the platform. He scooted right — skimmed along the edge — nothing but thirty feet of air cushioning his fall if he tripped. The car clacked, meeting the platform as he pushed off, skirted onto the tiny square a second before the train raced past, barreling toward the truck.

No time to celebrate as he hit the deck, covering Greer as the freight car slammed into the truck. The pickup exploded, metal and glass shooting into the air, the trestle rattling like bones in a drum. The platform trembled, nails popping loose as more support beams cracked and fell.

Fire erupted down the line as the car jumped the track, grinding down the ties, chewing a chasm in the wood. The front end fell through, hanging precariously from the rear, dropping a chunk of the structure into the water.

Chase held on, shielding Greer from the raining debris, the river smashing the frame below. The platform tilted, dropping twenty degrees before catching on one of the beams — stabilizing.

Greer moaned, her eyes fluttering a bit before she drifted off, head lolled to the left, skin paler than before.

He pushed onto his knees, staring at the wreckage when Carver walked onto the deck, arms thrown wide, his shrill laugh echoing down the river.

Royce picked his way along the remaining ties, stopped halfway, shaking his head as he played with the detonator. "Wow. Talk about a comeback. I gotta say. I didn't think you could pull it off." He cocked his head to one side. "If only you'd been this motivated five years ago."

Chase positioned Greer across the ties, then stood. Blood stained his clothes, pieces of wood and metal poking through the fabric. "It's over Royce. No collars, no bombs. Just you and me, and my team's already rallying." He pointed to the unit in the other man's hand. "That detonator's useless."

Royce laughed. "I never said it was hooked up to Greer or Buck. Those were more for show. A distraction of sorts. This one…" He waved the small box. "I rigged the entire bridge to go, one support beam at a time."

"So, that's your Plan B? We all die?"

"You left me to die once. I wasn't leaving anything up to chance, this time."

"I never wanted to leave you behind. That missile strike took us all out. I would've died, too, if Rhett hadn't dragged my ass back to the chopper."

"You never should have left us in the first place. You saw the blood. Heard Dalton's breath rattling through his chest. And Rios…" Royce shook his head. "He was dead before the strike even hit."

"What about Dalton? Is he mulling around here, too, like Hodges? Is he the real mastermind?"

Royce stilled, his left eye twitching, some of the color draining from his face. "He isn't a true believer. Never saw the light — never earned his salvation. He'll never be free."

Chase edged forward. "Are you implying he's still alive? Back in that compound? Did you leave him there to die?"

"I left him because he betrayed us, too."

Chase clenched his jaw, images of that night playing like a movie in his head. Thinking Dalton could still be alive, that maybe he wasn't broken beyond repair... "I'm sorry, Royce. If I could go back, do it over. I'd find a way to save everyone, but I can't, and what you're doing here... This won't change the past. Bring any of them back."

"That's where you're wrong." Carver took a step. "After years of suffering. Of having the truth beaten into me, I finally understand. I can shed this skin. All I need to do is cleanse *your* soul. Bleed the honor out of *you*. Consider it the mercy you never showed me because even if you pull a miracle out of your ass, Greer's never gonna make it to a hospital in time. She's lost too much blood." He shrugged. "Guess I wasn't quite as proficient at saving people as I thought."

Royce grinned. "But then, saving her was never part of the plan."

CHAPTER TWENTY-THREE

Chase inhaled as Royce hit the button on the detonator, then launched across the narrow space, KaBar glinting in the light, the blade slicing through the air in clear, sharp arcs. Chase dodged left, getting in a strike to Carver's ribs as he rolled past, gaining his feet before he slipped off the side.

Until the far support beam blew, shaking the entire structure. Smoke rose up from below, that freight car creaking as it tipped a bit lower. The resulting vibrations knocked Chase onto one knee, the surging water glaring up at him from below.

Royce regained his balance, tossing the knife between his hands before he glanced at Greer. Grinned. Chase read the man's intentions before the asshole took a step. He lunged, slid across the space, caught Royce a few feet back. Knocked his legs out. The guy hit hard, shoulder falling in the gap, the knife clattering free before slipping over the edge — disappearing beneath the water.

Another explosion.

More smoke. Flames. Wood and metal blasting through the air, hitting the platform like tiny spikes. The bridge swayed as parts at the far end cracked and heaved, crumpling into the water, the resulting impact causing massive flooding along the bank.

Royce rolled, tripped Chase onto his back, then launched on top, hands cinched around Chase's neck, fingers digging into his flesh. Chase punched the bastard's elbows, knocked them apart as he lifted his hips, tossed Royce over his shoulders.

They scrambled to their feet, neither one backing down. The next explosion dropped the freight car. The metal screeched as it scraped across the tracks, hitting the water, nearly taking the rest of the bridge with it. The power running the lights winked off, just Chase's headlamp mapping out what remained of the bridge.

Royce staggered to his feet, a couple pieces of shrapnel embedded in his thigh. Just like that night in Eastern Europe. Blood stained his fatigues, more dripping from a slice across his temple. Chase took a step as Royce shook his head — pulled out a Glock from an ankle holster.

He tsked when Chase edged toward him, nodding toward Greer. "I always knew it'd come down to this. You and me in a stalemate. Her life in the balance. I can kill her fast or slow, Remington. Your choice."

Chase looked him dead in the eyes. "At this distance, you'll only get one shot. If you're smart, you'll try to eliminate the threat. But you'd better hope it drops me because anything other than a lethal hit, and you'll be the one heading to the other side."

Royce laughed. "Guess you want her to suffer, too."

He spun, aimed at Greer, when claws clicked against the wood a second before Nyx appeared out of the night, nothing more than a shadowed blur amidst the darkness. Running full out. Skipping along the ties as if they were solid ground. No fear. No hesitation. Nyx took two more steps and jumped — hit Royce square in the back.

They tumbled forward, a single shot going wide as they skidded across the short expanse and onto the edge, gravity pulling at them as everything froze. That crazy hang time as they clambered for a hold.

Chase dove, snagged Nyx's harness before catching a handful of jacket. The momentum carried him forward, the sheer weight nearly taking him over until a hand wrapped around his ankle — held him steady.

Greer. Blood soaked through her jacket, hands shaking, but she held firm, reached for Nyx. It took a few tries and the dog scratching at the wood, to get her over the lip, handed off. Greer grabbed her harness, tugged her the last few feet as her grip waned, eyes rolling back before she tanked, hitting the deck.

Chase grunted, one hand gripped around the track, the other barely keeping Royce from falling — landing on the twisted wreckage burning beneath them. "Damn it, Royce, give me your hand."

Royce looked up, raised his arm, his weapon shifting into place. He aimed just as his jacket ripped, slipping free from Chase's fist. His eyes bulged wide, arms pinwheeling through the air before he dropped, body skipping off the metal shell, then slowly sinking beneath the surface.

Chase stared for a moment, chest heaving, hand grabbing at air, before he pushed off, scrambled over to Greer.

She blinked a few times, glimpses of green in the circled light. "See? You totally jinxed it."

He shook his head. "Guess I owe you pizza and dessert."

"Don't forget the beer." Her voice stuttered, breath shallow, choppy.

"Hey, eyes on me, sweetheart. I hear the helicopter. Just, hold out another few minutes, and I'll get you fixed up."

She nodded, eyes drifting shut. "Sure."

"Greer."

Nothing.

"Greer!"

He heaved her onto his shoulder, using the position to put some pressure on the wound as he tripped across the ties, Nyx guarding his ass. They got twenty feet away before the next bomb rocked the bridge, that platform they'd been on cleaving off — crashing into the water below.

The force knocked him sideways. He managed to turn at the last second — keep Greer from hitting the deck, as he slammed into the wood, everything winking out for a moment before he gave himself a mental shake — cleared his vision. Nyx crawled in beside him, licked his face, then barked. Her version of telling him to move his ass.

He groaned. "Christ, you're as annoying as Kash."

The dog yipped, again, tugging on his sleeve until he staggered to his feet. The bridge tilted, whether from the explosion or the ringing in his ears, Chase wasn't sure, but he took a step, froze, waiting for it all to settle.

Greer groaned, the muted sound proof he hadn't lost her yet. That if he just got his damn legs working, she'd have a chance.

He managed another foot, took a breath, then went again. If he didn't reach the ground before the next bomb detonated…

They'd never make it. Never outrun the collapse. Even now, chunks cracked behind him, rocking back and forth before breaking off — dropping into the river.

He suspected he had about thirty seconds left when Foster roared into sight, rotors humming, engines whining. His buddy banked the helicopter to one side, skimmed past the hill, then dropped in over the river, bleeding off all the speed before planting the skids across the track ten feet in front of Chase. Not quite landing, the machine still holding its weight, but enough Chase just needed to step up — jump inside.

Kash appeared a moment later, limping along the tracks, a noticeable gash on his cheek. He reached the chopper and threw open the rear doors, motioning for Chase to pick it up.

Chase grunted, then moved. One leg, then the other. Agonizingly slowly, all that time ticking down in his head. He reached the chopper with nothing to spare, accepting Kash's boost before stumbling inside — setting Greer down across the rear seats.

Kash jumped in behind Nyx, shutting everything tight, then yelling to Foster. Foster lifted the machine, tipped it off the bridge a second before the entire structure blew, a thunderous clap echoing around them. The helicopter shook, spinning twice before Foster wrestled it into submission, a few alarms still sounding as he banked it north — picked up speed.

Kash didn't ask what Chase needed, just handed him some plasma and saline, readying the crash cart, just in case. Nyx laid off to one corner, head resting on her paws, eyes wary as Chase got Greer's bleeding under control, got those IVs dripping.

Foster's voice sounded above the hum of the blades a moment later. "Providence is on alert. They've got a full team waiting with an operating room cleared and ready."

Chase grunted, watching her heart rate dance across the monitor, just like Rhett's had. "She's crashing."

He pushed some meds, started compressions when he lost her pulse. "C'mon, sweetheart. You can beat this."

Kash handed him the paddles.

Chase placed them on her chest, pressed the button. Her body jerked, hitting the seats with a low thud. "I've got a rhythm. Foster… brother every second counts."

Foster sighed. "I'm pushing her as much as I can. Any more, and we won't make it before the engines crap out."

Chase administered more meds, kept checking her vitals, hitting her with another shock when she faded, again, that familiar tone mocking him. Images of Rhett and Eli looping through Chase's head. Foster yelled something about being on short final, then the doors flew open, a swarm of white coats and scrubs rushing in.

A quick transfer onto a gurney, and they were racing for the building, running down those same white halls into the treatment room beyond. A nurse barred Chase from following, Kash's hand around Chase's arm holding him back. Chase shook it off, nearly tanked into the wall before Kash grabbed him — leaned them both against the wall.

Chase blinked, the floor shifting left and right beneath him. "I need to be in there."

Kash shook his head. "You need to sit your ass down. You've got pieces of that damn bridge everywhere." He physically stopped Chase from breaking free. "You know this team. They'll do everything they can, but you going in there and passing out on the floor will only distract them from what needs to be done. You got her here still breathing. She'll pull through."

Chase closed his eyes as he let his head fall back against the wall, her steady heartbeat carrying to him from the other room. Not the rhythm he'd like, but it was still a rhythm. A glimmer of hope that he'd done enough. That this time, it'd end differently.

He blinked to find his back on a gurney, bright lights blinding him from above. He groaned, rolled, only to have someone stop him. Chase looked up, Foster's wary gaze staring down at him.

His best friend tsked. "You're determined to kill yourself, aren't you?"

Chase tried to sit up and failed. "Greer..."

"In surgery. And before you undo all the hard work of yanking a thousand damn pieces of shrapnel from you, everything's going well. They should be closing up soon, and she's expected to make a full recovery."

Chase relaxed against the thin mattress. "You're not lying to me just to keep my ass in this bed, are you?"

"I'm hurt you'd even suggest that."

"Foster..."

"Fine, while I *would* do that, I'm not in this case. Kash has been hovering outside the operating room getting constant updates." Foster chuckled. "He looks more than a bit intimidating when he's on a mission, especially with Nyx growling at his side. And they all know he'll bust right in if provoked, so..."

Chase nodded. "How's Buck?"

"Fine. He's being treated for moderate hypothermia, but there shouldn't be any lasting effects."

"Buck really came through. We should help the guy out. The way he disarmed those bombs..."

"We'll brainstorm some options. See if any strike a chord with him."

"And Royce?"

Foster rolled his shoulder a few times as he shook out his right hand. "Zain and Saylor retrieved the body."

"I can't believe he did all this. Killed Rhett, Eli..."

Chase swallowed, coughed. "Is Nick still heading this way?"

"Should be landing in a couple hours. Bodie's picking him up. Why?"

"We need to talk. I've got a mission for him. And this time, we need a damn win."

* * *

Pain.

Clawing at the darkness, eating away the numbing sensation until she managed to drag herself to the surface — open her eyes. Machines beeped in the background, a metallic voice echoing over speakers. Something cool dabbed her forehead, hazel eyes stared down at her when she let her head roll to the side.

Chase smiled, dipping down until he was level with her. "I definitely jinxed it."

Greer grinned, hissing out her next breath when simply thinking about moving ricocheted pain through her chest.

More voices, footsteps tapping closer, then a warm sensation in her arm — everything fading back to black.

She drifted, a comforting weight holding her hand until she roused, again, the pain not quite as white-hot. She blinked, winced, then squinted at the room. Flowers and cards filled a table at the far end, way too many chairs cluttering the remaining space. A sigh sounded off to her right, Chase's handsome face blurring into focus.

God he was gorgeous.

From his tousled hair to those brilliant hazel eyes, she knew she could stare at him forever and never tire. Never take for granted what she'd found.

He smiled, and her stomach fluttered. "Hey, beautiful. Welcome back."

He squeezed her hand, dropped a gentle kiss on her temple.

She shook her head. Not a lot, but enough he paused, arched a brow. "More."

"Still making me earn it, huh?" He leaned in, planted a soft kiss on her lips. Not much more than a brush of his skin over hers, but it meant everything. Eased the jumping feeling inside her chest.

She wet her lips, accepting the water he offered her. "Where…"

"Providence. You were moved from the ICU a couple days ago."

"Couple?" She frowned, her head too thick to figure anything out. "How long?"

Christ, a couple words and everything derailed. Just stopped working, those shadows at the corners of her vision slowly creeping in.

"Four days, though, they said you'd likely be out for a full week." He grinned. "They don't know you like I do. But… it's early. Sleep. I'll be here when you wake up."

"Promise?"

"Wild horses, sweetheart."

She nodded, closed her eyes. She could worry about

how everything had turned out later. When she remembered all the details — what questions to ask. Until then, Chase's hand in hers was enough.

CHAPTER TWENTY-FOUR

"You're insane. Certifiably crazy."

Greer sighed as Chase paced the small room, shaking his head as he glanced at the machines behind the bed then her. Eyes narrowed, brow furrowed, he looked more than a bit pissed.

She reached for him, smiling when he instantly took her hand. No hesitation. No questions. "Chase. I'm fine."

"You're fine?" He leaned in close, and it took all her strength not to tug him the last few inches, taste his mouth. "You nearly died on me. No, scratch that. You did die on me. A few times. I was just lucky enough to get you back."

"It wasn't luck. And that was a week, ago."

"You weren't supposed to be awake for a week, let alone wanting to go home."

Greer held his hand when he began to turn away. "I know, I scared you. Scared myself. But it's not like I'm asking to go back to work or even my old apartment.

And it just so happens my new place has this kickass medic living there, full time."

That got her a roll of his eyes and a smile. "I appreciate the vote of confidence, but—"

"No buts. And before you start, I can list all the times you've discharged yourself early."

Chase placed his other hand over his heart. "Direct hit." He relaxed a bit and rested his hip against the edge of the bed. "I just want to make sure you're okay."

"Which will be a whole lot easier if we're sharing the same space." She urged him a bit closer. "The same bed without twenty possible," she made air quotes, "tangos walking through the door every day, who you practically tackle to the floor." She pinned him with a hard look. "The staff's talking, and they're not being kind."

"Don't really care whether they like me or not. I'm not apologizing for ensuring your safety. Not after almost losing you. When Royce called…" He swallowed, paled. "I'm not letting you down, again."

"You never let me down. I should have trusted your paranoia wasn't wrought out of fear. Though, you're gonna end up in traction if you keep switching between holding me on the bed until I pass out, then moving to that chair."

"First, I didn't have any proof to back up my worries, and second, I can handle some uncomfortable nights, I wasn't shot."

"No, you just got stabbed with a thousand pieces of trestle bridge."

Chase stared at her, then laughed. "Damn, I love you."

"Then, show me."

He shook his head as he closed the scant distance, slanting his lips over hers. The kiss was soft, gentle, and it touched her down to her toes.

Chase palmed her cheek. "You don't fight fair."

"I need you holding me all night. Not having these machines buzzing in my ears." She smiled. "I just need you."

He rested his forehead on hers. "You'll follow whatever the doctor says, right? No bitching or moaning."

"Oh, there'll be moaning…"

A throat cleared off to the left, boots scuffing the floor before stopping.

Chase eased back, shook his head, then peered over his shoulder. "Nick."

Nick Colter leaned against the doorframe, hands shoved into his pockets, a bemused smile curving his lips. "Don't you two have any restraint?"

Greer leaned against the pillows. "Trust me, that was us being restrained."

"Then, I agree with Greer. Get her home so the rest of us don't have to watch."

Chase narrowed his eyes. "Have you been standing in the hallway, listening?"

"Of course, I have. I work for the CIA. It's literally in my job description." He padded into the room. "Besides, I had to wait until you stopped sucking face."

Greer laughed. "Kids, today, call it kissing."

"Whatever, I wasn't convinced you wouldn't take it farther."

Greer smiled when Chase rolled his eyes. She'd been a bit anxious when she'd realized Nick had hopped on a flight — had arrived in Raven's Cliff shortly after Chase and his teammates had rescued her and Buck. Nick had never really played well with others, but he'd merely clapped Chase and his buddies on the back and thanked them for saving her life.

Then, he'd apologized for missing Royce's involvement. That he should have scoured the available footage faster. Chase had brushed it off, and they'd all fallen into an easy friendship since.

Nick moved over to the end of the bed. "You're actually starting to look human. How's the pain?"

Greer eyed Chase. "I'm fine. Pain's mostly gone."

Nick laughed. "You know your nose scrunches up when you're bullshitting, right?"

Greer flipped him off. "I'm well enough to go home."

"By home, you mean Chase's place, right? Because Foster's been letting me crash, and the last thing I need is another perfect couple walking around being happy all the time."

She frowned. "Sounds like there's something you need to share about you and Kate."

Nick's smile fell. "Another time. Unlike Chase, I'm not here for a social visit. At least, not fully."

Chase inhaled. "You've got news?"

"Wait." Greer shifted on the bed, careful not to visibly wince. "Why would you have news?" She looked at the door when Foster and the crew walked in carrying a few paper bags, the scent of fresh bread wafting through the room. "What did I miss?"

Nick eyed Chase, and she knew they had an internal conversation.

She tossed a pillow at Nick. "Don't look at him to see how much you should tell me because you're spilling all of it."

Nick laughed. "You always were a straight shooter. Grabbed everyone by the balls whether they deserved it or not. And yeah, you missed a few things. First, I had a friend pick through all the lodge video from when Rhett was abducted. She couldn't recover much, but she was able to capture a few stills, and Royce definitely took him. Looked as if Hodges took Rhett's place for a while – kept all those machines beeping — so it took longer for the staff to realize your teammate was missing. Not that I'm excusing them, but…"

He shifted on his feet. "Second, I've had a team retracing Hodges and Carver's steps. It took a while to get the appropriate clearance, but we traced them back to a similar compound south of that mission. We'd been led to believe the entire echelon had been eliminated, but it looks like enough of the leaders survived, they simply moved camp. Started fresh."

Zain inched forward. "Are they still there?"

Nick nodded. "Their numbers were reduced, but we just sent a drone overhead, and the live feed wasn't encouraging. Looks like they're gearing up for some kind of massive strike. Which means Carver and Hodges did us a favor. We can send in a team before our friends realize they've been compromised."

Chase crossed his arms. "What about Dalton? Royce made it sound as if he might be alive."

Greer inhaled. Carver had hinted that Dalton was still alive?

Nick shook his head. "No visuals on anyone fitting his description, but it's been five years. I'd expect him to look different. Either way, I'll be tagging along, and I'll make recovering any viable hostages my prime directive."

Greer coughed. "You're going into the field?"

Nick grinned. "I know. Damaged goods, but this one's personal."

She shook her head. She could argue, but Nick rarely wavered once he had his mind made up, and she knew the old injuries still haunted him. "When's the team going in?"

"Unsure. I'm heading back to Virginia tomorrow. I need to assemble a team — get eyes on our group. Maybe some boots on the ground over there. But it won't be long when it's evident they could launch an attack at any time."

Nick glanced at Chase's team. "I'd gladly take all of you but... I have a feeling you and the CIA don't quite see eye-to-eye."

Foster shrugged. "We haven't killed you, yet."

"I'll take that as a win. I'll keep you all in the loop as much as possible without getting arrested for jeopardizing national security. And I'll personally tell you whatever I discover about Dalton, good or bad, but I'm confident that the immediate threat's over."

Greer arched a brow. "You're sure?"

"Would I lie to you, Greer?"

"Yes. Especially if you were worried about my physical and mental well-being."

"Rude." Nick laughed. "True, but still rude. And yeah, it's over. Between the photos your pal Buck shared, and all the intel my team's gathered, we've confirmed they didn't contact anyone else."

Nick cocked his head to the side as he tapped his chin. "I can have one of our satellites do constant sweeps of the town if you're worried, though. Spy on all of you…"

Foster stepped forward. "I think we're good. And we'll all be more vigilant for a while. Just to be safe. Which brings me to our next issue. Are we busting Greer out before or after we eat, because I'm starving."

Chase groaned. "God, not you, too."

Foster scoffed. "Please, you were planning on breaking her out, yourself. You're just pissed she beat you to it. So, let's eat. Then, we make a run for it."

* * *

Three weeks later…

"I'm not ready for this."

Greer paused, her uniform half-buttoned, as she eyed Chase in the mirror. "For your shift to start?"

He crossed his arms. "For yours."

She sighed, slipped two more buttons through the holes, then turned, leaning against the counter. "We've talked about this."

"And I promised to be honest about how I felt, and this," he motioned at her, "scares the shit out of me."

She smiled, crossed over to him, stepping into his arms. "It's over."

Chase held her tight, his heart thundering against hers. "We think it's over, but…"

"No buts. Nick's had two agents in place for a couple weeks. They've confirmed Carver and Hodges were the last people to leave the compound before the leaders issued a lockdown. Started preparing for this massive attack. And based on how Nick phrased a few of his messages, they're launching their assault any day now, so… We're clear."

Chase blew out a rough breath. "And if we're wrong? If Dalton's been part of this from the start and is biding his time, waiting for us to get complacent so he can strike?"

"Chase." She eased back, looked him in the eyes, her heart skipping at the shadows staring back at her. How he'd been when Rhett had first died.

She reached up and brushed some hair off his forehead. She'd ruined any kind of styling when he'd surprised her in the kitchen, and they'd had a quickie bent over the dining room table. "What do you need?"

Chase stilled, eyes wary, breath held before he gestured toward her. "To know you're safe."

"And how can we achieve that without me locked in our house?"

His mouth quirked at the use of *our* house. "I never said we had to lock the doors all the time."

"Chase…" She mulled it over. "Can you get someone to cover your shifts for a few days?"

"Sure, but… How does that solve the issue?"

"You can ride shotgun. Be my human shield if any crazies show up."

Chase coughed, hitting his chest a few times before tilting his head. "You're going to let me ride shotgun? The whole day. Then, again tomorrow, and the day after that?"

"Just like a proper deputy, assuming it's enough to stop you from crawling out of your skin."

"But, what about protocol? The mayor? All the reasons you were worried about us pitching in when all this started?"

"I'm the sheriff. Fuck protocol, and the mayor can kiss my ass." She shrugged. "The fact Bodie uncovered he's having an affair has no bearing on my decision, whatsoever."

Chase laughed. "Did you just admit you'll blackmail the mayor if he puts up a fuss?"

She tiptoed up, drew her finger along his lower lip. "I prefer to think of it as strategic negotiating. Besides, it's the least I can do after everything you've done. And I don't just mean saving my ass. All the nightmares and the guilt over Troy…" She smiled. "It's better. Fading, I guess, and that's because of you."

She swallowed, then winked at him. "Well? Do we have a deal?"

He scrunched up his face as if he was considering the offer, then eased her back. "On one condition."

"What's that?"

"You say, yes."

She furrowed her brow. "Yes? To what?"

He took her hand. "To marrying me."

She inhaled, staring up at him, wondering if she'd imagined the words when he smiled. Dropped a kiss on her mouth. She reached up, fisted his shirt and drew him down for another round. Deeper. Longer, until all that heat from earlier threatened to smother her. "Are you nuts?"

He nuzzled her nose. "Yup. About you."

"We've only been living together a month, and that's pushing the definition."

"Don't care." He shushed her with another quick kiss. "I love you, Greer. Have since I realized you mean more to me than anyone ever has, including my brothers, so… I don't want to wait. To live by someone else's idea of the right amount of time before we jump. You're my world, and I jumped ages ago. All I need is a safe place to land."

Tears welled in her eyes then slipped down her cheeks. "You just had to prove you love me more." She smiled. "And I'll always be your safe haven because you've always been mine."

"Is that a yes? Because I honestly don't know."

She shoved him. "Yes, it's a yes, *Einstein*. Now, can we go to work, or am I breaking out the handcuffs?"

Chase chuckled, then lunged at her, hiking her up on his shoulder. "Looks like it's the handcuffs, because I need one more taste of you before we can leave."

He carried her over to the bed, launching them both onto the mattress. They bounced once, then he loomed over her, hair a mess, love shining back at her. He reached behind her and grabbed her cuffs, slipping one on his wrist before he dipped his shoulder, rolled them.

He held his arms over his head, nodding at her. "You've got the key, right?"

She jiggled her keyring. "Right here."

"Then, do your worst, Sheriff. Just know this…" He levered up. Kissed her. "Tonight, it's my turn."

"Whatever you say." She locked the other cuff in place. "I love you."

"Love you more. Now, let's get this party started, or you'll be late for your first day back."

Greer shrugged. "I won't tell the sheriff if you don't. Now, get comfortable. This could take a while."

EPILOGUE

Several months later...

"I knew hiring your team would be a giant pain in my ass."

Chase leaned against the door frame as Atticus surveyed the new setup in Foster's house. The grand opening of Raven's Watch's official headquarters. Chase wasn't sure when Foster had gotten onboard with the idea. But somewhere between all of them getting married and Mac giving birth to a healthy baby boy, he'd reconfigured the back half of the manor house to accommodate a permanent dispatch center.

Foster walked across the room, taking the radio mic out of Atticus' hands. "Pretty sure, you're the one who's a pain. And everything's live, so... Don't start chatting on the airways for fun."

Atticus rolled his eyes, grumbling under his breath when Mac entered the room, holding Sean Joshua Rhett

Beckett. Sean cooed, little hands waving beneath a blue onesie.

Atticus' gaze softened, and he smiled down at his grandson, talking gibberish in some weird voice that made Chase laugh.

The older man snapped his gaze to Chase's, frowning. "You got something to say, Remington?"

Chase removed his phone and snapped a photo. "Just wanted proof that your mouth actually curves upwards."

Atticus glared at him, then looked back at the baby, another smile gracing his face.

Mac joined Chase, leaning into Foster when he wrapped his arms around her. "It's kinda scary how smitten my dad is with Sean. I wasn't sure what to expect."

Foster leaned in. "I'm just happy he hasn't eaten him, yet."

Mac elbowed Foster. "He's not that bad."

"You keep saying that, sweetheart."

The floor creaked, Kash and Jordan slipping through, Nyx bounding along beside them, their newborn daughter swaddled in a pink blanket.

Mac inhaled, then darted over, smiling at the tiny face sleeping in Jordan's arms. "You've both got to be exhausted. You didn't have to come over."

Kash scoffed. "And have Atticus rip me a new one? Besides, Jordan threatened to shoot me in the ass if I stopped her from getting out of the house."

Jordan shook her head. "He's exaggerating, though, I was looking forward to a change of scenery." She walked over to Chase and motioned for him to hold the baby. "Not to mention a few more arms to utilize."

Chase froze. It wasn't that he hadn't been around babies, but... She was so small, so fragile.

Kash laughed as he nudged Chase. "Relax, you're not going to break her."

"Says the guy who sent out a blanket nine-one-one to us when faced with the first diaper change."

"Fair." Kash glanced down when Nyx sat at Chase's feet, gaze locked on the baby. "She's fine, Nyx. No one's hurting her." Kash sighed. "And I thought Nyx was protective of all of us. You should see her when we put the baby in the crib. Who needs a laser grid when you've got eighty pounds of muscle and teeth."

"Who's getting a laser grid?"

Chase turned as Greer ambled into the room, Saylor and Zain trailing behind her. Greer darted over, grabbing one tiny hand as Chase held the newborn against his chest. "It's for the baby's room, not that they're paranoid."

Kash shook his head. "We're not paranoid, we're proactive."

Jordan moved into Kash's arms, looking more than a bit radiant. "We're still discussing it, but with my past..."

Kash kissed her temple. "No one's getting to you or the baby. Promise."

Greer straightened. "Especially now that we have a few more recruits. I already have them making extra rounds out this way, just in case. Though, speaking of the baby, any thoughts on a name, yet?"

Kash glanced at Jordan, smiled. "Just one. Ember."

Jordan bit at her bottom lip, a rare moment of indecision. "Unless, that's too…"

"Perfect." Greer motioned for Chase to hand her the baby, instantly rocking back and forth as soon as she cradled her in her arms. "I think it's perfect."

Chase grinned. "Very fitting. Just remember, kids have a way of growing into their names, so… I'm thinking a double laser grid. One inside, one outside for when she starts trying to sneak out."

"She can't even roll over yet, jackass. I think we've got some time." Kash glanced over at Saylor and Zain. "Someone looks green."

Saylor glared at Kash, then raced off, nearly hitting Bodie as he ambled through the doorway.

Zain sighed. "Way to jinx it, brother. She only just stopped puking."

Kash held up one hand. "Don't blame the messenger, buddy. You're the one who knocked her up."

Zain beamed, the ass, looking more than pleased with himself. "I'll just be happy when this phase is over."

"Assuming it ends." Kash shrugged. "Some women puke the entire pregnancy."

"It's like you just can't help yourself." Zain motioned to the door. "I'll go check on her. Make sure Atticus doesn't break anything before we get a chance to use it."

"I heard that." Atticus made those weird 'watching you' fingers at Zain as he followed after Saylor.

Chase tapped Foster on the arm. "When do Keaton and the Florida crew arrive?"

Foster checked his watch. "They should be here any minute. Along with Nick." He nodded at Greer. "Did Nick tell you why he'd changed his mind and decided to visit? Because I thought he was on some top-secret assignment."

Greer shook her head. "All he said was to make sure everyone was here."

Chase smiled when Greer nuzzled Ember closer, his chest tight. They'd talked about starting a family. Not full on trying, yet, but she'd suggested removing her implant. That it was coming due, anyway, and maybe they should just let nature take its course. See what happened.

He'd agreed, secretly terrified he'd turn out like his old man — carry on the curse he'd always feared lived inside him. Greer hadn't called him on it, a fact that had made him love her even more. That she accepted him, flaws and all.

Now, watching her rock Ember in her arms, it all clicked into place, that curse finally fading into the past. Overshadowed by the sheer joy on her face, the way she looked up at him — smiled. Her face practically glowing. And he knew, no matter what happened, he was finally free.

Greer snugged in beside him, leaning against his chest as she rocked the baby. "We need to do something about Bodie."

Chase frowned, glanced at the man in question as he laughed with Kash and Foster as if he'd been part of the team all along. "That sounds ominous. What happened? Did you discover he's a sleeper spy or something?"

Greer elbowed him. "He needs someone."

Chase laughed. "You sure? Because women are a lot more work…"

His voice trailed into a grunt when Greer elbowed him, again. Harder. "I thought he was seeing that nurse from Providence."

"They broke up. Something about him being too military. Not that I know what that even means. Sure, he's got that situational awareness you all have, and I guess he can be a bit intimidating if you're on the wrong side of the law, but…"

Chase sighed. "I'll chat with Jordan. Maybe she knows another Shadow Ops agent looking to switch gears."

"You're an ass."

"The one you know and love. Though, that reminds me. How's Buck doing?"

Greer beamed. "He's like a new man. Or maybe more like he used to be. But as soon as Bodie offered to have him do some tracking for his security company, it's like a switch flipped. He's still… adjusting. But he's solved half a dozen crimes already. Has this uncanny ability of being in the right place at the right time to gather evidence. If he does any better, I might have competition for my job."

"I doubt that but… I'm glad. The guy saved our asses."

Greer looked up, beckoned him down for a kiss. "You saved my ass that night. A few times over."

Chase smiled, dipped in for another. "Purely selfish reasons."

Kash groaned. "Are you two kissing in front of Ember?"

Chase flipped him off. "Like you two haven't been doing that non-stop. Though, why the hell aren't you taking advantage of us holding Ember? You could have a quick make-out session on the couch. Make Atticus' blood pressure rise."

Kash grinned. "Every now and then, brother, you actually come up with a great idea. Jordan!"

He struck off, yelling out his intentions, Atticus already rolling his eyes.

The day wore on, Foster's cousin, Keaton and the rest of his crew arrived in a flurry of chaos. Fletcher and Bailey's two boys ran through the house, playing tag and hide and seek while Nyx followed on their heels, ever the nanny. Bailey looked happy, despite running off to pee every hour, her pregnancy nearing the end.

The toddlers stumbled around on the floor, Dawson and Keaton diving left and right when one of them teetered, somehow catching them before they tumbled. Hayes stood beside Chloe, his hand resting on her rounded belly, looking as if he enjoyed the noise and the mess. Not that Chase blamed him. After everything both teams had been through, they'd earned this moment.

The sun was already heading for the horizon, when the front door creaked open, Nick walking into the room, bringing a swirl of cool spring air with him. He stopped just inside, nodding at Chase before tugging Greer in for a hug. The man seemed harder, colder, his face more weathered than Chase remembered. As if time had spun faster for him.

Greer stepped back, tilted her head to the side. "You look like shit."

Nick chuckled. "Thanks, Greer, you look great, too."

"You know that's not what I meant." She glanced back at Chase for a moment. "Are you okay?"

Nick plastered on a fake smile. "Dandy."

"Right. I don't suppose this haggard look has anything to do with you and Kate splitting up? All those missions you've been going on despite claiming you're not a field agent, again."

"Not a single thing. And those were just temporary. I had a few loose ends I needed to tie up before I stepped back."

"And did you? Tie up all those ends?"

Nick grinned. "Mostly, though, there's one that turned out better than expected. Chase? Brother do me a favor and get your buddies."

Chase arched a brow but headed off, rounding up Foster, Zain and Kash. They stopped in the middle of the sitting room, Keaton's crew gathering on the fringes.

Nick nodded at them. "I hope it's okay. I brought a friend with me."

Nick darted back out the door, footsteps pounding along the main path. A door chimed in the distance, two footfalls heading back up the walkway. Nick appeared first, holding the door as another man shuffled in. Thinner. Rough, but steady.

He looked over at them, grinned. "Sorry it took so long. I got tied up."

Frozen.

All of them.

Standing in Foster's house, staring at Eric Dalton as he stood in the foyer, looking haggard and frayed, but his eyes clear and bright.

Chase took a step, stopped, then laughed as he closed the distance — pulled the man in for a hug. His buddies followed suit, clapping Dalton on the back, as they moved into the kitchen, grabbed Dalton a beer and some pizza.

Foster made the introductions, the noise level climbing as they talked about old missions — how they'd found their way to Raven's Cliff.

Dalton took a long slow swig of his beer, looking them all in the eyes. "I'm really sorry about Rhett. About everything. If I could have stopped Carver and Hodges…"

Chase waved him off. "You made it. Rhett would have been thrilled."

Dalton smiled, though it didn't quite reach his eyes. "Nick said you started a foundation in his honor."

Foster beamed. "The guy had more money than he knew what to do with. When he left it to us… We wanted it to help people. We'll be funding men and women who want to dedicate their lives to search and rescue, either as tech specialists or medics, but who don't have the finances to take the courses — get the experience. I think Rhett would approve."

"I think he would."

Foster nodded at him. "What's your next move?"

Dalton shrugged. "Right now, I'm just happy to get through a day without losing my mind. Haven't really thought about much else."

Saylor inched forward. "Well, there's an apartment over my boathouse. It's been designated for crew, but you're welcome to it, if you'd like. Maybe some salty air and gray skies would help. Lord knows it's helped all of us."

Dalton's eyes widened. "You're serious?"

Zain grinned. "Can't think of a better use. And you could hang out at the hangar once you're settled. Maybe come on the odd ride. If you want. No pressure, brother. We're just happy for the win."

Dalton glanced at Nick. "I might just take you all up on that."

Zain glanced over at Nick. "That goes for you, too, Colter. Judging on the rough appearance, it might be time to consider a new vocation. Chuck the CIA to the curb."

Nick glanced at Chase, then Greer, scrubbing a hand down his face. "I'm not really the search and rescue type."

"What about security?" Bodie shouldered up beside him. "Always looking for a few more good men. I might even forget you're a Spook."

"Now, you're just being mean. But…" Nick sighed, a few of the shadows lifting from his eyes. "We'll talk."

Bodie nodded as the party continued, Atticus chatting with Dalton, the kids finally passing out before everyone ambled off to bed, Foster's house packed full of family.

Chase held Greer's hand as they made their way back home, snuggling under the covers not long after. They'd just turned out the lights when Greer bolted up, scrambling over him before racing for the bathroom — hurling into the toilet a moment later.

Chase moved in behind her, holding her hair until she'd finished. He didn't ask any questions, just kept her close, waiting until she seemed ready before helping her to her feet. She spent a few minutes brushing her teeth, looking as if she wasn't sure whether to collapse or go in for another round, before finally heading back to bed.

He helped her climb under the covers, gathering her in his arms as she sighed against his chest. "Something you want to share with me?"

Greer snorted. "You're absolutely shit at surprises, you know that?"

"I'm not the one who just gave it all away. Literally." He looked down at her. Smiled. "You sure?"

Greer pushed onto her elbow. "Seven tests don't lie. At least, I don't think they do."

"Seven? The first two weren't enough to convince you that you were pregnant?"

"I didn't want to chance it might be a false positive, especially since I hadn't gotten the implant removed yet. Though, apparently, it ran out of juice, or so my doctor claimed when he removed it this morning. But I didn't want to get my hopes up only to find out I was wrong."

"Six other times?"

She gave him a swat. "That's not the takeaway here." She drew patterns along his skin. "The real question is… are you okay with this?"

Chase relaxed as any remaining doubts vanished into the green of her eyes. The image of her holding their baby. "All-in, sweetheart. Just like I am with you. Though, you realize this means you'll actually have to take some time off, right?"

Greer smiled. "Then, it's a good thing I hired extra deputies. Though, I intend on going back. You'll be okay with that, right?"

"Will you let me ride shotgun for a while?"

"I'll see what the sheriff thinks. I've heard she's a real ball buster."

"That, she is." He tucked some hair behind her ear. "A baby. Now, that's the way to end the day."

"And start tomorrow. I love you, Chase."

"Love you more, Greer. Now, get some sleep. I have a feeling the next twenty years are gonna be extremely busy."

SECRETS IN CALUSA COVE

EVERGLADES OVERWATCH BOOK #1

New York Times & USA Today
Bestselling Author

ELLE JAMES

USA Today
Bestselling Author

JEN TALTY

EVERGLADES OVERWATCH

SECRETS
in
CALUSA COVE

USA Today & NY Times best selling author
ELLE JAMES
USA Today best selling author
JEN TALTY

PROLOGUE

Sixteen Years Ago…

"Seriously, Dad." Audra McCain huffed as she climbed into her father's airboat in the dead of night. "I believe you, so no need to prove it to me." Only, she didn't believe. Not really. Not anymore. She'd accepted that her dad was a little left of normal long ago. His quirks—while annoying—were something she'd learned to live with because, at the end of the day, no one loved her like her daddy. He'd taught her how to survive in Calusa Cove.

Especially when the kids and their parents had started calling her a Stigini. Or an Owl Witch. At first, she hadn't known which was worse. *That*, or having a father the town considered a loon because he believed in conspiracy theories. But what difference did it make?

No one but her father—not even Ken—would ever see her as a whole person.

However, just because she listened to his crazy theories didn't mean she believed a single word. Those days had died when they'd buried her mother.

Truth be told, her mama's Native American heritage, and her ties to what some confused with witchcraft, were where the rumors of Audra being an owl-like creature had started. No one understood that her mom hadn't been a witch. Her mother had been tethered to the earth, to all the elements, and believed humans needed to be spiritually grounded.

Audra's dark freckled skin and red hair resulted from her combined one-quarter Seminole and three-quarters Irish heritage, giving her a unique look. But as she'd become a teenager, that mixture had only made her feel more like an outsider.

"I want a witness, and you have that smartphone thingy to take pictures," her dad said. "Just humor your old man. Before you know it, you'll be flying the coop." He arched a brow. "You'll probably run off with that boyfriend of yours."

She cringed, remembering the fight she'd had earlier with her dad, right in the center of town for all to see, hear, and judge. The argument where she'd told her dad what a whack job he was and she wished it had been him who had died six years ago and not her sweet, kind, and loving mother. Ken had a lot to say about that.

It was rare that she and her dad fought, but when they did, the words that tumbled from her mouth were harsh and were meant to hurt.

And she'd cut him to the core. She hadn't meant to. But he'd pushed her buttons. He used the past to force her hand. To make her feel guilty for choosing something other than him. Had it only been in front of Ken, Baily, and Fletcher—it wouldn't have been as devastating. They understood the dynamic. But her dad had done it in front of half the school. It wasn't even that the entire school had heard his crazy rant because everyone knew her old man thought weird shit happened deep in the Everglades. It was a running joke, and no one believed him. Not anymore. She was just tired of being looked at as though the crazy would rub off on her.

However, everyone still enjoyed the old stories. The ones this town had been made on. The myths and legends that made people stop for a hot minute on the way to their posh vacation destination to stroll through Calusa Cove and take in one of the sights. Maybe even go on a tour of the Everglades. But no one wanted to hear this new insane crap about things that went bump in the night, about the boats carrying bad men with bad things that came and went every couple of months.

She sighed. She was stuck in this small town for so many reasons, destined to be nothing but a redhead with a mouth as fiery as her hair.

"You did bring your phone, didn't you?" her father asked, his voice laced with a sense of desperation.

"Yes, Daddy," she said softly.

It was odd that he was fixated on that. He wouldn't allow the internet in the home because someone could listen. Someone was always listening. Spying. Looking into what he was doing.

She was lucky that her dad allowed her to have a television with cable, though he did ask her to unplug every electronic device when she wasn't using it—her computer included.

He'd gone ballistic when he found out she bought a smartphone with her own money. He demanded she power it off when she wasn't using it. Actually, he'd asked that she only use it outside, but she didn't listen. It was her only connection to the world outside of Calusa Cove.

And to her boyfriend. Though, currently, Ken was being a selfish asshole. She understood. This was Ken's opportunity to get an education. His family couldn't afford to send him to college, but the military could provide one.

Plus, his best friend was going with him—making it a no-brainer for Ken.

However, Ken failed to comprehend that he broke her heart every time he smiled and spoke gleefully about leaving Calusa Cove in the dust. Following him, even after she graduated high school, wasn't something she could just up and do. Who would watch after her old man in this backward town? For years, her father had cared for her, ensuring she had everything she needed and could fend for herself. It was her turn to take care of the man who loved her more than he loved anything.

Even his stupid conspiracy theories.

She took the ear protection her father handed her and placed it over her ears just as he reeved the engines.

Raising the spotlight, she helped her dad navigate the wilds of the Everglades. They could be so beautiful and peaceful at night. The stars and the moon hung in the sky like an umbrella. The water danced as if it didn't hide death and destruction. Eyes and tails everywhere, slinking through the water, waiting for their next meal to fall in.

Audra respected the Everglades and its ecosystem. Humans might be afraid of alligators, but people were their biggest predators. Mankind destroyed more gators than there were alligator attacks. If you didn't bother them, they'd leave you alone.

Just don't go swimming with one bigger than you.

This wasn't the first time her old man had dragged her out in the middle of the night to hunt for something other than gators and snakes. The first couple of times, it had been like going on an adventure, like her and her pops were pirates searching for treasure. It had helped her cope with the death of her mom.

But nothing was going to help her dad. Without his beloved bride, he had no one to ground him—not even his precious daughter, whom he loved dearly—could do that. No, he needed his Elana.

Her dad slowed the boat as they entered Snake River, a windy, narrow section of the Everglades. It was like the water version of *Sleepy Hollow*. Dark, creepy, and with a blanket of branches, blocking the light from the bright moon.

She took off her ear protection and studied her dad's profile. He'd aged so much in the six years since her mom had died. It was as if the best part of him had left along with his wife.

He went through the motions of living. He got up and shaved, though not very well. He went to work—only his business wasn't profitable. Thankfully, the house and land were paid for. But they still barely managed to put food on the table, and Audra, at almost seventeen, was getting tired of it. She wanted more for herself.

As a small child, she'd thought she wanted to work for Parks and Rec. Or maybe Fish and Wildlife. Now, she dreamed of being a photographer and journalist to see the world through a different lens than what she'd lived.

But she couldn't leave her father.

Without her to cushion the blows, Calusa Cove would destroy him. It would eat him alive and spit out his bones.

Very few people liked her dad. Less respected him. They saw him as a crazy old man who believed in conspiracy theories.

They were right about that.

But he was also kind, loving...gentle. He knew his brain wasn't quite right. He got that. But he also knew he still had one foot firmly planted in reality.

Only, you never really knew what you were getting when you talked to her old man. It was always a mishmash of both fantasy and reality.

"Daddy?"

"Yes, darling," her father whispered.

"I'm sorry about what I said earlier today. I didn't mean it."

"I know, pumpkin. I know," he said. "Forget about it."

"So, what are we looking for?" She leaned against her dad's arm and rested her head on his strong shoulder, the annoyance of being woken up on a school night long gone. Who cared about a stupid stats test? She wasn't going to college. And no matter how much Ken pleaded, for as long as her dad had breath, she wasn't leaving Calusa Cove.

As she stared at the lush trees hanging above while they took the last bend in Snake River, she wondered if she'd ever leave this place. What people thought of her didn't matter. The call to the Everglades was stronger.

"I've always found it interesting that we've named almost every island back here but one, though at high tide, it's not really an island, but a mush peninsula." Her dad kissed her temple. "But it's like Florida has dug its heels in and said, *We're not going to know. It's the island with no name.*"

"Well, then it kind of has a name." She smiled. "No one comes back this far or down this way much. Not even on airboats." She reached for her cell phone. No service, but she could snap pictures. "Though, Ken told me once he knew a few guys who came down from Fort Lauderdale through this section."

It had taken them two hours to get to this spot, and they had hauled ass. But she absolutely enjoyed the ride. It hadn't been too balmy—or too buggy.

Time with her dad always trumped the weird ways in which it happened.

"More people come back here than you think." He touched her hand, lifting the spotlight toward the clearing. "Some avoid it because they don't like to navigate through Snake River and Alligator Junction—especially at low tide—because too many boats have gotten plants and stuff caught in their engines."

"But that's why we have cages."

Her dad laughed. "That's for bigger debris, and we've had this conversation a million times."

"I know." She hugged his arm with her free hand. "Look at those eyes in the water over there. Got to be at least four gators just hanging out."

"This is a prime location for them," her dad said. "I knew a guy when I was in high school who came back here and wrestled three of them at once."

"I remember." Audra shivered. "Hector Mendoza. He died back here."

"No. He disappeared," her dad said, "on a night much like tonight about ten years ago. He told his wife he was going out early because he saw someone doing something fishy back here, and he never made it home. Some people believe he got eaten by an alligator. Others wonder if a swamp monster got him—or if he came face-to-face with Edgar Watson."

She laughed. "I love that tale."

"So do I, child." Her dad nodded. "However, there are some who believe that Hector was murdered back here for what he thought he saw."

She'd heard this a million times. "You're the only

one who believes that." She glanced up. "Why are we out here?"

"I swear I saw something." He pushed the lever and turned the boat toward the island with no name.

At night, everything looked different in the Everglades. During the day, it was rich in vegetation. Rich in beauty. One could get lost in the decadence of it all.

Once the sun dipped below the horizon, it was like stepping onto a horror set. Cue the music for *Psycho*. And yet, it was still the only place in the world she felt at home.

That thought made her chuckle. She'd never been anywhere else but Naples, which was a cesspool of tourists, snowbirds, and traffic.

"Give me the spotlight," her father whispered—as if someone could hear them. He scanned the mangrove, finding the tree line near a clearing about fifty feet in. "Look. There. Do you see that?"

She moved toward the bow of the boat, crawling on her hands and knees. Why? She had no idea. No one was watching. Only a fool—like her father—would be out here at three in the morning. She squinted, but sure enough, a small shack and some crates with strange markings came into view. "I need my phone."

"What the hell?" her father exclaimed. "What are you doing—"

A searing pain tore through her body from her head to her toes. It rattled her teeth. She dropped to the hull of the boat. Blinking, she pressed her hands flat on the boat's bottom, trying to push herself up, but instead, stars filled her vision.

Another sharp stab to her head. It was as if a bomb had exploded inside her brain.

And then the world simply turned… black.

* * *

Gripping the sides of the boat, she pulled herself up. It took all the strength she had.

A man's muffled voice drowned in her ears. It was like every sound bubbled underwater, unable to break through the throbbing in her skull.

A second voice. Or maybe it was the same one. She couldn't be sure. She craned her neck toward the chatter. The tone and texture of the voices were hauntingly familiar. It prickled her ears and tormented her mind. No matter how hard she tried, she couldn't place it.

The voice separated. Splintered into separate sounds. It was definitely two people. She knew that now. She blinked. The horrifying pain dancing on her temples made it impossible to see anything but the blackness of night.

Splash!

She leaned over and stared at the rippling water.

The men tossed chum overboard. She knew it was chum because she could smell the blood. Smell the raw, dead meat as it hit the brackish water.

She blinked.

Tails and eyes.

Eyes and tails.

The water flipped and flopped.

Mouth and teeth lurched from the waterline. Then a tail. It slapped the side of the boat.

More teeth.

Another tail. Two gators fighting over breakfast.

Her breath caught in her throat. Something…an arm…fingers… reached up from the murky water.

The sound of an engine roared in the distance.

Bolting upright, she screamed.

She huffed, sucking in a deep breath. She clutched the sheets as her chest burned for more oxygen.

"Hey. It's okay. I'm right here," Ken said, taking her hand. "Same nightmare?"

"Yeah." She sighed, fluffing the pillow and sitting higher in the hospital bed. Every time she closed her eyes, it was the same. It was like her father was reaching out of the water, begging her to save him.

And she'd failed.

"Whoever clocked me—"

"Audra, you've got to stop telling that story. It makes you sound as crazy as your dad."

She pursed her lips. "Are you going to sit there and tell me the bumps on the back of my head aren't real?"

"No. But it makes more sense that it was an accident, and that's the tale you need to tell. There was damage to your dad's airboat. Before someone found you, you had to use an oar to get close to the docks. You and your dad ran into something out there, and you fell and hit your head. It's a miracle that you didn't fall into the water yourself. You go off the rails about someone trying to kill him…" Ken let the words trail off as he let out a long sigh.

Thank God. Because she would have popped him in the mouth if he'd kept talking.

But that wasn't going to stop her from laying into him either.

"Are you kidding me? Explain to me how my father got dumped into the water if he was the one driving and I was crawling on the bow of the boat?" She held up her hand. She didn't want to hear his excuses. "Also, please enlighten me how so many gators ended up swarming that boat." She cocked her head. "Because that doesn't happen unless you chum the water."

"Babe. You're basing the alligator swarm on a nightmare."

"Don't you dare 'babe' me," she mumbled. "Maybe my dream isn't completely accurate. But someone hit me over the head. I didn't fall. Why don't you believe me? You're supposed to be on my side."

"I am," Ken said. "You have to understand how crazy this sounds and how people are going to—"

A tap at the door thankfully shut him up because she couldn't listen to another word. "Come in." She adjusted her covers.

"Sorry to bother you," Chief of Police Trip Williams said, "but I need to interview you, and sorry, young man. I need to do it alone."

"No problem." Ken squeezed her hand. "I'll go get you a milkshake."

Ken and his stupid milkshakes. They didn't solve anything, and they weren't going to make their problems go away.

Trip pulled up a chair and made himself comfortable.

She'd known Trip her entire life. He was a decent man who treated the people of Calusa Cove with kindness, her father included.

But sometimes Trip could be a hard-ass.

He had that hard-ass look about him right now.

Crossing his legs, he rested his hands in his lap. He gave her a weak smile.

Yeah, this wasn't going to be fun.

"There are a few things we need to clear up," Trip said. He pulled out his notebook and tapped his finger on one of the pages. "I'm concerned about a couple of things."

"I've told you everything I remember." She rubbed the side of her head, careful not to hit the stitches. "Someone murdered my dad."

"You see, that's the problem," Trip said. "It appears the boat hit something. It appears everything's an accident."

"This was no accident, Trip. Someone—"

Trip held up his hand. "Here's the thing. I believe you when you say it wasn't an accident. However, getting anyone else to believe your story will be a struggle, and let me tell you why without you going off on me. Can you do that?"

"That depends." She cocked her head and folded her arms. She might be a teenager, but she'd never had a problem speaking her mind with adults—not even the law. "Are you going to say something that's going to piss me off?"

Trip leaned forward. "I've known you since the day you were born. When you came out with fiery red hair, I told your parents that you were going to be a pistol, and you're more like a stick of dynamite." Trip laughed. "I don't believe anything I'm about to say, but I'm the law, little girl, and I must look at every angle. So, I'm going to tell you how this will go. You'll let me haul you down to the station when they release you. You're going to get a lawyer if it goes too far, and I'll do my best to make sure it doesn't."

"You're being a jerk," she mumbled.

"I'm being the chief of police." He lowered his chin. "And right now, the town gossip is that you killed your dad, tossed his body into the Everglades, and crashed the boat on purpose so that you'd fall and hurt yourself. Then, for dramatic effect, you made sure the fuel line was damaged so the boat wouldn't be drivable. Some are even saying they heard strange noises last night. Owl noises. And that you've been practicing witchcraft." He arched a brow. "While that's all bull, there is some circumstantial evidence that points to a possible homicide, but I've got no body. And the motive? Well, it's weak. However, you opened yourself up when you threatened your dad in front of the entire town."

"I did no such thing."

Trip waggled his finger. "I don't have much to make anything stick. Nor will the State, but they will ask questions of you and everyone in this town. You know they will. Do you know what they will find?" He didn't wait for an answer. "A town full of people who remember you poking your father in the chest and telling him you wished he was dead instead of your mom." Trip dared to shrug. "Outside of talking with me,

I'd stop the conspiracy theory crap. It doesn't help you. It only makes you look like you're a chip off the old man's shoulder and will add fuel to a fire you don't want to be ignited. You let me control the narrative. You let me work the accident angle. I'll handle everything else."

"You want me to sit back and say nothing? You want me to let this town believe I killed my dad?"

"That's what you heard me say?" Trip shook his head. "No, little girl. That's not what I want you to do. I need you to let me do my job, but knowing you, you'll be out there in the middle of the night again. I can't have that. It's going to be hard. Damn hard. People will talk and whisper worse than they ever have. But only if you give them something to talk about. I'm a good cop. I know what I'm doing. Let me put this to bed so you don't have this hanging over your head for the rest of your life."

"Can I ask you a question?"

Trip nodded.

"Is your goal to prove this was an accident or that my father was murdered by someone other than me?"

Trip drew his lips into a tight line. "Your father was my friend. So was your mother. They'd want me to protect you. That's my first order of business. So, I want to direct this town into believing it was an accident. I'll continue to dig. I'll find out what really happened, but you, little girl, need to keep that big fat mouth closed."

"Screw that," Audra muttered. "Someone either took my dad or killed him. That should be your focus. I don't give a shit what people think of me. Never have. Never will."

"That's a mistake." Trip stood. "That train of thought will land you in prison for murder."

Everglades Overwatch Series
Elle James with Jen Talty
Secrets in Calusa Cove
Pirates in Calusa Cove
Murder in Calusa Cove
Betrayal in Calusa Cove

A NOTE FROM KRIS

I wanted to take a moment to express my gratitude and appreciation to those who've helped make Raven's Cliff a success.

To Elle ~ All I can really say is WOW, it's been a wild ride. One I know I'll never forget.

To Jen ~ I feel like we both jumped onboard runaway trains, hair flying, pulse thundering. But we made it safely to the final station, sister, and that means everything.

To Chris ~ You're amazing and the words, "I'm going to call you on that," will forever live rent free in my head, all in your voice.

To the readers ~ I can't thank you enough for taking this journey and falling in love with the men and women of Raven's Watch. It's been a true honour to bring their stories to life.

One final note ~ if you're wondering about Bodie and the other men who've become brothers to Foster's crew, never fear. They might just get their own stories... Because who doesn't want to return to the misty, fog-covered coastline of Raven's Cliff.

See you on the flip side.

ABOUT ELLE JAMES

ELLE JAMES also writing as MYLA JACKSON is a *New York Times* and *USA Today* Bestselling author of books including cowboys, intrigues and paranormal adventures that keep her readers on the edges of their seats. When she's not at her computer, she's traveling, snow skiing, boating, or riding her ATV, dreaming up new stories. Learn more about Elle James at www.ellejames.com

Website | Facebook | Twitter | GoodReads | Newsletter | BookBub | Amazon

Or visit her alter ego Myla Jackson at mylajackson.com
Website | Facebook | Twitter | Newsletter

Follow Me!
www.ellejames.com
ellejamesauthor@gmail.com

ALSO BY ELLE JAMES

Raven's Cliff Series
with Kris Norris
Raven's Watch (#1)
Raven's Claw (#2)
Raven's Nest (#3)
Raven's Curse (#4)

Everglades Overwatch Series
with Jen Talty
Secrets in Calusa Cove
Pirates in Calusa Cove
Murder in Calusa Cove
Betrayal in Calusa Cove

A Killer Series
Chilled (#1)
Scorched (#2)
Erased (#3)
Swarmed (#4)

Brotherhood Protectors International
Athens Affair (#1)
Belgian Betrayal (#2)
Croatia Collateral (#3)

Dublin Debacle (#4)

Edinburgh Escape (#5)

France Face-Off (#6)

Brotherhood Protectors Hawaii

Kalea's Hero (#1)

Leilani's Hero (#2)

Kiana's Hero (#3)

Casey's Hero (#4)

Maliea's Hero (#5)

Emi's Hero (#6)

Sachie's Hero (#7)

Kimo's Hero (#8)

Alana's Hero (#9)

Bayou Brotherhood Protectors

Remy (#1)

Gerard (#2)

Lucas (#3)

Beau (#4)

Rafael (#5)

Valentin (#6)

Landry (#7)

Simon (#8)

Maurice (#9)

Jacques (#10)

Cajun Magic Mystery Series

Voodoo on the Bayou (#1)

Voodoo for Two (#2)

Deja Voodoo (#3)

Brotherhood Protectors Yellowstone

Saving Kyla (#1)

Saving Chelsea (#2)

Saving Amanda (#3)

Saving Liliana (#4)

Saving Breely (#5)

Saving Savvie (#6)

Saving Jenna (#7)

Saving Peyton (#8)

Saving Londyn (#9)

Brotherhood Protectors Colorado

SEAL Salvation (#1)

Rocky Mountain Rescue (#2)

Ranger Redemption (#3)

Tactical Takeover (#4)

Colorado Conspiracy (#5)

Rocky Mountain Madness (#6)

Free Fall (#7)

Colorado Cold Case (#8)

Fool's Folly (#9)

Colorado Free Rein (#10)

Rocky Mountain Venom (#11)

High Country Hero (#12)

Brotherhood Protectors

Montana SEAL (#1)

Bride Protector SEAL (#2)

Montana D-Force (#3)

Cowboy D-Force (#4)

Montana Ranger (#5)

Montana Dog Soldier (#6)

Montana SEAL Daddy (#7)

Montana Ranger's Wedding Vow (#8)

Montana SEAL Undercover Daddy (#9)

Cape Cod SEAL Rescue (#10)

Montana SEAL Friendly Fire (#11)

Montana SEAL's Mail-Order Bride (#12)

SEAL Justice (#13)

Ranger Creed (#14)

Delta Force Rescue (#15)

Dog Days of Christmas (#16)

Montana Rescue (#17)

Montana Ranger Returns (#18)

Brotherhood Protectors Boxed Set 1

Brotherhood Protectors Boxed Set 2

Brotherhood Protectors Boxed Set 3

Brotherhood Protectors Boxed Set 4

Brotherhood Protectors Boxed Set 5

Brotherhood Protectors Boxed Set 6

Iron Horse Legacy

Soldier's Duty (#1)

Ranger's Baby (#2)

Marine's Promise (#3)

SEAL's Vow (#4)

Warrior's Resolve (#5)

Drake (#6)

Grimm (#7)

Murdock (#8)

Utah (#9)

Judge (#10)

Delta Force Strong

Ivy's Delta (Delta Force 3 Crossover)

Breaking Silence (#1)

Breaking Rules (#2)

Breaking Away (#3)

Breaking Free (#4)

Breaking Hearts (#5)

Breaking Ties (#6)

Breaking Point (#7)

Breaking Dawn (#8)

Breaking Promises (#9)

Hearts & Heroes Series

Wyatt's War (#1)

Mack's Witness (#2)

Ronin's Return (#3)

Sam's Surrender (#4)

Hellfire Series

Hellfire, Texas (#1)

Justice Burning (#2)

Smoldering Desire (#3)

Hellfire in High Heels (#4)

Playing With Fire (#5)

Up in Flames (#6)

Total Meltdown (#7)

Take No Prisoners Series

SEAL's Honor (#1)

SEAL'S Desire (#2)

SEAL's Embrace (#3)

SEAL's Obsession (#4)

SEAL's Proposal (#5)

SEAL's Seduction (#6)

SEAL'S Defiance (#7)

SEAL's Deception (#8)

SEAL's Deliverance (#9)

SEAL's Ultimate Challenge (#10)

Texas Billionaire Club

Tarzan & Janine (#1)

Something To Talk About (#2)

Who's Your Daddy (#3)

Love & War (#4)

Billionaire Online Dating Service

The Billionaire Husband Test (#1)

The Billionaire Cinderella Test (#2)

The Billionaire Bride Test (#3)

The Billionaire Daddy Test (#4)

The Billionaire Matchmaker Test (#5)

The Billionaire Glitch Date (#6)

The Billionaire Perfect Date (#7)

The Billionaire Replacement Date (#8)

The Billionaire Wedding Date (#9)

The Outriders

Homicide at Whiskey Gulch (#1)

Hideout at Whiskey Gulch (#2)

Held Hostage at Whiskey Gulch (#3)

Setup at Whiskey Gulch (#4)

Missing Witness at Whiskey Gulch (#5)

Cowboy Justice at Whiskey Gulch (#6)

Boys Behaving Badly Anthologies

Rogues (#1)

Blue Collar (#2)

Pirates (#3)

Stranded (#4)

First Responder (#5)

Cowboys (#6)

Silver Soldiers (#7)

Secret Identities (#8)

Warrior's Conquest

Enslaved by the Viking Short Story

Conquests

Smokin' Hot Firemen

Protecting the Colton Bride

Protecting the Colton Bride & Colton's Cowboy Code

Heir to Murder

Secret Service Rescue

High Octane Heroes

Haunted

Engaged with the Boss

Cowboy Brigade

An Unexpected Clue

Under Suspicion, With Child

Texas-Size Secrets

ABOUT KRIS NORRIS

I'm just a small town girl, living in a lonely world. I took the midnight train…oops, sorry. Got off-track.

Author, hobbit, and crazy lady running in the woods, I'm either madly creating masterpieces in my dungeon, or out chasing Bigfoot with my dogs.

I see myself as unapologetically Canadian, and I love all things maple syrup.

I loves connecting with fellow book enthusiasts.
You can find me on these social media platforms…

krisnorris.ca
contactme@krisnorris.ca

- facebook.com/kris.norris.731
- instagram.com/girlnovelist
- amazon.com/author/krisnorris

ALSO BY KRIS NORRIS

SINGLES

Centerfold

Keeping Faith

Iron Will

My Soul to Keep

Ricochet

Rope's End

SERIES

RAVEN'S CLIFF with Elle James

RAVEN'S WATCH

RAVEN'S CLAW

RAVEN'S NEST

RAVEN'S CURSE

'TIL DEATH

1 - Deadly Vision

2 - Deadly Obsession

3 - Deadly Deception

BROTHERHOOD PROTECTORS ~ Elle James

1 - Midnight Ranger

2 – Carved in Ice

3 - Going in Blind
4 - Delta Force: Colt
5 - Delta Force: Crow
6 - Delta Force: Phoenix

TEAM EAGLE
1 - Booker's Mission
2 - Walker's Mission

TEAM FALCO
Fighting for Fiona

TEAM KOA — ALPHA
Kian Unleashed

TEAM KOA — BRAVO
Flint's Battle

TEAM RAPTOR
Logan's Promise

TEAM WATCHDOG
Ryder's Watch

COLLATERAL DAMAGE
1 - Force of Nature

DARK PROPHECY
1 - Sacred Talisman
2 - Twice Bitten
3 - Blood of the Wolf

ENCHANTED LOVERS
1 - HEALING HANDS

FROM GRACE
1 - GABRIEL

2 – MICHAEL

THRESHOLD
1 - GRAVE MEASURES

TOMBSTONE
1 - MARSHAL LAW

2 - FORGOTTEN

3 - LAST STAND

WAYWARD SOULS
1 - DELTA FORCE: CANNON

2 - DELTA FORCE: COLT

3 - DELTA FORCE: SIX

4 - DELTA FORCE: CROW

5 - DELTA FORCE: PHOENIX

6 - DELTA FORCE: PRIEST

COLLECTIONS

BLUE COLLAR COLLECTION

DARK PROPHECY: VOL 1

INTO THE SPIRIT, BOXED SET

COMING SOON

DELTA FORCE: FETCH

MCGUIRE'S TARGET

GHOST GRID

NEEDLE LINE

Made in United States
Cleveland, OH
04 November 2025